"WHY, SWEETHEART, YOU AREN'T AFRAID OF ME, ARE YOU?" HE ASKED THICKLY.

"Yes!" said Katie. "I mean no! I daresay that you will be terribly angry, but I must tell you that . . . "

Linden stopped her mouth roughly with one hand laid over her lips. "I'm devilish drunk, girl, so if you've got something to say, you'd better be coherent."

Katie swallowed and looked up into the heated eyes so close to hers. "My lord, I . . . I don't want to do . . . that." She could hardly recognize the hoarse, panic-stricken whisper as her own voice.

"Then you shouldn't go to men's houses, sweeting. Especially not the houses of men like me." There was no soft mercy in the sable eyes. Then, surprisingly, the eyes lightened and Lord Linden rolled on his back and laughed. "Lord, child, it's been a long time since I heard anyone refer to it as . . . 'that'!"

Free of the steely arms, Katie quickly threw her legs over the side of the bed and stood trembling on the rug. "But Lord Linden . . ." Katie shook her head and played her last card. "I'm a virgin."

"That, at least," he snapped, "I can do something about."

Also by Laura London

THE WINDFLOWER
A HEART TOO PROUD

And in the months to come, look for

THE GYPSY HEIRESS
LOVE'S A STAGE
MOONLIGHT MIST

THE
BAD BARON'S
DAUGHTER

Laura London

A DELL BOOK

Published by
Dell Publishing Co., Inc.
1 Dag Hammarskjold Plaza
New York, New York 10017

Dell ® TM 681510, Dell Publishing Co., Inc.

ISBN: 0-440-10735-0

Printed in the United States of America

One Previous Edition

New Edition
First printing—April 1985

With love to Elizabeth Peterson

The
Bad Baron's
Daughter

Chapter One

Outside the gin shop lay one of the most wretched slums in London; it was an area of boarded windows, barefoot begging children, and the desperate hacking cough of consumptives. The dirty winding alleys teemed with pickpockets, and prostitutes with matted hair plucked slyly at the sleeves of passersby and exchanged insults with men and women sitting slumped in doorways or lounging against the rough-grained brick buildings. The stucco frame of the gin shop sat squat between two of these raw brick giants with the half-mischievous, half-bored air of a schoolboy squashed between two plump matrons on a public carriage. A rectangular wooden sign hung outside the doorway announcing *The Merry Maidenhead* in amateurish italic lettering with the line drawing of a bottle labeled "gin" below.

It was, without doubt, the last place anyone would expect to find a young lady of gentle birth, and yet there was Baron Kendrick's daughter standing behind the French-polished mahogany bar, her head framed on either side by an assortment of bottles with such titles as "The No-Mistake," "The Real Knock-Me-Down," and "The Out-and-Out."

The evening was unusually humid for May, and moisture from the still air had settled into her hair, causing springy ginger wisps to curl damply against her high forehead. There were freckles on that forehead and across the short, shapely nose and soft cheeks, too, scattered in a soft radiant dappling. Her mouth was wide and untemperamental, and her eyes, now darkened slightly with apprehension, were the soft pastel blue of a robin's egg. She was tallish and fine-boned, so slender that the casual observer might be pardoned for thinking that he beheld a boy, particularly as the young lady was indeed dressed in men's clothing: gray leggings, breeches of indeterminate color with one patched knee, an old-fashioned tricornered hat, an olive jacket riddled with grease spots, and a square apron tied around her waist. It was *haute couture* from Mrs. Coalbottom's second-hand clothing cart on Monmouth Street.

The young lady, Kathleen Janette Kendricks, as she had been christened; Katie, as she was known, was engaged in a careful survey of the gin shop, or at least what she could see of it, for the sun had fled some hours past and the only light in the narrow, high-ceilinged room came from the smelly tallow candles set in brass sconces widely spaced along the smoke-discolored walls. The Maidenhead was crowded on Katie's first night on the job; the airless tenements had disgorged their contents into the streets and gin rooms.

At the end of the room, the doors swung in soft rhythm from the steady arrivals and unsteady departures of the patrons. A group of truculent Irish laborers had staked out a territory in the far corner and were alternately boasting, toasting, and threatening to carve one another. Occasionally the group would band together and hurl loud insults at the nearby table, where some sailors on shore leave were beginning to relax, adding dribbled tobacco juice to the salt stains on their tight-fitting reefer jackets. A few scattered clusters of students were enjoying the ambiance; their blasé expressions were belied by the speculative looks they directed at the table where a convivial band of gaudy prostitutes camped. As Katie watched, the oldest prostitute, gray-haired and naked to the waist like her younger sisters, collapsed face forward on the table, upsetting her flagon. She was none too gently conveyed by her friends to the pile of straw at the rear of the room to join others in her condition, where she restlessly nodded off into an alcoholic dream of what might have been and certainly never was.

If you hadn't any dreams of your own, *The Merry Maidenhead* could supply them. For the price of one penny, you could get drunk, for two pennies dead drunk. Some called it Blue Ruin, some called it Strip-Me-Naked, but it was little more than raw alcohol flavored with juniper. Katie's responsibilities in the scheme of things had been summed up thus: "Fill their empty flagons, collect their money 'n mop up the floor after they casts up their accounts." This occurred frequently, but not as often as the foul quality of the brew merited, thought Katie. She would have as soon drunk sewage.

The swinging doors opened again, causing a wash of moist night air to freshen the atmosphere in the shop, and a group of young men entered. The impeccable cut of their clothes, the polish of their boots, the snowy whiteness of their cravats, and the self-assured arrogance with which they carried themselves marked them, even to Katie's inexperienced eyes, as slumming aristocrats. Her attention was drawn to one man in particular. That he was a figure of some distinction was obvious. He attracted deferential attention from his companions, and was popular with the crowd, who cheered his arrival and opened ranks magically, allowing him to make his way, accompanied by his cohorts, to a corner table.

He was the most attractive man Katie had ever seen. Once, as a little girl, when Katie's father had been teaching her how to ride, typically on far too large and temperamental a horse for her tiny size, he had sent her to jump a five-barred gate. The horse had refused, sending Katie flying to the ground with a force that drove the air from her lungs. She felt that same breathless confusion now, as the crowd parted to allow her a clear line of sight.

His face was too young to look so cynical. There was restless intelligence in the rich brown eyes, and a contemptuous tilt to the unsmiling lips. The copper candlelight warmed the crisp onyx curls that fell over one eye.

He took his place, having dislodged a sleeping old man, and crossed his long legs on the table in front of him, causing a clatter of overturned empty bottles, then rocked back on the hind legs of his chair, seemingly oblivious to the stir his entrance had created. A large plebian crowd quickly gathered to watch as a pair of dice rolled out onto the table, the tattered clothing of the spectators contrasting with the cut and color of the gentlemen's attire. Shouts of laughter and excited comments arose from the throng as the dice began to tumble and pound notes began to flash.

Katie had been leaning her elbows on the smooth surface of the bar, her small chin cupped firmly in one palm. She was joined by a tall, twentyish youth, clad, as she was, in a bartender's apron. His thinnish black hair hung lank to his shoulders where it curled under slightly against a gray cotton shirt with cutoff sleeves. He tugged at the dirty blue and white dotted kerchief knotted around his neck, regarding Katie with amusement in his cunning gray eyes.

"Hankering after the nation's heartthrob, eh, Katie? You and every other female in London."

"Was it so obvious?" asked Katie. "Who is he, Zack?"

"That's Lesley Byrne, Lord Linden. His earldom's English, of course, but his mother's from the old French aristocracy—hates Bonaparte. Linden's our latest romantic hero, back from the French wars, where he was pursuing a line of God knows what skullduggery on behalf of His Majesty. That was until he almost got himself killed about a dozen times. He's a prime favorite with the prince, and old 'prinny' decided that good drinking companions were harder to find than good spies and ordered Linden home. But damned if it wasn't a lot easier on Merry Old England when Linden was off among the Frenchies. Like caging a panther, if you ask me. The boy's a regular hellion. Been back only two months and already he's killed a man in a duel, seduced a string of society lovelies, and caused more riot and rumpus than Beelzebub spittin' in holy water." Zack rubbed a hollow cheekbone with the back of his hand and began wiping down the bar with a bleached muslin rag.

"Zack, do you think Lord Linden is like Papa? Easily bored, I mean?" asked Katie.

"Ain't no doubt o' that. Rumor barely gets out that Linden's playing with one woman, but what she's dropped and he's picked up someone else." Zack collected the empty bottles from the bar and bent down to put them into a wooden crate. "Still worrying over your papa's absence, are you? The baron'll turn up, Katie, he always does."

"You can call it absence, if you please to, but I call it disappearance," said Katie unhappily. "He hasn't sent me a letter in weeks, not a line, not a word. And if even *you* don't know where he is . . . Zack, something's happened, I know it."

Zack straightened and gave Katie a few consoling swats on the shoulder. "Oh, aye, something's happened, like a cock fight or a boxing match or a congenial card game. Katie, you know your old man has no more sense of time passing than the rock of Gibraltar. And if you think that because he and I crony around together he keeps me informed of his every turn and sway, then you're dead wrong. The last I heard from him he was off pursuing some damned intrigue or other with a married woman in Dorset."

"Zack, if only you knew her name, then we might . . . "

"Oh, no, we might not!" said Zack quickly. "Your father wouldn't thank us for bustling into his affairs, and anyway, I don't know the wench's name. Damme, Katie, do you think I keep a list of your father's particulars?"

Katie transferred her chin to her other palm.

"No. But Zack, perhaps if you thought very hard, you *might* remember the lady's name? I mean, this is an emergency."

"Oh, is it, Miss Mousemeat?" said Zack, pretending amazement. "You'll have to explain to me why."

"I've already explained so many times that I think my head will spin from my shoulders if I say it again," said Katie with pardonable exasperation. "I've been evicted from our cottage in Essex for nonpayment of rent. Not only do I not have a penny to my name, I'm monstrously in debt to the tune of ten thousand pounds to that man with the gold tooth who came to the cottage and said that he would put Papa in prison if I didn't give him the money immediately. Plus there's the fifty pounds Papa and I owe in back rent and the fourteen shillings outstanding on the butcher's bill."

"Bugger the butcher's bill!" advised Zack. "I keep telling you that you're not the one who's ten thousand pounds in debt, it's your father! And if there's some weasel trying to get that much money out of your father, then all the more reason for him to play least in sight. I can't see what good you think it would do if your old man was to walk through the door right this minute. You'd still be evicted from that shack you call a cottage, you'd still be stone broke, and the shark with the gold tooth would still be waiting for his ten thousand pounds. Name one time that the baron's ever gotten himself, much less anyone else, out of debt."

Struck by the undeniable truth of this statement, Katie lapsed into a short, depressed silence.

"Things do look dismal, don't they?" she said looking at her reflection in the polished surface of the bar. "I don't know what I would have done if you hadn't given me this job in your shop. I know you didn't want to on account of your not hiring women, but thanks."

"I could hardly throw you out on the street, could I? Your old man did keep my mother in style for a few years. While the winnings lasted." Zack took a coin from a customer's grubby hand and slid a glass of gin across the bar.

"I wish he could win more often," said Katie.

"The man already wins more than Lady Fortune intends for him to, Katie. But that's the way things are with a gambler, more ups and downs than the peg of a butter churn. As for my not employing women, Katie . . . has it ever occurred to you why I don't hire them? Because it's too much trouble to be responsible for them. Do you know what I mean by that? No, I can see you don't. Now listen. You have no way to make a living. You're not employable. You have no talents that I know of. You've got only one asset." He reached over to straighten her second-hand cravat. "You've got the kind of looks that make a man want to take you to bed."

Katie blushed until her freckles disappeared. "Za-ck!"

"Well, Katie," he said matter of factly, pinching her chin. "It's about time somebody pointed it out to you. We bought you those boy's clothes this afternoon and that may put off some of the bigger beefwits, but not for long. People are going to start catching on. How long do you think I can protect you? Sooner or later, and probably sooner, there's bound to come a time when I'm not there at the right moment—or the wrong moment. And you know what's going to happen to you? You'll get it whether you want it or not, probably from a dozen rascals at once."

"Za-ck!" she repeated. Her blush turned into a blanch.

"There you go again! I know my own bloody name!" He gestured toward the drunken prostitute slumbering on the strawpile. "Take a good look, Katie. That's your future if you stay in the Rookery, unless you let your . . . looks work for you instead of against you. Listen to me, Katie. I have a lot of connections who could help us find someone to look after you. It wouldn't be hard to get a generous settlement, enough so you could set up a comfortable house, pleasant circumstances, maybe even a few servants. Now don't stare at me as though I'd smacked you in the mummer, it ain't as bad as that. The fellow doesn't have to be old and ugly. We could arrange for you to meet him first, before anything's settled, and then if you didn't like him or the arrangement, we'd look around for someone else. I wouldn't want you to be with someone you couldn't like. What do you think?"

"You want to know what I think?" asked Katie, her fists clenched, fire blazing in her eyes. "I think you took off your hat and your brain stuck to it. That is *the worst idea* I've ever heard. You're saying that I ought to become someone's mistress, aren't you?"

"Don't have to shout in my face, Mousemeat, I'm only two feet away. Damned if I know how a whipsy-gypsy rabblerouser like your old man ever hatched a chick so full of whims and prudery as yourself," said Zack, reaching behind him to retie

17

the slack strings of his apron. "Take my mother, for instance. She lived with your father for six years after your mother died—can you tell me that we weren't as happy as any legal family? And look at my mother now, set up in Vienna in a bloody villa, mind you, by that German fellow, having the time of her life and enough money left over from her housekeeping accounts to send me the bacon to purchase the Maidenhead."

"I don't want to live in a villa in Vienna and I don't want to buy *The Merry Maidenhead*," said Katie. She frowned and patted Zack on the chest. "The trouble with you, Zack, is that you have no morals."

"Sure, Katie. Fine, upstanding morals and a penny'll get you a glass of gin. What good have morals ever done you? Anyway, you're not in any position to be able to afford a satchel of morals. Save it 'til you're sixty-five and have 'em then." Zack leaned back against the bar's brass railing and studied Katie's angry face. "What are you doing, saving it for marriage? Anyone who'd want you, you wouldn't want. Who's going to marry the impoverished daughter of an outcast peer? On the other hand, there's a pretty good field of men who would want you as a mistress."

"That," said Katie, in a hurt voice, "was not a kind thing to say."

A lanky, doe-eyed girl with a red kerchief on her head came up in time to hear the last, and leaned over the bar with one hand on her hip, a saucy smile revealing the lack of one front tooth.

"'Ey, Zacky, m'man. Are ya bein' unkind to yer little friend 'ere and 'er jest arrived this afternoon? That's a record even for ya."

Zack leaned over the bar on his elbows and met the new arrival's offered lips with a quick kiss of greeting.

"Hullo, Winnie. How goes the revolution?" said Zack.

"Not as good as th' gin business looks. 'N ya can stop makin' fun o' me chosen avocation. Ain't ya interested in th' struggle fer th' rights o' man?" replied Winnie.

"There's only one man's rights I'm interested in," said Zack. "My own."

"Aye, it's a 'eartless self-seeker, y'are," said Winnie, mischievously. She turned to look at Katie. "Oi see ya changed genders since oi left this afternoon. Are ya all rested up from yer ride out from Essex this day on 'at rattle-trapsy stagecoach? Was a fair piece ta come by yerself, wasn't it? So. You talked Zacky around ta employin' ya 'ere."

"Yes, with difficulty. Now Winnie," said Katie, with a quick glance toward Zack, "tell the truth. Zack says people will be able to see through this disguise and be able to tell I'm a girl. Even with my hair up under my hat like it is. Is he right?"

Winnie subjected Katie's trim form to a critical appraisal. "Oi'll tell ya, sis. Yer so blisterin' pretty even as a boy 'n there's some 'at come in 'ere won't matter to 'em one way or t'other."

Katie was shocked. "It seems to me, Zack, that you've set up your business in an awfully wicked part of London."

Zack shook his head. "That's what I've been telling you, Mousemeat. It's no place for the likes of you. There's some bad people down here."

"Yes, and if it was up to you, I'd be one of those bad people," said Katie.

"Ooh, my, speakin' o' bad people," exclaimed Winnie. "Lookee there who jest walked in th' door. It's Nasty Ned Fabian 'n 'is nasty friends."

Katie followed Winnie's gesture to the front of the shop, where a rough-looking bunch of foul-mouthed, dirtily dressed men were wading their way through sloshing tankards and sloshed customers and hailing a barboy for some gin. They set themselves up at a table near the gambling aristocrats and immediately began spitting gin on each other, "accidentally" dropping and breaking their flagons, and creating a loud disturbance. They were led by a nasty-looking brute indeed, well over six feet tall, with a crude, heavy face, glowering red-rimmed eyes, and a muscular, top-heavy look.

"Damn," said Zack in a low voice. "Why does he have to pick my place?"

"Who is he?" asked Katie.

"Those lads likes t' mill, oi'm tellin' ya," Winnie informed her. "See 'at big bloody rampsman in th' middle, there, talkin' louder than even th' rest o' 'em? That's Nasty Ned. 'E's tried fer years ta make it in th' ring 'n was almost top man a few times, but they say 'e played too rough 'n never really caught on. Now 'e's got nothin' ta do but lead 'is bloody gang o' troublemakers 'round 'n bust up gin shops. 'E's so mean 'e'd spit in 'is own mother's eye!"

"He's a lot more than mean," said Zack. "He's a hired fist. If he's in here, that means only one thing, that he has some business with someone. Katie, if he calls for anything, let me or one of the boys handle him. You stay away." He glanced worriedly toward Katie. "If I had any sense, I'd send you up to your room now."

"Zack, you can't send me upstairs every time the clientele gets a little rough, or how am I going to be able to work here? And if Winnie can live in the Rookery, why can't I?"

"Oh, pshaw," said Winnie good humoredly. "Oi can take care o' meself from point go. Anyone bothers me, oi jest tell 'im oi got th' French pox, or 'at it's me time o' th' month.'"

"Kate, you can't compare yourself to Winnie," interjected Zack. "She was born and raised here. Do you know that Winnie carries a knife in her garter? Do you think you could learn to do that? Or more to the point, do you think you could ever use it on anyone? I remember going fishing with you, and you couldn't even hook the worm because you felt sorry for it. Katie, Katie, you can't work in *The Merry Maidenhead* the rest of your life."

"I'm not saying for the rest of my life," protested Katie. "It's only until I find Papa, or he finds me. Besides, it's not the only possibility, not even considering your unmentionable idea of a few minutes ago. I could be a governess, for instance."

"People don't marry the daughters of outcast gentlemen," said Zack, "and they won't hire them to raise their children either."

Katie tapped her lips thoughtfully with one finger. "All right then, I could be a chambermaid. That's honest work."

"Ha," said Winnie. "Wi' yer looks, girl? Oi can see ya trippin' up ta change 'is lordship's sheets and findin' yerself between 'em instead."

"I'm tired," said Katie, "of hearing disparaging

comments about my looks. If my looks are going to be a problem, I'll take Winnie's knife and cut off my nose."

Zack grinned widely. "Believe you me, no one will hire you if you don't have a nose." He tapped the dainty member under discussion with one smudgy finger.

Katie drew herself to her full height. "If you will pardon me," she said with a dignified smile, "I have not the time to dally. Someone's signalled for service, and I'm going to wait on him. Pardon me." Katie brushed past Zack, who watched as she walked through the hinged gate out of the bar and made her way across the crowded shop to the customer.

"Plucky, yer little friend," said Winnie, making her fingers walk lightly up Zack's bare arm. "And ya'd like ta turn 'er into a playmate fer some baldin', bloat-bellied banker? Seems a shame, y'know. Couldn't ya jest let 'er stay upstairs 'til that father o' 'ers comes back ta look after 'er?"

"Winnie, the Baron looks after Katie the way a thunderstorm looks after a picnic. Not that he ain't fond of her, in his way, but the man's so God-awful irresponsible that he's barely aware of Katie's existence six days out of the seven," said Zack, grimly. " 'Sides, it won't make a ha'penny's worth of difference to Katie's future whether the baron shows up or not, because it wasn't my idea to set Katie up as some rich man's light frigate. It was his."

"What? A 'ell o' a father 'e is," said Winnie, with disgust.

"Can't argue about that. The baron came to me some time ago and made me promise that if anything happened to him, I should make sure Katie goes to a decent protector. Said that when she was old enough, he meant to set to finding someone for her himself, but it's more like him to disappear like this and leave me to do the dirty work," said Zack bitterly. "Still, some provision's got to be made for Katie—can't leave a chit with her face wandering about the street."

"What about Katie's mother's family? Wasn't there money there?" asked Winnie.

"Aye, but the baron fought like badgers with his father-in-law years back and the two decided that if they ever saw each other again, it would be too soon. That grandpa never took much interest in his own daughter and none at all in Katie, but Katie wrote to him anyway after the baron disappeared. Clutching at stars, so to speak. She told him that he could get in touch with her here if he liked, but apparently he hasn't liked. No help from that quarter."

"Maybe not, but there seems ta be one thing missin' from these nice little plans you 'n th' baron got fer Katie. 'Er consent. Ya know, Zacky, oi'm thinkin' that yer Miss Mousemeat may not go along wi' it."

"She will, Winnie," said Zack with finality. "She'll come around."

Never, thought Katie, never, never, never. She set down one glass of gin on the table she was serving as punctuation for each "never." She made a mental list of the numberless things she would rather do than join the muslin company. This list encompassed the impractical to the ridiculous, and she considered and abandoned a dozen schemes while trying to think of words powerful enough to forever drive from Zack's mind his infelicitous plan for her future. She'd known Zack before she had been able to say his name, and knew him to be not easily dissuaded from a set course. In fact, she thought with misgiving, she had never been able to talk him out of anything. She glanced at the bar where Zack and Winnie were engaged in an animated political conversation with a group of Winnie's friends; Winnie was gesturing theatrically.

A group of students had vacated the table near the aristocrats, leaving a crop of half-empty bottles and thumb-printed glasses. Katie set her tray down and began a clinking harvest. It was a pleasant chore because Lord Linden sat no more than four feet from where Katie was working, and she was in a good position to observe him. Hankering, she thought. Myself and every other girl in London. She watched as he caught the dice thrown to him. He shook them in one long white hand and tossed them into the center of the table with a negligent graceful flip. A nearby companion rallied him at the unfavorable result of the toss, and Linden responded with a slow, attractive smile that caused Katie to take in a quick breath of the reeky air. She reflected ruefully that she had been pierced by a foil not meant for her.

A bottle crashed from a nearby table and Katie turned toward the sound.

"'Ey, wot's a bloke ta do ta get some service around 'ere!" Nasty Ned bawled. He was gazing angrily at her, conspicuously waving the neck end of a broken gin bottle.

Katie took a hurried step backward. "I'll go call Zack," she said hastily.

Ned snaked out one hairy, muscular arm and pulled Katie in front of him. The tray she had been carrying was upset; the glasses and bottles dumped and rolling on the floor.

"Wot do we want wi' 'im?" Nasty Ned growled. "Yer all th' 'elp oi need." One finger of his left hand was gone to the first joint, and he roughly caressed her cheek with the stub, "Oi've 'ad me eye on ya, me boy. Oi likes yer looks. We could go fer a walk in th' alley."

His fingers dug into Katie's wrist through the wilted cloth of her coat. She looked down the length of the room toward Zack and Winnie, who were still deep in conversation with their friends. It seemed as if the walls of the room were expanding, carrying her farther and farther away from them. She tried to call Zack's name, but the words were without force, inaudible above the raucous buzz of conversation. Her mind searched for an escape.

"All right, sir. But, um, first let me take off this apron," said Katie hesitantly. Ned relaxed his grip for an instant, and Katie broke from him and began to race toward the bar. She was brought up short by one of Ned's companions, who stood grinning evilly, blocking the narrow pathway. She turned to see Ned rising from his chair to follow her. Her foot knocked against a metal slop bucket, and as if in a dream, she took it in hand, and reaching up, overturned the disgusting contents upon the surprised features of Nasty Ned, placing the bucket over his ears as she did so. The fulsome mess that habitually lurked inside the slop bucket oozed and dripped down the clothing and person of the ruffian, who roared hollowly in the bucket like a wounded bull. Ned disentangled himself, revealing a besmirched countenance ugly with vein-popping rage.

"Oi'll cut yer heart out 'n eat it, ya young wretch! Talk ta me blade 'ere if ya won't talk ta me!" he roared, the repulsive slime from the slop bucket dripping from his eyebrows. From out of his pocket, he produced a thick-bladed butcher knife. He lifted it into the air and sent it whirling at her. Katie, her legs weak from fear, stumbled sideways and she felt the blade's steely breath as it passed very close to her ear.

Lord Linden had been concentrating on his dice when the silver gleam of the knife whipped on its path through his field of vision to land with a crack in the wall in back of him. This drew a roar of disapproval from the crowd, which had been indifferent to the little argument until now. Linden looked casually toward the blade where it jutted from the wall. He directed a short, indifferent glance at Katie and then a slightly longer, slightly less indifferent glance at Nasty Ned.

"Hey, slum rat," said Linden, and pulled the knife out of the wall with a backhanded jerk. "If you want to practice your aim, don't place your target in front of me. There's more room for this kind of game outside." He tossed the knife negligently toward Nasty Ned who caught it in one hand.

"Oi'll go outside, all right, 'n oi'll take this little barboy wi' me. We'll play a game 'e may never've played before." Ned looked viciously at Katie, who quailed and clutched frantically at Lord Linden's arm as though to anchor herself to the relative safety of *The Merry Maidenhead*. Linden looked down at her fingers in some surprise and made a sharp movement to disengage his sleeve from their desperate clasp.

"Have I attracted a barnacle?" said Linden impatiently. "Let go of me, child."

"Aye, let go o' 'im," exclaimed Ned angrily. "Yer comin' wi' me."

One of the bawds from a nearby table unexpectedly raised her gin-cracked voice in Katie's behalf. "The poor young'un don't want ta go wi' ya. Leave 'im alone, ya big bullock."

Lord Linden made another attempt to pry off the little fingers, and then stopped to scan the soulful blue eyes raised pleadingly to him. He gave an exasperated sigh.

"Very well, if you don't want to go with him, you don't have to go with him," he told her. "Detach yourself." Katie didn't move, so he spoke again, more gently. "I won't let him take you outside. There is no need to cling to me as if you were drowning. That's right, let me go. Thank you." He slowly lifted his long legs from their resting place at the table's edge, stood and took a few steps toward Nasty Ned.

"It's a very small fish," Linden said quietly. "Why not throw it back in?" A single ruby solitaire twinkled wickedly from his left hand, but it shone with less brilliance than the clear coffee shade of his eyes.

"'At little maggot dumped a bucket o' slops over me 'ed," Ned said furiously, his eyes red with rage. "Don't let it cozzen ya wi' 'em big blue eyes. Oi knows its type, the two-faced little piglet."

"Possibly," said Linden. "But I've decided that you two should be separated, as you can't seem to get along. So you'll simply have to find someone else this evening."

"And oi sez oi ain't gonna," said Ned, tightening his hands into melon-like fists.

The answer to this was not verbal, it was physical. Linden placed a hand on Nasty Ned's chest and gave him a quick powerful shove. Ned fell backward heavily, upending a table in the process. He rose to his feet again, the blade gleaming.

"Ya panty-waist swell. Oi'd as soon skewer ya as anyone," Ned threatened.

Linden raised his eyebrows. "Would you? I wonder. You won't fare so well with me as with yon beardless weanling," he sneered, nodding toward Katie. "I'll tell you what, my homely friend. Shall we make this more interesting for our audience? Loser buys drinks for the house."

"Fine with me," snarled Ned, raising his voice to be heard above the clamor of approving yells. "Too bad ya ain't goin' ta be around ta enjoy th' party."

The crowd cheered as Linden removed his coat and tossed his hat into the hands of a companion. "'Ave at 'im, Lord Lesley, 'at's th' lad," came the calls from the onlookers. A veritable arsenal of knives, brass knuckles and truncheons began piling up on the table in front of him. Lord Linden ignored the pile of weapons and walked across the floor to stand carelessly in front of the enraged brute. A light, self-assured smile played with the corners of his lips as he spread his hands mockingly and said softly, "Now then, baboon. Come skewer me."

Ned feinted twice with the shining blade as Linden stood before him, a study in cheerfully arrogant nonchalance. Suddenly, Ned lunged for blood. Quick as quicksilver, Linden shot out a strong wrist, pulling Ned off balance, and in a series of swift, graceful movements, he brought his knee up to batter Ned's face, and then with one hand on Ned's belt and another on his collar, he threw the failed pugilist into the wall with long practiced ease. The wall and Ned's head collided with a thud that shook the room, and he fell heavily to the floor.

The room erupted with a resounding cheer. Byrne's friends swarmed around him in a congratulatory huddle, clapping him heartily on the back with cries of "Capital move, Lesley, absolutely tops!" Drinkers surged toward the bar, demanding their drinks (to be charged to Nasty Ned) and shouting toasts to Lord Linden. As the hubbub died down, Linden and the other aristocrats turned their attention to the fallen adversary.

"Have I broken his neck?" inquired Lord Linden indifferently.

"Unfortunately, no," replied one of his companions, prodding the man's unconscious head distastefully with his boot. "I fear the ease of civilian life has put you a trifle off your touch."

"A trifle," agreed Linden. He turned to an admiring group of onlookers. "Perhaps you could drag this sleeping ox over to the straw? I think he may not wake for some time and he blocks the way."

"Glad to, guv'nor," came the response. Several pairs of filthy hands pulled Ned away and tossed him unceremoniously into the strawpile. Linden gingerly plucked Ned's sweat-stained jacket from where it lay across a chair, walked over to the recumbent bully, and threw it over his shoulders.

"*Bonne nuit*, baboon," said Linden, laughing under his breath.

Katie was leaning weakly against the table abandoned by Nasty Ned and his friends, when she felt someone pinching her elbow. She turned to find Zack beside her. "I've been standing here trying to think of a tactful way of saying I told you so," he said mildly.

"And found you couldn't?" said Katie. "Zack, did you see that? He was trying to kill me."

"I saw. In fact, I was trying to get a better view but the good seats had been taken. Did you ever try to make your way across a gin shop during a knife fight?" Zack tilted his head to one side. "You're fortunate I'm too generous a man to remind you that I told you to stay away from Nasty Ned."

"I couldn't help it, Zack. Before I knew it, he was smacking me against the wall and trying to drag me outside with him. And then he threw that knife at me."

They were joined by Winnie, who finally succeeded in elbowing her way through the crowd. "Trouble yer best friend, young'un?" she asked with concern. "Ya jest made yerself an enemy ya don't need."

"She did. But she found herself a friend she *does* need," Zack replied, cocking his eyebrows and nodding toward the table occupied by Linden and his entourage.

"Lord Lesley?" Winnie cried. "Aye, 'n where's

'e gonna be when Nasty Ned wakes up? Probably 'avin' 'is din wi' th' Prince Regent!"

"True," said Zack. "So it might be a good idea if she went over and thanked him for his trouble. The word might get around if it looked like she was having a chat with him."

Katie looked at Zack with trepidation. "Zack, I don't want . . ."

Winnie clapped a hand over Katie's mouth. "If ya don't want, then ya shouldn't go pickin' fights wi' th' likes o' Nasty Ned." She pushed the reluctant Katie firmly in the right direction. "Better get right to it. It 'pears they're gettin' ready ta take their leave."

The group of young aristocrats had indeed decided that they had exhausted the possibilities of *The Merry Maidenhead*. There was a general scraping of chairs and commotion; one of their number was raising his glass to the ceiling and draining his last drops of gin, and Lord Linden stood up restlessly, looking around for his hat.

He was shrugging into his immaculately tailored black coat when he felt a light hesitant tugging at his sleeve. "My lord?" said a sweetly musical and very feminine voice. Linden turned to find himself looking down into Katie's unthinkingly worshipful blue eyes.

"Well?" he inquired, without warmth.

Katie flushed at his tone and hung her head. "I wanted to say thank you, my lord," she whispered.

"It's nothing," he replied. He tapped her chin with his knuckle, reached up to ruffle Katie's hair and then stopped. Thoughtfully, Linden took one bright thick curl and felt its creamy texture. He let his gaze wander gently over her slender body and then return to Katie's delicate face. His smile was slow and sensuous.

"What's your name, child?" he asked, the words stroking Katie like silk.

"Kat . . . oh," stumbled Katie, as she remembered too late that she was supposed to be posing as a boy. His hand still played inside her curls and she felt as though her hair had sensation, could feel Linden's touch.

"I see," said Linden softly. He released the captured curl and let his hand linger on Katie's cheek. "Do they make life difficult for you at *The Merry Maidenhead*, your *beaux yeux?*"

"My—? Was that French?" she asked, confused.

"Yes, that was French," he said and then grinned. "How old are you? Sixteen, seventeen?"

"Seventeen."

"Seventeen," he repeated. "Let me give you some advice, little one. If you want to see eighteen, the next time you decide to dump the sewer bucket over someone's head, make sure he's smaller than you."

Katie felt his caressing finger leave her cheek, and when she opened her eyes, he was gone.

Chapter Two

It had been a hot day, and the cool breath of night had not yet brought relief. Shadows were lengthening, the rays of the setting sun blocked by the lean tenements packed together like the trees of a giant pine forest; crowds of people scurried beneath like so many busy forest creatures. The streets of St. Giles' Rookery were decorated with a septic array of decomposing refuse.

"That's th' last o' th' lot," said Winnie. She set down the empty paste bucket, pulled a plaid handkerchief from her waist, and wiped her perspiring brow. "Thanks fer carryin' th' posters fer me, Katie."

"The pleasure was mine. Zack won't let me out alone since Nasty Ned picked that fight with me in the gin shop. Believe me, I've had enough of the hermit's life the past few days. I'd help you carry hot coals with my bare hands to get out for a bit." Katie stepped back and read the brightly colored rectangle they had affixed to the streetside wall of a skittle alley. "In fact, I believe I have been carrying hot coals. 'The tree of liberty must be refreshed from time to time with the blood of patriots and tyrants,'" she read aloud. She smiled at Winnie. "Did you write that?"

"No, some bloke from th' colonies. Zack is doin' th' cautious thing not lettin' ya out alone. Best ta be wary."

"Do you think we still have to be wary? Ned hasn't been back in two days," said Katie. "Maybe he's forgotten about it."

"Oh, 'ell," said Winnie, grabbing Katie's arm and pulling her into the shadows. 'At was bad luck, sayin' 'at. Look over there." She pointed.

Katie blinked and looked twice, squinting her eyes into the late afternoon shadows. Her heart sank. There, across the busy street, leaning against the black brick wall of the tenement opposite, were Nasty Ned and a gang of four other persons of the ruffian persuasion, lounging false-casually, their arms folded menacingly across their chests. There was no mistaking Ned's loutish, thick head and his muscular shoulders, even in the fading light. It was remarkable how well-acquainted she felt with him, even though they hadn't been properly introduced. She briefly considered walking out into the street, hailing him, and asking him how his head felt this fine day, but rejected the possibility for fear he would give her an overly detailed explanation. Winnie chuckled fatalistically.

"Our gentleman friend, Sweet Ned, is 'ere, 'n oi don't think 'e's payin' us a social call."

"What should we do?" Katie said.

"Well, oi'll tell ya," said Winnie, biting her nail. "Oi don't think they've seen us, 'n there's a chance 'at they ain't even after ya. But we don't want ta take 'at chance." She paused. "There's a cock pit around th' corner. Rather than try ta make it back ta the Maidenhead, it gettin' dark 'n all, oi think we should walk ta th' cock pit 'n if they follows us, we kin lose 'em in th' crowd. 'Ow does 'at sound?"

Katie nodded dumbly.

"Let's start walkin'," said Winnie. They stepped together into the street. Katie threw a nervous glance over her shoulder, and saw Ned and company leave their place of rest and come after them at a fast walk.

"We better cut 'n run," said Winnie. "Follow me. It's right around th' corner."

Directly in front of them a large crowd was surrounding swinging double doors, their faces illuminated from a subdued light inside the building. Clouds of clay pipe smoke were billowing out of the doors, which were in constant swinging motion as patrons made frequent entries and exits. Loud hurrahs and contentious arguments came floating into the night air. This was the cock pit. Katie had been in one as a child. Her father, experiencing a rare spasm of paternal attention, took her to one of these brutal places where she had sat rigidly, eyes averted while beautiful fighting cocks sliced each other to ribbons for the entertainment of sweating, smoking, profane onlookers.

Katie and Winnie were jostled by the crowd, then suddenly they were separated. Katie looked frantically for her companion. She could hear Winnie calling her name, but it was impossible for her to make a reconnoiter in the crush. She could see that she was near the swinging doors and ducked into them.

Katie found herself in a large pavilion. Gray smoke swirled and eddied near the low ceiling, which was held up by rough wooden pillars. The place was packed with spectators, their cheers sending a hollow roar reverberating against the dirty wooden walls. The floor was scattered with grimy sawdust. She elbowed her way toward an area which seemed not quite so congested, past young apprentices, butchers, tradesmen, sporting young bloods, pimps, and a prostitute or two. She turned and craned her neck in time to see Ned and his group breaking through the crowd, Ned's red face scanning it—for her.

There was a door behind her. She wrenched it open and slid through it in the frantic hope that it would lead to the alley. Instead, Katie found herself in a stuffy room, its corners mysteriously veiled in regular lumpy shadows. The only available light was a subdued streak from a shuttered lamp beside the door. Katie stood still, trapped. Outside, the crowd was shouting excitedly, but much more real was the sound of her own ragged breathing. She became aware of muffled murmurs and rufflings coming from one side of the room.

"Who's there?" whispered Katie. "Please say." No response.

Trembling, Katie bent down to lift the shutter from the lamp. Suddenly the room's cramped contours were rent with a shrill, earpiercing clamor that sounded as though Katie had loosed fifty screaming devils. This was the resting area for the fighting roosters of the cock pit. Along the walls were lined a score or more wooden cages, housing game cocks from every corner of the British Isles. Pirchin Ducks, Dark Grays, Spangles, Shropshire Reds, and Red Duns, indignant at this invasion of their private domain, gave shrill vent to their wrath in a manner that poor Katie was convinced could be heard as far away as Holland. And certainly as far away as the cock pit in the next room.

"Oh, don't, don't squawk so," cried Katie, lifting one shaking finger to her lips. "You stupid creatures, you're giving me away . . ." Katie's voice died into the gaunt melody of angry cackles. Given away. For there, stepping into the fetid little room, were Nasty Ned and his entourage. Katie's heart plummeted to her feet.

"Well, well. Fancy meetin' you 'ere wi' all th' other scrawny chickens," said Ned, a menacing grin on the thick rufous face. "You 'n me's got ta talk, maggot. Me blackjack 'ere's got somethin' real private ta say ta th' side o' yer 'ead."

Katie fearfully backed several steps and stopped. It was no good. Ned's friends were blocking the only escape. In a pitiful little gesture, Katie dropped her hands to her sides and closed her eyes to await the blow that would bring darkness. But the blow never came. Instead, incredibly, Katie heard the casual, accented drawl of Lesley Byrne, Lord Linden.

"Turn around, toadface. I want to see if I made any improvement in your appearance two nights ago." Nasty Ned wheeled and Katie opened her disbelieving eyes to look toward the voice.

Lord Linden was lounging by the door, negligently tossing a small box-lock pistol up and down in the palm of his hand. His head was tilted slightly to one side, his dark hair painted with the flickering lamplight. Ned looked warily at the bright steel of the gun and spoke, his voice cracking nervously.

"Now look 'ere, guv, this ain't yer fight. Oi was drunk 'at night or oi wouldn't 'ave 'ad 'at set-to wi' ya 'n 'at's a fact. Oi don't want no trouble wi' th' likes of you. Your Lordship could go on now 'n leave this 'ere maggot ta me."

Linden's pure teak eyes were unreadable as he shifted his gaze to Katie's disheveled form. He studied her lovely blue eyes, filled with fatigue and fear, the sculptured lips pale in contrast to her flushed cheeks. Then he looked back at Ned.

"To be honest, *mon ami*," said Linden calmly. "I'm thinking of killing you." Ned's mouth opened perceptibly and he swallowed.

Linden sneered. "Yes, I can see I am gaining a reputation with you, *n'est-ce pas?* Good." He caught up the gun and pointed it at Ned's chest. "Listen to me, my hideous friend. I don't care for the style of your attentions to this young person. It's bad form, you understand? If you continue them," he said, without emotion, "I will kill you."

Ned nodded, a hunted look on his face. "As ya say, guv. Never meant anyone no 'arm, oi didn't. Jest a bit o' fun, ya might say."

"*Bien.* So get out, baboon, and take your *canaille* with you," Linden stated flatly. Ned availed himself of this invitation with a coward's haste. The door swung shut behind the last of the thugs and Katie found herself alone with Lord Linden and the twenty-odd fighting cocks.

Chapter Three

Lord Linden redeposited the pistol into a small pocket in the lining of his jacket and smiled at Katie.

"So. Now what, child?" he asked.

Katie returned the smile shyly. "Now I make another inadequate thank you." She lifted her palms, spreading her hands expressively. "You are goodness itself, my lord."

"What a trusting little creature you are. And a very bad judge of character," said Linden, amused. A high wooden platform ran across one wall, and Linden leaned back with his elbows resting on its ledge, his eyes glittering strangely in the lamplight. "You travel in dangerous company, *petite*."

Katie sank down on the edge of an empty cage. The cocks were quiet now, peacefully pawing, stretching and rustling their feathers. "Not always, my lord. I grew up in the country, in Essex mostly, and there aren't any dangerous people there. Except when there's a fair in Colchester and some of the farmers have too much ale and get into fights." Katie passed a hand abstractedly over her eyes. "London, I think, is a whole different pot of potatoes. Do you think that Nasty Ned will be frightened and decide to leave me alone?"

"No," said Linden, who was not a man given to pretty untruths. "I think that he's probably waiting around the next dark corner for you."

Katie sighed, unsurprised. "That's what I was afraid of. T'would be quite in keeping with my luck lately, what with the man with the gold tooth and the butcher's bill. But how did you know I was in here?"

"I saw you run into this room from where I sat by the pit, and I saw that you were followed. Did you drop another slop bucket over his head?"

"No," said Katie despondently. "I suppose he is still angry about the last one. He seems to be more of a subscriber to 'an eye for an eye, a tooth for a tooth,' than to 'turning the other cheek.' I daresay you will think me sadly lacking in spirit, but I very much wish that it might be otherwise. I'm not much of a fighter," Katie pondered this statement and then added, "at least not in the physical sense."

The orange lamplight had spun a soft halo around Linden's hair and etched clear shadows about his smiling lips. "No," he said, "but then, that would be too much to expect, don't you think?"

"Oh," said Katie, wrinkling her nose slightly in perplexity. "I think that means . . . well, that you may have guessed that I am not a boy? Was it because when you asked me my name at *The Merry Maidenhead*, I said Kat and it sounded like Kate?"

"That," he said, "and your long eyelashes. Where do you live? I'll take you home."

"Would you really?" said Katie gratefully. "I—it

would be a great relief to me if you would, though I hate to have you thinking I am a barnacle."

"My dear child, don't waste your energy worrying about what I think of you. I don't think anything about you, except perhaps that you're too damned beautiful for your own good." He dropped his hand to Katie's cheek, feeling the heat from her blush warm against his fingers. "Cheer up, little flower, life will get easier for you once you learn the right way to use those . . . long eyelashes of yours. And you will learn."

Far from cheering Katie up, Linden's calm statement made her feel more depressed, as it came chillingly close to Zack's uncomfortable remarks on her first night at *The Merry Maidenhead*. Katie swallowed and put her palms on her knees, rising numbly to her feet.

"Come then, child," said Linden, removing his fingers from her cheek. "I think our feathery friends would like to be left to their rest." He opened the door into the cock pit and Katie bent conscientiously to reshutter the lantern.

As they made their way through the crowded room, Katie trotted at Linden's heels in a manner that reminded him of the way his springer spaniels had followed him through the lush woods and fragrant meadows on his estate when he was a child. The thought made him feel vaguely uncomfortable and he put it firmly from his mind as he elbowed his way through the crowd.

When they stepped outside, the air had cooled with night. Linden summoned a hack with an imperious movement of his hand and assisted Katie in, asking her where she lived. He followed her, directed the jarvey, pulled the carriage door shut after him, and then leaned back at his ease, his arm resting on the carriage seat.

"Why *The Merry Maidenhead*?" he asked.

"Do you mean why do I want to go there now or why did I ever go there in the first place?" inquired Katie.

"Both."

"Well, I live there in a bedroom upstairs, or I have since I came to London. You see, Zack is the owner—oh, and he lives upstairs too—and he is my good friend," said Katie. "Though he has some odd ways of showing it sometimes."

"I believe it," said Linden, without expression. "And your wearing boys clothes . . . ?"

"Because Zack doesn't hire women."

Linden tilted his bicorne to the back of his head. "I see. You put on boy's clothes and instantly become a boy. Hocus pocus. What fun it must be to be seventeen." There was mockery in his voice, but a trace of seductively sympathetic amusement, as well. Katie felt as though she had been stroked. She leaned her bent elbow on the smooth cool edge of the hack window and rested her head wearily on her arm.

The carriage moved forward at a slow trot through twisting streets thronged with pedestrians, carts, and carriages. The air reeked with a thousand urgencies of sight and sound. Rows of colorless tenements marched shoulder to shoulder like platoons of an ill-fed army. Once they passed a ragged group of men lounging idly beneath the marbling glow of a streetlamp, and Katie imagined for one frightened moment that she could see Nasty Ned's lumbering form among them. It was not he, though, and Katie blinked, shuddered, and shifted her head slightly, glad for Lord Linden's presence beside her as the horses' hooves clicked on the brick street. She felt the light touch of a finger on her cheek and then, briefly, on her lips.

"Tired, child?" Lord Linden asked.

"I think perhaps I am. I was thinking how glad I am to be here with you," Katie answered naively.

"Dear me," said Linden drily. "I feel compelled, in all honesty, to point out that I am not 'goodness itself,' that I rarely, if ever, do anything without the strongest possible motives of self-interest, and that I am no more a fit companion for someone your age than that baboon who seems intent on delivering the *coup de grâce* to your svelte little body."

"What motives of self-interest prompted you to save me from Nasty Ned at *The Merry Maidenhead*?" asked Katie curiously.

"You were clamped on my dicing arm. And I don't think you could have been disengaged without some damage to my jacket. Don't romanticize my actions, chit, I didn't care what was going to happen to you, I just didn't want it to happen in front of me."

"It may not have meant much to you," said Katie in a small voice, "but it was awfully important to me."

"Without doubt, *chérie*, but don't, for God's sake, thank me again. You sound as though you might be building up to it."

The hack took a last lurching turn and came to a jiggling halt at the stucco front of *The Merry*

Maidenhead. Linden handed Katie down, and tossed a coin to the jarvey as Zack came through the door, pulling on a light jacket, followed by an agitated Winnie.

"Mousemeat! Oh, Jesus!" cried Zack. "I was coming to look for you. Winnie got here a minute ago and . . ." Zack stopped and looked at Linden. "What happened?"

"Nothing!" said Katie. "At least, I was almost killed, but Lord Linden saved me. I ran into the cock pit, you see, and they made the greatest roar, like lions, except that they were chickens. And Nasty Ned came in behind me and was going to hit me but Lord Linden came and . . ."

"I can figure it out from there, puss," said Zack, putting a proprietary arm on Katie's shoulder and hustling her inside. "And if you're going to stand outside here like a target, then you might as well let me paint a bull's eye on your chest. Winnie, take her upstairs."

"Yes, but Zack, I'd like to tell you about . . ."

"You shall, pet, but later. Upstairs! And no more buts."

Katie managed a last wistful look at Linden as Winnie dutifully shepherded her toward the stairs and out of sight. Zack turned back toward Linden and motioned to an adjacent table.

"Have one on the house, my lord?" suggested Zack, observing Linden closely.

Lord Linden met and held Zack's stare and lowered himself leisurely into a chair. He shrugged.

Zack went to the bar and returned bearing a bottle and two glasses. Linden watched with an evident lack of interest as Zack set down the glasses and filled them.

"Well," said Zack, seating himself opposite Lord Linden, "the girl has reason to be grateful to you."

"Neat," observed Linden. "A little abstract, perhaps, but neat."

Zack held up his hand. "All right. I can be more concrete, if you like. Gratitude can have a material expression."

"Can it?" A faint amusement glimmered in Linden's coffee eyes. "Enlighten me."

Zack paused and took a quick swallow of gin. "I could arrange for her to express her gratitude in a way that you would find . . . uh . . . satisfying."

"And how much would I have to pay for this 'satisfying' gratitude?" Linden picked up his glass.

"Fifty pounds?"

"Expensive," said Linden, raising his eyebrows slightly.

"You think so?" asked Zack. "She's a virgin."

Linden smiled. "Of course. They're all virgins. Do you think virginity makes a woman more appealing to me? Unthink it, friend."

"Very well," said Zack cheerfully, "she's not a virgin."

"A versatile creature. She loses her virginity in one breath," said Linden, grinning. "I only wish it had been that easy for me to lose mine."

"I might as well lie," retorted Zack, "because you have no way of knowing whether I'm telling the truth or not. Unless you find out for yourself."

"*Very* neat," said Linden, draining his glass and rising to his feet. "If I'm ever in the market for a slum brat of questionable virtue, I'll contact you. But don't count the minutes." He turned toward the door and added, as a disinterested afterthought, "Don't despair, my pimp friend, with her looks you won't have any trouble unloading her elsewhere."

"I know," said Zack, making a detailed study of his none-too-pristine fingernails. "Nasty Ned was in this afternoon and offered me twenty-five guineas for her delivery this evening. I'd rather you than him, but if not you, well. . . ."

Linden stopped and turned, looking at Zack, his eyes expressionless. He slowly drew a bill from his pocket between thumb and forefinger, and allowed it to drift to the table like a falling leaf. Zack watched it land.

"She'll need some time to pack," Zack said. "I know where you live. I'll bring her there in an hour. Is that all right with you?"

"Yes," said Linden quietly. "But *you* I never want to see again."

Less than an hour later Katie found herself again riding cross town in a hackney carriage with her cloth traveling bag on her knee and Zack slumped in the seat beside her.

"Zack, are you sure your friend won't mind me coming to stay? It's such short notice . . . you'll come in with me and explain about Nasty Ned and everything, won't you?" asked Katie anxiously.

"There's no need. I sent a message. Don't start fussing, Mousemeat, this is only a temporary arrangement to keep you safe until I can get things straightened around with Nasty Ned."

Katie looked at Zack's silhouette hopefully. "Do you think you'll be able to do that?"

"It'll take some doing, but we'll work it out," said Zack soothingly.

"And you'll . . . oh!" Katie lifted her palms to rub her eyes. "The world began to spin for a moment . . . but it's all right now, I think. I feel so tired. But what was I going to say before . . . oh, yes. You'll send for me right away when it's safe to come back? Or if you hear any word of Papa?"

"The very minute," promised Zack. He sat up and leaned over to Katie. "Close your eyes and hold out your hand."

Katie scrunched her eyelids together and gingerly presented an upturned palm. "It's not something horrid, is it? Oh, it's only paper." She opened her eyes. "Zack! It's a note for fifty pounds! Zack, no, you can't mean me to keep this."

"I do. It's your wages."

"Wages?" asked Katie. "But I've hardly worked at all. Zack, where did you get so much money? You haven't robbed anybody, have you?"

"I don't know, that remains to be seen. Anyway, whatever happens, I sure as hell don't want that money. And don't start asking me what I mean, Katie. I'm not in the mood to start in on a lot of damned difficult explanations," said Zack irritably.

Katie stared at his shadowed face in amazement. "I shan't if you don't like me to, but I must say that you are behaving very mysteriously."

"Not mysterious," snapped Zack. "Abstract. And neat."

And obscure, thought Katie, shifting Zack's odd words through her mind. The effort was too much for her, though. The dim interior of the hack had blurred and melted into a splotched opalescent screen. She made a concerted attempt to focus her vision and it improved somewhat.

"What a night," said Katie. "You're acting strange and I'm feeling strange."

Zack patted her hand. "Getting dizzy, eh? It's the laudanum starting to work."

"Laudanum?" asked Katie, with a sinking sensation. "What laudanum?"

"The laudanum in that milk you drank before we left. I only put in a spoonful, so I don't think it'll have too much effect."

Katie felt her throat tighten. "But Zack, isn't laudanum to calm people? I was already calm."

"You don't look calm to me. Besides, I thought you might have trouble getting to sleep."

"I never have trouble getting to sleep."

"Tonight," said Zack, "you might."

The hack stopped before a long row of depressingly well-groomed townhouses. Each was an intimidatingly precise copy of the next: fashionable balconies of cast-iron scrollwork, tall double-hung windows, and immaculate stucco exteriors. Katie looked uncertainly at Zack as she jumped unsteadily onto the clear swept pavement.

"You have a friend who lives here?" asked Katie. "It looks very . . . respectable."

"Looks can be deceiving," said Zack. He ran lightly up the four front steps and banged on a heavily paneled oak outer door. "Come on, Katie. There's nothing to get yourself worked up about. Just do whatever he says without making a melodramatic, missish pother over the business, and things'll flow sweet as spring water."

"He?" cried Katie dazedly. "I thought your friend would be a woman. Oh, Zack, you haven't done something dreadful, have you?"

"Trust me, Katie. I've got your best interest at heart."

Since Zack's ideas of what was in her best interest were so different from her own, this was hardly reassuring. Zack was starting back to the coach; she tried to follow him, her eyes wide and pleading.

"Where is this? Zack, please don't leave me here alone."

He propelled her back to the door, his hand on her elbow. "It's all right. Do you think I'm delivering you to a brothel? There's nothing in there that will hurt you, pet. It's not like you to be so ruffled. Listen. Someone's coming to answer the door. Keep your chin high, Mousemeat." Then he was gone. She heard the horse's hooves clapping away into the night as a muffled rattling came from the other side, and the door was opened by a middle-aged, gray-templed gentleman dressed in funereal black.

"Come this way, miss," said the gentleman, looking through her. He allowed her to enter a small candlelit hall with a magnificent sweeping stair leading up to another floor. She followed him up the stair, afraid to touch the banister for fear of leaving a hand print.

"Were you expecting me, sir?" she said, her voice shaking. She felt like a small, furry, miserable creature padding behind this imposing personage, as if her ears had become long and pink and she had sprouted a hairless tail.

He paused and half turned, "Yes, miss. If you'll follow me, miss."

There was a long hallway at the top of the stairs, and she padded after him to a tall black walnut door. A feminine voice was speaking on the other side of the door in shrill staccato bursts. The distinguished gentleman paused for a fraction of a second, knocked quietly, and pushed the door open, motioning for her to precede him into the room.

"Your guest has arrived, my lord. If it is convenient for you, sir, I shall depart for my holiday. I shall return Monday morning."

"By all means, depart, Roger. I envy you."

Lesley Robert Emmett Byrne, Lord Linden, was draped across a low couch covered in cocoa plush, his long legs stretched in front of him. A half-empty wine glass dangled from his left hand. He waved the butler on his way. The room itself was high-ceilinged and airy, the walls lined with bookshelves on two sides. Between the books were many small exotic statues quite removed from Katie's limited experience. She felt a forceful impression of an impeccable taste in decoration supported by ample wealth. There was a third person in the room; a fine-boned creamy-complected woman, dressed in a gown of beige watered silk, the décolletage barely concealing a small but beautifully rounded bosom. She was far more than merely attractive, but her best feature was her hair, which fell in wheaten hills down her bare back. She held the center of the room, standing in front of Lord Linden, tapping her foot, with hands on curving waist, her full rosy lips open in astonishment. "How utterly bizarre!" exclaimed the woman, gesturing at Katie. "Is this a taste you acquired in France?"

Linden smiled maliciously at the blonde girl, and then studied the remaining wine in his glass. "You think it's a boy? It claims to be a girl, but I haven't confirmed that yet. Would you like to stay and assist me in determining its gender?"

"Thank you, no," said the woman, tossing her head. "I'll leave you to enjoy your perversions in peace. Find your little heaven wherever you please."

"I will, Laurel, I will," he said. "But really, my dear, you are well served for coming here unbidden."

"Go to the devil," she hurled at him. "Though I doubt he'd have you." She stormed out past the paralyzed Katie, slamming the door behind her. Her steps receded down the hallway, and a few seconds later, the door to the street was slammed as well. Linden glanced at Katie and then leaned his head back against the wide cushions, closing his eyes.

"Poor child. You look scared out of your wits." He drained the wine glass.

"My lord, I have to tell you . . ." began Katie urgently.

"Not now, blue eyes," said Linden. "I've spent the better part of a quarter hour listening to Laurel shrilling, and I'm in need of five minutes of golden silence. Sit down and shut up."

It suddenly occurred to Katie that Lord Linden had been drinking heavily. She had noticed in the cock pit that he wasn't sober. Linden hadn't slurred his words; his step had been steady and graceful; but Katie had seen her father in every possible stage of intoxication and could recognize its signs as surely as she knew mare's-tail clouds meant rain. And Linden, it was clear, had drunk more since she'd seen him last. Katie sat down.

She remained perfectly still for a while, her eyes tracing the mystically swirling pattern of the oversized oriental carpet, her thoughts seeming to twist and circle into themselves like the design, in willful rhythmic disorder. What had Zack told Lord Linden about her? That she was willing to become his mistress? She knew that she should never have followed the butler inside; that had been mistake number one. No, trusting Zack had been mistake number one. Her next mistake had been not turning and running away down the stairs as soon as she saw Lord Linden—surely it now looked as though she had planned to stay. Katie could feel the laudanum tightening its languorous chains around her mind until thinking became as hard as trying to slice through a forest of sinuous vines. How clever Zack had been and how cruelly unscrupulous. Katie stared at a small Roque clock, intent on marking off five minutes. She blinked her eyes, and when she opened them again, eight minutes had passed. How could the hand of the clock jump like that? She realized she had been asleep.

Of all the awkward moments to nod off, thought Katie, and rose to her feet, rubbing her numbed cheeks. Linden, she could see, hadn't moved from the couch and didn't appear any more amenable to hearing any explanations from her than he had eight minutes earlier. Trying to blink the sleep from her eyes, she moved across the room to the wide statue-lined bookcase. She looked, in drowsy fascination, at a tiny bronze figurine of a cloaked dancer.

"How did it get broken?" Katie wondered aloud as she frowningly regarded a hairline crack in the dancer's flowing robe.

Katie heard a movement behind her and then

Lord Linden's voice. "I don't know, child. It happened a long time ago."

"How long ago?" asked Katie rather sleepily.

"Mm-m, a thousand years, perhaps."

Katie had been stroking the statue's smooth contours with one loving finger but at his words she drew back her hand quickly, aghast that she had touched an object of such value.

"A thousand years! Is it from Egypt, then?" Katie's knowledge of antiquities was sketchy.

"Greece," said Lord Linden. He walked to Katie, who was investigating the mysteries of another statuette. This time it was the elaborate ivory portrait of a young prince.

"Is this from Greece, too?"

"No, my dear. India. Turn around." She obeyed him without thinking and he lifted his hands to rest them lightly on her shoulders. A curious, sweet smile tugged at the corners of his lips. "Do you know that I would like very much to remove your hat?"

Katie's eyes grew very wide. "W-would you, my lord? I daresay that my hair is sadly rumpled beneath it." But he pulled it off anyway and tossed it carelessly on a nearby library table.

He stared at Katie, and something in his look brought the blood to her cheeks with an almost blistering intensity. Linden reached out to thread one of Katie's warm pliant curls through his fingers, his gaze caressing her. Her mouth felt strangely swollen, as if her lips had become suddenly conspicuous, and she parted them slightly. Katie felt his hands touch her hips; there was no physical pressure, he was only resting them there, yet her muscles tightened involuntarily, became taut and rounded. He was running the side of one long finger down her cheek, and she felt it skim the surface of the silken hair. She wanted to lean backwards, against the hard hand that was cradling her hips, and relax, to lift her face to the warmth of him. She was floating and lost, her swollen lips aching to be touched and soothed and opened.

She felt a slight pressure, cool and dry, on her lips; she felt relieved. Then it was gone, and she was searching for it blindly. She found it again, and yearned to trap it and hold it. But then she was the one trapped and held, by the pressure of Linden's steady hand against the back of her neck, and her breath was caught and aching deep in her throat as his lips marauded the softness of her tender mouth. His fingers played in the velvet curls at her neck, and then slipped gently around to open the top button of her shirt. He removed his mouth from hers to place a soft kiss on the translucent skin above her collarbone, and moved his lips down the swelling mound of her breast.

Katie reached her hands up to push shakily against Linden's hard chest. He stepped back, supporting her with his hands on her shoulders, and watched her silently, enjoying the delicately flushed contours of her face, the fantastic auburn stream of her hair and the slender graceful line of her hips. Then because she didn't seem to know what to do next, he lifted Katie gently into his arms and carried her to his bedroom. The bedclothes were drawn back and he placed Katie on the smooth white sheets, her glorious hair spreading into satin bunches on his pillow. He sat beside her then, and gathered her near him so that he could bury his face in the shimmering silk that framed her face. Katie, almost faint with shock, tried to turn her face from him but he caught her curls with one hand and placed the other underneath her chin. He lifted her face to his and touched his lips once more to hers, tenderly at first, then firmly and urgently.

It took Katie several glorious minutes to wake from her dream world to a very unwelcomed reality. She had heard before how quickly and easily a girl could be seduced, and now she knew how true that was. Now was a fine time to tell Lord Linden she didn't want to become his mistress, after her innocently eager response to his kisses. Lord Linden, Katie realized unhappily, was not going to take well to being interrupted now. She searched her mind for inspiration, and remembered something Winnie had said that first night at *The Merry Maidenhead*.

"Lor—Lord Linden . . . I have the French pox."

He didn't stop kissing her. "Thats all right, sweetheart. So have I."

Katie fairly shot up with alarm. "What! Lord Linden, I was lying. I don't really have the French pox."

Linden pulled her down beside him again, imprisoning her head between his arms, and smiled sardonically.

"I appreciate your honesty, sweetness. In honor of it, I'll confess that I don't have the French pox either. What's your real name?"

"K-Katie."

"How charming. Come; kiss me, Kate."

Katie, who knew even less about Shakespeare than she did about ancient history, found it was several minutes before she could speak and this time her voice sounded frighteningly weak and far away.

"My lord?"

"I know. You've contracted bubonic plague," he said huskily.

"N-no. But it's my time of the month."

Lord Linden's hand was engaged in a sensual caress of Katie's thigh and she could feel his breath warm on her cheek.

"Kate. Sweet Kate. Bonny Kate. I don't care."

It was daunting. Since Lord Linden was too intoxicated with passion or alcohol to respond to hints, she would have to be more direct. Katie tried to arm herself by remembering the more depressing stories of ruined virtue she had heard; they had gained a frightening new realism after Katie had seen the drunken bawds at *The Merry Maidenhead*. She might be transported to a dream world with Lord Linden's embraces, but when he tired of her (which would be soon if his past career was any indication) she would have begun a path that seemed to reach its inevitable conclusion at *The Merry Maidenhead* where she would be forced to accept any man who wanted her. Like Nasty Ned. The thought filled Katie with such horror that she found the strength to push hard against Lord Linden's chest in a scared attempt to gain his attention.

"Please, my lord. Please, please stop," she said desperately.

Drunk Lord Linden might be, but his senses were not so dulled that he failed to hear the fright in Katie's voice. He had been kissing the curve of her neck, but at her words, he looked up.

"Why, sweetheart, you aren't afraid of me, are you?" he asked thickly.

"Yes!" said Katie, rendered quite breathless and stupid with anxiety. "I mean no! But I don't want ... that is, I hope you won't ... I daresay that you will be terribly angry, but I must tell you that ..."

Linden stopped her mouth roughly with one hand laid over her lips and rested his chin on his other hand.

"I don't see anything," he said. "I'm devilish drunk, girl, so if you've got something to say, you had better make it coherent. Now I'm going to take my hand away from your mouth and you've got one sentence to say whatever you want and then I'm going to stop listening. Understand?"

Katie nodded quickly under his hand. His long fingers slipped away from her mouth until they were cupping her face. Katie swallowed and looked up into the heated eyes so close to hers.

"My lord, I don't want to do ... that." She could hardly recognize the hoarse panic-stricken whisper as her own voice.

Linden caressed her delicate jawline with his thumb. "Then you shouldn't go to men's houses, sweeting. God, especially not the houses of men like me." There was no soft mercy in the sable eyes. But then, surprisingly, his eyes lightened, and Linden rolled onto his back and laughed. "Lord, child, it's been a long time since I've heard anyone refer to it as ... 'that'!"

Free of the steely arms, Katie quickly threw her legs over the side of the bed and stood trembling on the rug. Lord Linden stretched out his hand to stroke Katie's forearm lightly.

"Katie, my poor child. Don't make me angry

now, you won't like it, I promise you. Come back to bed." His voice was soft, friendly, and utterly pitiless.

"But Lord Linden, you see it was Zack . . ." She felt his fingers encircle her wrist painfully.

"Katie," said Linden calmly, "I don't want to hear about your problems with your pimp. If you raise that subject again, I'll do something to make you wish you hadn't. Do you want me to be more specific?"

Katie shook her head and played her last card.

"Lord Linden, I'm a virgin."

Apparently Lord Linden was not among that admirable fraternity who consider the preservation of virginity a laudable aim.

"That, at least, I can do something about," he snapped. Lord Linden's temperament, never noted for its sweetness in sobriety, had about as much forbearance as a striking adder's when he was drunk. He twisted her wrist harshly, and she cried out. He ignored her. "Look. You came here by your own choice. It's too late for second thoughts. Because you don't seem to have much experience, then I had better explain that I want you. Now. And if you don't come back to bed, then I'll bring you and you'll be hurt. You don't want that, do you? No. Neither do I. And if you're thinking of crying, I had better warn you that nothing makes me lose patience faster."

Katie stared at him, her face amazingly free of anger, condemnation, or rancor. She merely looked tired, perhaps a little forlorn and frightened, but also oddly trusting. She looked sadly at the ruthless fingers guarding her wrist. Then, trembling very slightly, she lowered herself to the bed.

"No, I won't cry," she said, "I never cry." In a gesture very like her reaction to Nasty Ned when he had raised the blackjack to strike her at the cock pit, Katie closed her eyes and lay her arms at her sides.

Linden studied her curiously, wondering what struggles in her life had schooled her to this final, unresentful fatalism. It was as though a long and overpowering experience with defeat had taught her the futility of resistance after she had recognized failure. Laurel, in a similar situation, would have fought to the end. Lord Linden's conscience rarely interfered with his pleasures and he was unaccustomed to denying himself, but neither was he cruel enough to bring this shivering child to her knees one more time. He stood up, walked to the door, and removed the key, throwing it onto the bed beside Katie.

"Lock it," he said, going out and pulling the door firmly shut behind him.

Chapter Four

Katie awoke the next morning by degrees that blended together in an idle, leisurely progression. After Lord Linden's abrupt departure last night, she had risen obediently to lock the door, loosened the string about her waist that served as a belt, and crawled between the crisp sheets of Linden's bed. I shall never sleep tonight, Katie thought, and that was the last thing she remembered until the clapping rattle of a wagon's metal wheels on the street below called her back to consciousness. At first she was aware only of the compact spongy mass of the mattress beneath her; it was the first time Katie had slept on a feather bed. Trance-like, Katie observed the angular, uncompromising lines of an old-fashioned mahogany cabinet, now muted by the bluish rays of the early morning sun. It was peaceful to lay so, without thinking, without moving, but the pointed shaft of one chicken feather had worked its way through the mattress ticking and prodded Katie's back with dogged persistence. When she could ignore it no longer, Katie sat up and turned to find the tiny spike, pulled the feather through the sheet's coarse weave, and blew it off her palm to watch it float languidly to the floor. There was no denying it now. She was awake.

Katie stood up, tightened the string-belt, and tried to finger-comb her heavy curls into order. There was a tripod basin stand near the bed, its low shelf containing a porcelain urn of cool fresh water, so Katie washed as well as she could. She looked around under the bed and behind an armchair for her hat and then remembered that it had come off in the drawing room. She also remembered how it had come off. There was nothing for it. Reality must be faced. Katie unlocked the door and tiptoed into the next room.

Reality lay sleeping heavily on an inlaid satinwood couch, unconsciously picturesque with one hand dropped to the floor and the other curled disarmingly against his forehead. A faint sleep blush ran across Lord Linden's nose onto either cheek and Katie would have liked to touch it softly with her finger but didn't dare. She had a fair amount of experience with men on a morning after an evening of too much convivial drinking; she guessed that a hangover would not greatly improve Lord Linden's temper, so she was in no haste to wake him.

Instead Katie went quickly to the hall, walked downstairs, and opened the large paneled front door to gaze into the street. London's ambitious corps of street vendors were already out, pushing their rickety carts laden with a fascinating array of merchandise. Flower girls, piemen, fruit sellers, and knife sharpeners advertised their wares with boisterous energy. Katie saw a barefoot lad pulling a clumsy ice wagon coming around the corner. She thought for a second, then ran down the steps and bought a penny's worth of chunky ice, and carried it back inside wrapped in her jacket. Downstairs she found a room that could only belong to Roger, the absent valet, and a neat kitchen with an adjacent pantry. Roger, Katie found, was a well organized gentleman's gentleman. She quickly found the items she required: an icebag, a threaded needle, and milk. The icebag was for Lord Linden, the needle for a jagged tear in her jacket that must have been made sometime during yesterday's adventures, and the milk was for herself. She had eaten only half an apple and one stale bun in the last twenty-four hours.

Katie loaded her plunder on a worked silver tray and carried it upstairs. Thus, the first view Lord Linden had that morning was of Katie sitting crosslegged on his Persian carpet with her elbows on her knees and her oval chin resting on the heels of her out-turned fists.

"Good God!" said Linden and shut his eyes with unflattering alacrity. It was some moments before he opened them again. Katie silently handed him the icebag. He laid it against his neck, wincing with an oath as the cold damp sailcloth made contact with his skin.

"Bad, is it?" inquired Katie sympathetically.

"Yes." Lord Linden shifted the icebag and looked at Katie. "God! I don't remember anything after that third bottle. Well, chit, did I bed you last night?"

"No, my lord. You—you said I should lock the door."

"The devil I did! I must have been as drunk as David's sow." Linden buried his face in the icebag. "*Merde.* I remember now." From the look on his face, Katie correctly divined that the recollection afforded him very little pleasure.

"I am sorry," said Katie meekly. "I'm afraid what happened was very much my fault. I should have explained that I didn't want to become your mistress at the outset, but Zack never told me . . ."

"Zack," said Lord Linden succinctly, "should be shot." Leaning one hand against the couch's scrolled back for support, Linden rose stiffly. "I'm going to bathe. I'm going to change. And then I'm going to come back. All right?"

Without waiting for Katie's assent, Linden strode into his room and closed the door behind him with a pronounced whap. He was gone at least an hour. Returning admirably *point-device* in a beige morning coat, tight breeches, and shining top boots, he found Katie seated tailor fashion on the floor before the wide bay window, scrupulously intent on mending a gaping hole in her faded jacket. She had just finished taking a small distasteful sip of a yellowish liquid in a clay cup set by her knee, and it had left a small blurry mustache on her upper lip which curved upward uncertainly as Lord Linden came in. Again, she reminded him of a friendly, shaggy puppy waiting for the kick.

"Good morning, my lord," she said, with her sweet, self-deprecating smile. "I hope you won't mind, but I borrowed a needle and thread from the pantry downstairs."

Lord Linden's interest in his valet's inventory was minuscule at best, so he waved a hand dismissively and leaned his broad shoulders against the ornate marble mantel where he stood regarding Katie without affection.

"I shall be done in a moment; then I'll leave. Unless you'd like me to go right now?" asked Katie.

"Finish."

Linden watched her as she again bent her curly head over the jacket, her brow furrowed in painstaking concentration. For all her effort, it was the sloppiest sewing he had ever seen; the stitches were large and uneven and the poor child pricked herself each time the needle cleared cloth. It had been Lord Linden's intention to remove this lovely but most unrewarding waif from his life with all possible haste, but as he watched her poke her finger for the fifth time and then, with weary patience, draw the needle again, Linden felt an unfamiliar sensation in his chest that he was quite unable to identify. It was an odd combination in a bar girl: gentle manners, cultured speech, and this disconcerting gallantry. Lord Linden did not want to get involved with Katie. But somehow he found himself asking, "Who are you?"

Katie looked up doubtfully. "I hate to say, my lord. I daresay you'll be shocked."

Linden folded his arms across his chest. "I will strive," he said drily, "to bear up. Who is Papa?"

"Baron Kendricks," said Katie regretfully.

"Kendricks!" said Lord Linden in a voice that made Katie jump and stick herself again. "I don't suppose it would have occurred to you to have included that somewhere in your gibberish last night? What in the fiend's name is a chit of your birth doing serving rag water at a place like the Maidenhead?"

"But I explained that," said Katie, puzzled. "You see, I persuaded Zack to give me a job there."

"What you haven't explained, my little idiot, is

how you came to know a man like Zack to begin with."

"Oh. We lived together. When we were children. Zack's mama and my papa were like this." Katie held up two crossed fingers. "But they never married because Zack's mama said Papa was too unsteady to make a good husband. One night Papa lost a great deal of money at play so she and Papa had a fight and she said that she was going to move on to greener pastures. She did, too. She lives in Vienna, in a villa."

"God! Zack should be shot, but what your father needs," said Lord Linden with feeling, "is to be drawn and quartered. Didn't you have any relatives to object to his lodging you under the same roof with his mistress?"

Katie made a jumbled knot and broke off the thread with her teeth. "Only Grandfather, my mother's father. But he was a merchant, and Papa told him that he'd be damned if he'd listen to the moralistic nonsense of a cit. That made Grandpa mad and he said that I'd be better off dead than raised like that and he never wanted to hear of my existence again. I did write to Grandpa before I left Essex and told him that Papa had disappeared and I would be at *The Merry Maidenhead*. Grandfather hasn't contacted me, so there you are."

"How often," asked Linden, "does Papa disappear?"

Katie sucked thoughtfully on her needle-stabbed finger. "Oh, all the time. But never before for so long and without leaving me *any* money."

Linden frowned. "Haven't you any idea where your father is?"

"No. The man Papa owes ten thousand pounds

to thinks he's gone to the Continent to escape his debts, but the more I think about it, I recall that Papa often talked about going to America—he said that there is a lot of opportunity for gamblers there."

"Mmm," said Linden, looking sardonic. "Isn't there anyone besides Zack to take you in until your father can be located? Friends?"

"I'm afraid not," said Katie sadly. "People tend to disassociate themselves from the families of card-sharpers, and we moved a lot to avoid Papa's creditors. I don't have any friends. Besides Zack."

"Did you come here last night because you decided I might be a better bargain than Zack?" asked Linden, regarding Katie steadily.

Katie flushed. "Was that how it looked? Zack only told me that he was taking me to the house of a friend where I'd be safer than at *The Merry Maidenhead*. You see," said Katie, the pain fresh in her voice, "I trusted Zack."

Lord Linden could not have looked less sympathetic. "Katie, a newborn infant would have known better than to trust Zack."

Katie regarded Linden with her astonishingly blue eyes. "Even if my father said I could trust him?"

"Particularly if *your* father said you could trust him, nitwit. I know I wasn't in much of a humor to listen to you last night, but don't you think you could have tried a little harder to tell me all this, considering what you had at stake?"

"Yes, but it wasn't easy for me to think clearly because Zack had drugged me with laudanum."

"Oh, you were drugged, were you?" said Linden

caustically. "That certainly adds an irresistibly sordid piquancy to everything. Do you feel all right now?"

"Oh, yes, thank you," said Katie. She set down her needlework and took another sip from the clay cup.

Linden scowled. "What are you drinking?"

"Milk. It was downstairs. I hope . . ."

"Yes, yes, you hope I don't mind." Lord Linden took the cup from Katie's hand and gazed at the curdled contents. "Jesus. This is sour. How long has it been since you've eaten anything? No, never mind, I don't want to know. Finish your jacket and we'll go out for breakfast. Sour milk. Are you trying to make yourself sick?"

"No, my lord. I never get sick."

"Truly? What a convenient creature you are. You don't get sick. You don't cry. Our little misunderstanding of last night aside, is there anything else that you don't do? Yes, you *ought* to hang your head, that's the closest I've ever come to raping anyone. Throw the milk out now, there's a good girl."

Katie walked over to the clear bay window, opened one hinged pane and dumped the milk outside. Unfortunately, it was not clear sailing to the pavement and Katie, hearing an indignant scream, looked out the window to find that she had tossed the spoiled milk squarely onto the lavender parasol of an elegant young lady who had been taking her morning promenade below.

"Oh, dear," said Katie, dragging her head inside hastily. Lord Linden joined her by the window.

"Oh, dear is right. Are you trying to have me

67

evicted?" said Linden, his dark eyes washed by laughter.

"But that's what they do in the Rookery, toss the garbage out the window."

"My dear child, this is not the Rookery, this is Bennett Street. And here 'they' do *not* toss their garbage out the window. What a life you must have led!" said Linden. "Tell me, *chérie,* who looked after you during those times that Papa disappeared?"

"Ladies that Papa hired, mostly, though none of them stayed very long because Papa forgot to pay them most of the time. When I got older, I stayed alone. Papa says that every tub must stand upon its own bottom."

Lord Linden pinched Katie's chin gently between his fingers. "Katie, if we are going to get along, I think you had better stop telling me what Papa says. Frankly, I am beginning to develop a profound dislike for that gentleman."

"Are we going to get along, my lord?" asked Katie wonderingly.

Lord Linden sighed, released Katie, and sat down in an open-backed armchair. He couldn't send the chit back to the Rookery and Nasty Ned. It would be nothing short of murder. "I'm afraid so, *petite.* At least until I can find your father and bring him to some sense of his responsibilities. That is, if he hasn't gone to America."

Katie had great faith in Lord Linden's powers of persuasion, but an intimate knowledge of her father's character told her that it was beyond the power of mortal flesh to bring him to a sense of his responsibilities. "It's not that Papa doesn't like me," she explained, "it's only that he doesn't think about me very often."

Lord Linden looked grim. "Then we'll just have to remind him."

Chapter Five

London shone rose that evening and on Bennett Street the bandtailed pigeons strutted to and fro on the rails of the ironwork balconies, chuckling softly to themselves. Katie could hear them as she lay on her stomach on Lord Linden's bed, watching him tie his white silk cravat.

"How did you know that I didn't have French pox?" asked Katie. She lifted her slim ankles from the bed and bounced them one by one against the mattress.

"Because," said Linden, immersed in the mysteries of knotting.

"Because why?" pursued Katie.

Lord Linden started to say something and then stopped as though he had changed his mind. "You really are very innocent, aren't you? If your friend Zack was so eager to introduce you into the muslin company, it seems to me that he ought to have used a little more energy making sure you knew the facts of life."

"Well, I do know them. Once I saw a cow and bull. Zack says that's all you need to know."

Linden gave a quick gasp of mirth. "Which partially explains your reluctance last night."

"Are you still angry with me about that?" asked Katie uncertainly.

"No."

Katie thought a minute. "Lord Linden, do you recall that lady who came into the restaurant while we were having breakfast? The one who is your grandmother's friend? I think she might not have believed you when you told her I was your nephew. She wasn't very friendly, was she?"

Linden smiled at some secret thought. "Don't worry, child, it was directed at me and not you."

Katie wriggled to the side of the bed and let her head hang over the edge. "How do you think she knew I wasn't your nephew?"

"Probably because she knows that none of my sisters would ever allow their offspring to traipse around London looking like the loser in a dogfight," said Linden crushingly.

Katie digested this in silence. Then she dropped her hands to the floor and rubbed her knuckles against the rug. "I think you look beautiful. Will it be much fun at the party you're going to tonight?"

"Lord, no, dull work, my dear. A *soirée* at my grandmother Brixton's, of all the damned things. Banal as a banker's bath water."

"Why do you go then?"

"Because *grandmère*'ll raise holy hell if I don't show up. And that means she'll send my mother a long, detailed letter about what a hell-bound babe I am and my mother will send *me* a letter, splattered with tears and lavender scent, begging me to stop breaking her heart with my wild ways. My mother can work herself into hysteria rapidly, I assure you. And, it not being possible to slap one's mother in the face, I'd have to endure a certain amount of it." He grinned suddenly and looked very young. "Actually, *Grandmère* and I have a lot in common. She's got Caligula's own temper, too."

"Was Caligula one of those Greeks?"

Linden gave his cravat a final pat and came to sit on the bed beside Katie. "No, barbarian. He was a Roman emperor." He tapped her nose lightly. What a problem this girl was. A short stop at Bow Street had set inquiries in motion concerning the whereabouts of Katie's father. They had found that there were others interested in this subject: the baron's creditors. Housing her until her father was found was a problem. Lord Linden could well imagine the reaction of any London hostess requested by him to provide shelter for a young girl of Katie's glowing beauty and present circumstances. No one would believe he hadn't made her his mistress. If that wasn't enough to damn her, her father's reputation surely would. Baron Kendricks was a notorious cheat, and nothing short of the sponsorship of a duchess would ever open society's doors to the Bad Baron's daughter. As he looked down into Katie's soulful blue eyes, he thought how unfair it was that Katie should be tarnished with her father's reputation. In spite of her rearing, the girl was an unfledged innocent. It spoke volumes for Katie's inexperience that she still trusted him after last night.

Katie sat up, hugging her knees. "Is your grandmother's house far away?"

"No, it's about four blocks down Bennett Street. Are you afraid to stay here by yourself?"

"No, but I don't understand why you don't want

to come back here after the party. It will be a lot of trouble for you to stay somewhere else and it would be so easy for me to sleep in the drawing room."

"Perhaps." Linden rubbed the back of Katie's hand with his finger. "Unfortunately, it would also be so easy for me to forget my good resolutions. I'm a dissolute creature, child, and you want to beware."

The big blue eyes smiled into his trustingly. "You've been kinder to me than anyone has before. You know, Lord Linden, about last night . . ."

"Yes?" He let his finger wander over her wrist.

"If I was going to be anyone's mistress, I would like to be yours. But you see, when you got tired of me, then I would have to be with just anybody, and I don't think I could do that."

Linden rose abruptly from the bed. "Don't tease yourself about it, child, it doesn't matter. I've got to be off now. Don't burn the house down while I'm gone. And don't open the door for anyone; I won't be back before morning, so if anyone knocks, it won't be me." He reached over and chucked her under the chin as she sat, crosslegged, on the bed. "Good-bye now."

She listened to his steps on the stairway and heard him lock the door behind him. She was alone. Her face brightened with an idea, and she bounced from the bed, skipped across the room, and opened the French doors leading to the balcony. The pigeons scattered with a wild flapping of wings as she leaned over the wrought-iron railing to look for Lord Linden. He was nearly at the corner, sauntering elegantly through the golden evening.

"Enjoy yourself!" she called through cupped hands, and waved. He turned and touched the brim of his top hat with the brass tip of his cane in a farewell gesture, and she watched him, hands on chin, until a slight bend in the street took him out of her sight. The late breeze ruffled playfully at her auburn hair and flapped at the curtains on the French doors behind her, ran in to make a turn around the room, and passed by her again on its way out. She stood idly, in reverie, as the pigeons returned to coo softly at her feet.

"Well," she said aloud. "Pigeons certainly make a more pleasant noise than fighting cocks." As if it understood her, one of the smaller pigeons walked stiff-legged between her feet and stood there, rubbing its wings against her ankles. "Dear little thing," she said.

She remembered then that the pantry had been freshly stocked that day from funds from Linden's ready pocket. They had bought bread, dried meat, fruit, cheese, and especially for her, he had said, a strange bundle of yellow, smooth-sided tubular fruit, connected together at one end in a way she thought was vastly clever.

"Bananas," he had responded to her query, smiling to himself. "From the Canary Islands. No, they aren't attached for shipment; they grow that way, in bunches. Little monkeys eat them in the jungle, they say."

So now I'm going to eat monkey food, she thought. Katie looked doubtfully at the oblong yellow fruit. If only there was a monkey around to tell her how to eat it. She brought it out of the pantry into the little kitchen, took a knife from the rack and cut it in half. She found it was filled with a delightfully scented white fiber. Possessed by a culinary brainstorm, Katie sliced two pieces of bread and squeezed both halves of the banana out onto them, carefully daubing the fruit around to make sure it was evenly distributed. She cut two pieces of cheese and laid them on top, poured a sparing glass of white wine and carried the snack upstairs. Katie changed into a comfortable old nightdress, and sat crosslegged in a giant overstuffed armchair that she pulled before the open French doors of the balcony. And there she had a royal feast, entertained by the flutterings of the pigeons and watching the comings and goings of the finely dressed passersby. It seemed everyone was going to a party somewhere, and she was having a party herself. The shadows grew longer and blacker, spreading across the street until they had diffused the sunset into darkness. The swallows and bats began to dart once again. Katie put aside her plate, having reduced the mongrel sandwich to a small pile of crumbs, and dozed contentedly.

She woke with a start some time later, thinking she had heard a knock on the door downstairs. It had been so real, so distinct; three sharp raps. Perhaps she had dreamed it. Her eyes were wide in the darkened room as she listened. Nothing. She closed her eyes again and tried to return to sleep. Seconds, or minutes later, it came again, the triple knocking.

Katie lifted herself slowly from the chair and winced as it squeaked beneath her. The dark outline of the key Lord Linden had left her was barely visible against the purplewood veneer of the small tier table in the corner. She reached out and touched it in passing, feeling its reassuring metallic coldness; then she crept down the carpeted stairway.

The doorknob was being rattled and turned by an unseen hand.

"Katie," came a sepulchral whisper from the other side of the two-inch oak door. It was a voice she had never heard before, a disembodied, menacing voice that drew out her name as if it would pull her soul from her body. Involuntarily, she backed from the door.

"Open the door, Katie."

She backtracked up the stairs, staring mesmerized at the twisting doorknob. Her mind raced frantically, attempting to attach a face, an identity, to that ghostly whisper. Linden had his own key. Anyone visiting Linden wouldn't know her name. If it were Zack, wouldn't he identify himself outright? Perhaps the voice had no face. The rattling of the doorknob ceased and Katie halted stiffly, poised in uncertainty, one hand clamped tightly on the railing. Seconds slipped into moments and breath returned to her constricted throat.

The French doors were open upstairs! A picture sparked into her mind of a now threatening breeze, gaining entrance to ruffle uninhibited through the exit to the balcony. Katie turned and ran up the stairs, intending to slam the doors. She rushed into Linden's bedroom and faced the starlit balcony.

A black-hooded head was rising over the iron railing; the faceless personification of the disembodied voice. A blade glimmered dully in the moonlight as the figure vaulted awkwardly over the railing and advanced across the room at Katie like a black shadow. In a blind panic, she grabbed the key from the corner table and ran from the room, her pursuer's footfall rustling heavily behind her. She skidded down the steps, and her shaking fingers refused to quiet themselves as she fumbled hysterically with the lock. Before, the door had sheltered her, but now it held her prisoner. Katie twisted her head to see her assailant bearing down on her, the blade held high. At that moment, the lock gave way and she tore outdoors, hearing the knife hissing as it searched for her. Her assailant stumbled over the threshold with an audible thud and she gained a few steps on him. Katie flew down the pavement without looking back.

Five houses down the block, a pair of grooms stood chatting next to an elegantly groomed, long-maned Arabian mare that pulled restlessly against the hitching post. The smoke from the groom's clay pipe curled and eddied in the rectangle of light thrown out from the open door behind them. Katie snatched the reins and threw herself into the saddle of the nervously circling horse just as the owner, dressed in formal riding clothes and carrying a crop, came out to take possession of his waiting animal. Katie was thundering down the street, hair streaming, expertly guiding the horse with her knees, before the groom or the outraged owner could prevent her.

"Horse thief! Stop!" Two grooms and the injured owner chased her as she galloped in the direction she had seen Lord Linden walking. Four blocks, he had said. Her pursuers puffed after her, the horseman waving his crop wildly in the air. Katie longed desperately for protection and there was only one man she knew that could provide it. A brightly lit mansion ahead and to her left, surrounded by waiting coaches, must belong to Lady Brixton, she decided.

It had been a rather uneventful evening for the footman tending Lady Brixton's door that night; one of your run o' the mill stuffy high society gigs, so he was taken completely off guard by the slim nightdress-clad miss who came galloping out of the night on a fine Arabian mare. The young Godiva reined in and fairly flung herself upon him, where he sat in his porter's chair, haughty in his white stockings and powdered wig.

"Is this Lady Brixton's?" asked the girl frantically. "Is Lord Linden within?"

"Yes it is, gel, and yes, he is—but you can't go in there! Hey! Come back! This is highly improper!" But she was gone, brushing past an astonished pair of new arrivals. Katie received a flashing impression of glittering ambiance; there was a sparkling crystal chandelier, bronze candleholders, a glistening marble and gilt porcelain mantel clock, and a rich variety of sterling silver spice boxes, fruit dishes, and coconut cups. A hundred fashionably dressed guests were cut in midsentence and stared open-mouthed at Katie. Lady Brixton, at the head of the reception line, a bastion of blue-blooded, bejewelled respectability, changed the glazed condescension of her facial expression to a mask of frostily horrified astonishment.

It was not an atmosphere that nurtured melodrama, and Katie, standing panicked and wild-eyed before a vast seat of London's most exalted citizens, suddenly felt that it might have been better to have taken her chances with her attacker's glinting knife. Words froze in her throat and she clasped her hands together fearfully.

Standing beside Lady Brixton was a short, rather plain girl in elegant mourning black, whose face also registered a planet-struck expression. There was a third person in the reception line; he was very young and very handsome with peach-blond hair and a friendly pair of pale brown eyes, which had widened with incredulous delight as Katie, *en déshabille,* came spilling into his grandmother's parlor. I'd like to have you for dinner, you luscious creature, he thought, and strolled forward to say quite kindly, "May I help you with something, my dear?"

"Oh, yes, please," whispered Katie apprehensively. "May I talk to Lord Linden?"

Linden, thought the young man. It would be. He turned to see Lord Linden striding through the crowd toward them and watched with frankly envious appreciation as Katie flung herself at Linden and clutched desperately at his tailored lapels.

"Lord Linden," gasped Katie, "a man came into your bedroom. He had a knife! Really! And that man thinks I stole his horse, but I didn't. And I think that I've lost the key to your house because I don't have it in my hand anymore. Is that your grandmother? I think she is very, very angry with me and I don't want to be here at all. I'm so unhappy. Please, please help me."

The tale of how Lord Linden's latest *chère amie* had gate-crashed one of Her Grace Lady Brixton, the Duchess of Hounslow's most select *soirées* was to spread like freed fire through the all-male echelon of London's finest clubs the next morning. And the story lost nothing in the telling, for those gentlemen fortunate enough to have been present at Lady Brixton's could not decide to whom they should award top honors; the dazzling titian-haired nymph who had so enlivened Lady Brixton's otherwise dull party, or Lord Linden, for what General Clappington had admiringly described as "the boy's deuced cool head under fire." Lord Linden had calmly disentangled Katie's fingers from his chocolate brown evening coat, grabbed the lacy tablecloth from a nearby supper table and, to the disgust of the other gentlemen present, wrapped it around Katie's too ravishing figure. Then, with charming aplomb, he had made a graceful bow to his hostess, thanked her for a most pleasant evening, assured her that he was her most obedient servant and made his exit, shoving Katie in front of him with a little more force than might have been strictly necessary.

Chapter Six

Lord Linden, attempting to remove Katie from his grandmother's austere residence, found himself having to run a gauntlet of indignant persons, from the disapproving doorman to the wrathful owner of the Arabian mare, all of whom seemed to feel that Katie should be conveyed, without delay, to the nearest jail and there incarcerated until such time as hell grew icecaps. Katie made a valiant, though muddled attempt to defend herself to these critics, which was cut short by Lord Linden, who told her tersely to shut her mouth if she knew what was good for her and bundled her urgently into the nearest hackney, warning her to wait for him there. It was some mintues later that Linden climbed in the hack, slammed the door behind him and lowered himself to the seat opposite Katie. The carriage shuddered and pulled forward.

"Talk," said Lord Linden, "and it had better be good."

Katie cleared her throat, convinced more than ever that she should have taken her chances with The Knife. "Lord Linden," she began, "I am so . . ."

"Katie. My dear child," said Lord Linden slowly.

"Do *not* tell me you're sorry or I will shake you until your teeth rattle."

Katie plucked at the tablecloth tucked about her knee. "Did that man believe that I wasn't trying to steal his horse, only borrow it?"

"The gentleman didn't appear to appreciate the distinction. However, he's agreed not to press charges. Now, tell me about the man who came into my bedroom with a knife."

Katie described everything; the persistent knock, the masked figure on the balcony and the hoarse whisper behind the door.

Lord Linden frowned. "Are you sure it was 'Katie' you heard? It couldn't have been anything else?"

"I'm sure. Do you think I should have stayed? I'm afraid that the hooded man may have robbed your apartments."

Linden reached over to tweak one of her tumbled curls. "No, child, you did right, though God knows social ruin stares me in the face. On the other hand, the sight of you in that disreputable nightdress gave Andrew's hot young blood a chance to simmer."

Katie groaned and dropped her face into her hands. Then she peeked up through her fingers. "Who is Andrew?"

"The ditchwater blond adolescent in the reception line who was drooling at you. He's my little brother. Eighteen. He's been enlivening *Grand-mère*'s household with his presence for the season. And itching to give a green gown to some lusty wench. I can see you're getting ready to ask me what a green gown is. Figure it out yourself."

"I—I could tell which lady was your grandmother. She looked exactly like a duchess—at least, she looks exactly what I've always thought a duchess would look like."

"A living cliché," murmured Linden wickedly.

"I thought so," said Katie seriously. "There was a young lady with her, wearing black. Is she in mourning?"

"Technically yes, emotionally no. She's my second cousin Suzanne. Her parents married her off at nineteen to some rustic Irish peer who was fool enough to get himself killed riding to hounds before they were married the half year. Suzanne's mourning period is almost up, and *Grandmère* has taken her in hand to ensure that any possible second marriage is not the disaster her first one was."

"But surely your grandmother couldn't blame Suzanne for her husband's hunting accident," said Katie.

"You underestimate my grandmother," he said wryly. "She blames whomever she can get her hands on."

That recalled to Katie's mind her own indiscretion. "She'll blame you for my ruining her party tonight, won't she? You should be very angry with me, you didn't want to have trouble with your grandmother, and she looked madder than a caged cat."

"Yes, she did, didn't she?" said Linden with a reminiscent grin. "The old hatchet. I imagine there'll be some fireworks, but it's a matter of perception as to whether you spoiled the party. The argument could be offered that you made it a success."

"Everyone will talk," said Katie, mortified.

83

"What do we care?" he said, with the nonchalance of someone used to being the center of gossip. "We won't hear 'em. Besides, it was all in a good cause, little Kate, so smile at me. Lovely. Now listen. After tonight, it's obvious that you aren't safe alone and I can't stay with you. No, don't argue with me, Katie. Once is happenstance, twice is coincidence, but three times is a pattern. You're too damned accident prone to be real, so I'm afraid that somehow you've made an enemy. Do you have any idea who . . . ? No, I can see that you don't. This attack tonight wasn't quite in Nasty Ned's style, was it? Still, I think I should pay him a visit tomorrow before we can securely eliminate that possibility. In the meantime, though . . ."

"Do you think I should go back to stay with Zack?" asked Katie, tucking her heavy auburn curls behind her ears.

"Absolutely," said Linden witheringly. "Then we could lay bets on which you'd lose first, your life or your maidenhead."

"Well, I don't see that I have much choice," retorted Katie, stung.

"No, you don't. So you'll have to do what I tell you if you want to save that lovely neck of yours. I'm going to take you to stay with Laurel Steele. Yes, the woman who was at my house when you arrived yesterday. God knows she's a self-indulgent immoral hellcat, but then, so am I, so you're just changing frying pans. And you'll be safe from your friend with the hood."

"No!" cried Kate, appalled. "Why, she hated me on sight. She said I was bizarre! She'll never have me, my lord."

"Yes, she will. She'll do what I tell her. She may not like it, but she'll do it."

"I won't go," said Katie determinedly. "I'd move in with Nasty Ned and lose my maidenhead fifty times first."

"Foolish chit," said Linden, unimpressed. "Losing your maidenhead fifty times is an anatomical impossibility. I don't think the house of one of the most notorious courtesans in London is the best place for you either, Katie, but frankly, I don't know any respectable ladies who would take you in, especially on my introduction. Staying with Laurel could hardly be worse than working at *The Merry Maidenhead*. Console yourself with the thought that your reputation can't get any worse than it is already."

"It may surprise you to know," said Katie crossly, "that I don't find that thought consoling in the least!"

Linden shrugged and reached for a straggling hemp cord near the hack's window. "All right, blue eyes, if that's what you want . . ."

"Wh—what are you going to do?" asked Katie nervously.

"Signal the driver to take us back to my house," said Linden amicably. "You don't want to go to Laurel, I don't want you to go back to Zack, and you are so all fired hot to lose your virtue that . . ."

"But I didn't really mean it!" cried Katie. "I'm sorry I was pettish, and I will go to Laurel, if that's what you want. But . . . Lord Linden, isn't she your mistress?"

"Lord no. Was that what was bothering you?" asked Linden, scrutinizing Katie's face closely. "We're . . . um, well, friends sometimes, when she's got some damned bill that she wants me to pay. But mostly we fight like demons in a dog hole. I make a point of offending Laurel on a bi-weekly basis, so this will be nothing out of the ordinary, believe me."

When the hack arrived at *la* Steele's expensive establishment on the edge of Mayfair, Lord Linden escorted Katie in and handed her into the care of Laurel's astonished French maid, with instructions that Katie be given a meal and a bed. The readiness with which he was obeyed told its own story of Lord Linden's power in this household. And so, by the time Miss Steele came home, Katie had long since been tucked into a luxurious guest bed and fallen into a reassuring dreamworld.

Laurel had not been among those honored by an invitation to Lady Brixton's *soirée*, but certain of the gentlemen who had been there had later joined a rather more free and easy party at a discreet establishment in Pall Mall, at which *la* Steele had chosen to appear. She had listened with great amusement to the tale of how Linden's latest toy doll had made him again the center of scandal and conjecture. A nasty little smile itched at her lips as she breezed into her foyer and tossed her cashmere shawl to her waiting maid.

"*Bonsoir,* Madame," said the maid, smoothing the shawl tenderly over the curve of her arm.

"'Lo, Antoinette. I shall retire right away, so you may have these lights snuffed," said Laurel, starting to mount her staircase.

"*Oui,* Madame," said Antoinette. "Shall I tell Lord Linden that he is to go upstairs?"

"Lord Linden? But surely he isn't here? They

say he left Lady Brixton's earlier, and with his hands quite, quite full. When did he come?"

"One hour ago, perhaps more. His lordship brought with him a *jeune fille* with great blue eyes and red hair. He said I was to put her to a bed, and *maintenant,* she is sleeping in the green bedroom. Madame doesn't approve?" asked Antoinette, seeing a slowly dawning fury on Laurel's face.

"Damnation, no! Madame does not approve! How dare he? Oh, when I get my hands on him . . . where is he?" stormed *la* Steele, no longer finding Lord Linden's conduct so amusing.

Antoinette indicated the library so Laurel stalked purposefully to that room, murder blazing in her eyes. She found Lord Linden comfortably established on a serpentine-top sofa with his shapely legs stretched out before him, boot heels resting on the fragile surface of a fine Jamaican tea-table. Miss Steele ground her teeth.

"Lesley, this is it! I won't have it, do you hear?"

Lord Linden had been engaged in a desultory perusal of a volume of execrable and rather smutty poetry but now he cast it aside to gaze up at his sometime mistress.

"I hear you, the servants hear you, and probably your neighbors down the street can hear you," said Linden, who rarely wasted energy on tact when he was not disposed to do so. "Lord, you keep late hours, Laurel. It's after three o'clock. Must be hell on your complexion."

There were times when Miss Steele could be diverted from the issue at hand by Linden's insults, but this was not one of them.

"Lesley, you're a provoking, promiscuous blackguard," said Laurel wrathfully.

"*Magnifique,* Laurel. You should tread the boards. You've always told me I'm a provoking, promiscuous blackguard. Why have apoplexy about something that's well established?" Lord Linden wore a faint, malicious smile.

"But this is the first time that you've ever dared to bring a . . . oh, Another Interest of yours into my home!" snapped Laurel.

"Jealous?" he asked provocatively.

"No! Lud, I pity the creature. At least I've never had the misfortune to be your financial dependent. Oh, Lesley, how could you bring her here?"

Lord Linden lifted his long legs slowly from the table and smiled disarmingly at Laurel. "My dear, I had no place else to take her."

"Well, Lesley, *my* dear," Laurel's voice dripped honey, "perhaps I could suggest something. Why don't you take her and dump her back into whatever gutter you pulled her from originally?"

Lord Linden unwound his long body from the sofa, crossed to a dainty wine cellarette and poured Laurel a brandy, saying casually that she'd been robbed if she'd paid more than a shilling a bottle for the insipid stuff. Laurel found herself fast approaching hysteria.

"Damn you, Lesley, will you listen to me?" she cried, stamping her foot. "I don't want to drink brandy, I don't want to talk about brandy and I don't want to think about brandy. All I want is for you to go upstairs, wake up your little doxy and get her out of my house!" This last sentence ended on a note bearing an unfortunate resemblance to a scream. Lord Linden handed the brandy to Laurel with a distinctly dangerous glint in his eye. He spoke calmly and deliberately.

"Don't, Laurel. Be mad at me if you like. But don't let it become a tantrum. My temper's never sweetened enough to accommodate them, as well you know."

Laurel hesitated. She knew from painful experience that Linden could only be tried so far before he was apt to forget chivalry. Laurel clearly remembered a time when she had nourished hopes of being enthroned as Linden's primary mistress. She had reproached him for one of his multiple infidelities. Finally, exasperated by his lack of response, she had lost her temper and slapped him, and Linden had retaliated automatically with a blow that had necessitated her retirement from company for some few weeks with a blackened eye. Uneasily she recalled that far from demonstrating the least remorse, Linden had callously expressed the pious hope that she would take the incident as a lesson governing her future dealings with him.

Fretfully, Laurel turned from him and twisted her hands together. "It's too much, Lesley. Truly. You can't expect me to house your light o' love." She turned back to him, trying hard to maintain control of her voice. "Lesley, the chit is too much *cause célèbre* after her appearance at Lady Brixton's. The tale is already common tongue. I'd be a laughingstock if it were known I'd taken her in."

Linden looked bored. "No one will hear about it from me. And if word gets out, you can think of some convincing tale. Besides, she's not my mistress, so you won't be lying. Not that I think that would bother you," he added carelessly.

Laurel gave an unladylike snort. "Not your mistress indeed! After the way the half-naked chit ran into Lady Brixton's parlor, clasping at your shirt and prattling on about your bedroom. I wonder that you've the nerve to hand me such a faradiddle."

"I didn't think you'd believe me, but it's true. I've never laid hands on the chit." The sable eyes sparkled. "Actually, I did lay hands on her, but it came to nothing because she wouldn't have me."

"A likely story," sneered *la* Steele. "Since when are there girls you lay hands on who don't become your lovers?"

"As a matter of fact, my sweet life, there are plenty of them," said Linden nastily, his voice hard with sarcasm. "You see, I only boast of my successes."

"I don't believe you." Laurel was unable to visualize a lady with resolution enough to withstand Lord Linden's charm, which she knew could be devastating.

Linden shrugged and flung himself into a large, winged armchair. "Then why don't we send for a physician so you can have her examined?" he said with an intensely unpleasant flippancy. "Use your mind, Laurel. If she were my skit, why would I bring her here instead of setting her up in a house in Chelsea? She's just a poor frightened baby with pitifully little knowledge of the world. She won't be here long, only until I can find her father—he's disappeared to God knows where."

"Oh, and hasn't your paragon any relations to see her through this crisis?" asked Laurel acidly.

"She's Kendricks's daughter."

"What! The Bad Baron? That wayward, unprincipled ivory turner? And you've brought his daughter into *my* house? My God, Kendricks is a pariah, blacklisted from every club in town. Lesley, I'll be ruined!" Laurel stamped her feet in good earnest.

Lord Linden watched her angry perambulations serenely. He knew her well and could play her like an angler would a hooked carp. The carrot and the stick; he had used enough stick, now it was time for the carrot. He looked up at her. "Come here." She stood still and regarded him hostilely. "Come here. Or do you want me to come to get you?" Misliking the look in his eyes, Miss Steele sullenly crossed to kneel by Lord Linden's chair. She folded her arms, lay them across Linden's knees and rested her chin on her wrists, looking angrily into his velvet eyes. Linden patted her forehead speculatively with one finger.

"Laurel, will you keep her for a few days out of, er, affection for me?"

"No!"

"Will you do it if I buy you something?" he said, trying not to smile and only half succeeding.

Laurel was avaricious to the very soul. She continued to pout, but a coy gleam entered her eyes that Lord Linden knew well. Silly, transparent jade, thought Linden. This is going to cost me.

"It would have to be diamonds at the very least," purred Laurel.

Linden grinned cheerfully. "Devil take it, Laurel. Do you think I'd sit and dicker with you like a damn bourgeois? You can have the crown jewels if you like, but mind, I don't want the chit mistreated."

"Oh, la, mistreated, is it? Why this sudden spate of philanthropy? So unlike you, my sweet rogue." Laurel reached up to run a finger gently over Lord

Linden's lips. She turned her face slightly to one side, letting her own lips graze his tantalizingly, and was pleased with the slow, sensual smile that darkened and tamed his opaque sable eyes.

Linden began, one by one, to remove the pins that restrained Laurel's elegant coiffure. His smile broadened and just for a moment, became heart-stoppingly boyish, though when he spoke, it was with his same cool derisive drawl. "I must be softening in my old age."

"Do you think so?" murmured Laurel. "I don't remember you softening the last time you mistreated me. . . ." And she raised her mouth invitingly.

Chapter Seven

It was an elegant room. The walls were hung in sculptured scarlet brocade ornamented with gilded girandole mirrors. The faded pastels of the seventeenth-century French tapestry which covered the far wall depicted the classical courtship of Zeus and Leda. A mammoth tent bed, however, was undoubtedly the *pièce de résistance* of the bedroom. Miss Steele, now lying among the cool satin sheets, was wont to confide happily that she had spent more money on that bed than on any other single piece of furniture in her townhouse. Indeed, it was a gorgeous object. Flanked with satinwood columns inlaid with green laureling, mounted with bronze capitals and bases, its massive canopy dripped streaming layers of cranberry silk and supported a silver-veined mirror positioned directly over the bed. The mirror itself was festooned with hundreds of nodding ostrich plumes dyed to an overbrilliant gold. Gorgeous.

This splendor was not wasted on Katie, who was silhouetted against the faint morning sunlight filtering into the bedroom through the tasselled velvet curtains. Lord Linden might say that the room resembled something from a sixpenny bawdyhouse, but to Katie, it looked like a queen's chambers.

La Steele, engulfed in multiple layers of an orchid negligee, was glaring at Katie. "When Lesley said he was sending your clothes, I had no idea your trousseau consisted of a few rags in a cloth bag. Is that—garment—the best you have to offer?"

Katie looked defensively at the shapeless expanse of gray that fell in untidy folds around her ankles. "Yes. It looked nicer when it was blue, but I put too much soap in the washtub once. I have another one, but it has an inkstain on the bodice. I've always dressed like this. Papa says 'fine whiskers cannot take the place of brains.' "

"I'm not interested in what you've always done. I'm interested in right now. And I never want to hear you mention your wastrel of a father in my house again! Any man who would thrust his only daughter into a Rookery gin shop ought to be clapped into Bedlam. I detest eccentrics! It's obvious that you're sickeningly beautiful, but I won't, won't have you skipping around my house looking like something from the circus. I've seen better looking coverings on a peck of potatoes. Even those breeches you wore at Linden's were more attractive. Look at you, your hair looks like unsheared lamb's wool and I have not the slightest doubt that you've got dirt beneath your fingernails. Antoinette! Have a tub of hot water fetched immediately!"

Katie might have bloodlines that stretched back to William the Conqueror, but her upbringing had been haphazardly plebian. Sponge baths were the rule in her life, and she had a peasant's conviction that those individuals so imprudent as to immerse themselves into a hip bath might soon expect their demise from an inflammation of the lung. Thus it took the unified and, at times, violent efforts of Laurel and her maid to bathe her. Katie suffered under their vigorously applied ablutions and tingled with frustration and embarrassment as they rubbed her dry with hard towelling.

"Now, observe, 'Toinette," said Laurel, circling about Katie where she stood forlornly in the middle of the room, tiny rivers of water coursing down her back from her wet head. "Observe how the charms of youth are wasted on the young."

Antoinette giggled. Katie fairly shriveled, her arms crossed modestly in front of her pink, blushing body. She gazed longingly at the gray frock crumpled in the corner. Laurel caught the direction of Katie's gaze and snatched the dress from the floor, holding it by thumb and forefinger.

" 'Toinette. Remove this thing and have it burned."

Katie groaned.

"Be silent!" snapped Laurel, and slapped Katie sharply on the cheek. "And I'll smack the other side, too, if you don't begin conducting yourself with a little dignity. Wrap the towel about you and come into my dressing room so we can do something about that pony's mane. And stop that choking; no one ever died from a bath."

The next hour, Laurel and Antoinette spent rectifying the grooming neglects of Katie's short lifetime. They brushed her hair until her scalp felt like a raked hayfield, rubbed her with scented skin creams, attacked her freckles with a concoction that Antoinette rather alarmingly referred to as virgin's milk, and recut, curled, coiled, and confined Katie's hair with topaz ribbon.

"Now," stated Laurel, "the dress. Oh, no, not that one. I've worn it at least twice. Do you think I want it said that I dress the chit in my castoffs because I'm afraid of the competition? Intolerable! Bring the new figured silk—ah, yes, the sea green. Now, raise your arms, girl. Oh, you don't obey me. All right then, how do you like this?"

"Ow!" said Katie, rubbing the spot Miss Steele had just pinched. "I'm sorry I seem disobliging."

"Oh, pray hush, and hold still. If there is anything I detest, it's someone who apologizes for being disobliging. If you were really sorry for it, then you wouldn't do it, would you? Stand straight! She's too slender, 'Toinette, you will have to take a tuck here. Yes, and here. Fine."

Laurel and Antoinette stood back to observe the fruits of their labors. Miss Steele, it appeared, did not find the fruit at all to her taste.

"I knew it," fumed Laurel, "the wench is stunning! Ah, Lesley, if you only knew how your bill is mounting. Before I might have settled for a diamond or two, but now, I'll have no less than a tiara and three pairs of earbobs."

"Poor Madame," said Antoinette. "But perhaps it is not so bad. That little nose, faugh! It is too short for the classic. And the freckles, mon Dieu, they are everywhere!"

"What of it?" Laurel waved her hand in angry dismissal of these handicaps. "Men don't want classical perfection. They want, oh, I don't know what the stupid creatures want but it's obvious that this chit has it. In abundance. Well, at least I shall be spared the mortification of having to introduce her into company; Lesley was adamant that he didn't want her to meet anyone here. Oh, but Antoinette, will the servants tittle-tattle? If this should get out, people will say that I'm aiding Lesley in the corruption of a daughter of a peer, or some such nonsense."

"No, no, Madame," reassured Antoinette. "Leave me to deal with the servants. Mademoiselle will be your little cousin from the country, *n'est-ce pas?* And she is not to be introduced into company because . . . because . . ."

"Because she is too damn beautiful and she shines me down," snapped *la* Steele, furiously.

"Now, Madame, you fret yourself without cause, *enfin*. We will say that she doesn't go among strangers because there has been a bereavement in her *famille, oui?* And in a few days, m'lord will take her away so you must not worry yourself. Perhaps Madame would like to return to bed *maintenant?*"

"Indeed I should. For one day I have already borne," said Laurel as she swept back to her fabulous tent bed, "enough!"

Katie watched as Antoinette tucked the sheets about her mistress, who rolled onto her side and nestled deeper into the pillows. "There," murmured Laurel comfortably. "Oh, and don't forget to feed the child sometime today, 'Toinette, or we will have Lesley saying I am mistreating her. *Au revoir*." Laurel closed her eyes and Katie followed the beckoning Antoinette from the room.

The next hours were long ones for Katie. A dainty luncheon was brought to her room on a silver tray with cut crystal plates, but Katie was too afraid of breaking a plate or spilling lemonade on the expensive fabric of her gown to enjoy it. Katie spent some time staring blindly out the window, worrying about her father, wondering about the man who had tried to attack her last night, and having wistful daydreams about her onyx-haired protector. Lord Linden, England's favorite son and *enfant terrible*, who had already ensnared so many feminine hearts, could add another pelt to his trappings. Katie put her hand to her cheek where his lips had been, then to the curls that he had ruffled, so careless of his effect on her. She wondered what his eyes saw when they looked at her. Probably a shabby, not-very-smart nuisance, inarticulate, undereducated, and adoring. Katie cringed inwardly and felt depressed. She walked over to stand square in front of her bedroom's full-length mirror and regarded herself curiously. It was as though she were looking at a painting of someone else—a tall, showy beauty to whom the artist had capriciously added freckles, red hair and then, as a final joke, her tiny, tilted nose. Whatever Miss Steele might say, she couldn't view these features as anything but an unfortunate disfigurement. And her body, whew! In the past, her clothes had been concerned with covering her body. This gown seemed to have been designed to reveal it. She was not used to seeing the graceful curves of her body so exposed, and to her, there was something almost obscene in their sudden disclosure. She decided that she looked like what Zack had wanted her to become, and this accorded so ill with her self-image that she began to feel like the sparrow who tied a daisy to her tail and tried to impersonate a peacock.

These unhappy thoughts were interrupted by Antoinette, who came to announce that Lord Linden was below and requested the pleasure of a few words with Mademoiselle. Would Mademoiselle care to accompany her downstairs? The last thing Katie wanted was to have Lord Linden see her in a get-up that she considered patently dedecorous, so she followed Antoinette reluctantly, stopping first to grab an eiderdown comforter from her bed and wrap it tightly about her shoulders. Antoinette shook her head and muttered something under her breath but forbore to do more than admonish Katie not to disarrange her coiffure.

Lord Linden was waiting in Laurel's small, walled garden, leaning back against a columnar pedestal supporting an antique stone urn. Beside the rather angular symmetry of the formal garden, he appeared somehow even more raffish than usual. He turned at the sound of Katie's footsteps and the hushed whiff of the comforter dragging the ground. Slowly, Lord Linden absorbed the splendid, artless arrangement of her soft hair, the tightly clutched covering, and the woebegone distress on her exquisite features.

"Poor Katie. Did they misuse you then, child?" asked Linden, his eyes so filled with sympathetic understanding that Katie's heart lurched sideways. She nodded, biting her lip.

"How unhappy you look. But it had to be, my infant. It's a censorious world, and wearing the clothing of the opposite sex is rather frowned upon." He patted her cheek gently. "Now, sweetheart, this is after all a Christian nation so there is no need for you to affect purdah just because you've readopted woman's clothing. You'll boil in that comforter, darling, so let me take it away and set it inside while we talk."

"To own the truth, my lord, I don't like to be without it, because you see, underneath . . ."

"I don't see underneath, my little fawn, but I should very much like to. Are you shy with me, child?"

"No. Well, perhaps. Laurel burned my own dresses. She said they looked like rags; then she made me wear one of hers and it makes me look hatefully . . . lumpy. And it shows most of my chest," said Katie, her brow knit. "Lord Linden, would you like it if someone made you wear a dress like that?"

Linden couldn't help the appreciative smile that sparkled in his eyes. "It would be disconcerting, I'll admit. But then, my dainty Kate," he said lightly, "I'm not a woman." He took one of Katie's pretty hands and raised it carefully to his lips. "And you are."

Katie gazed innocently into his eyes. "But I don't feel like a woman."

It would have been very much to Lord Linden's taste to assist Katie toward her realization of that goal, so it was not without a severe struggle with himself that he released Katie's hand and said, with studied nonchalance, "Never fear, you'll get in the way of it soon. Hand me that thing, that's a good girl. Now see, was that so . . . my God!" The Bad Baron's daughter had been a pretty boy, but the stylish gown transformed her into a marvel of nature. Laurel had certainly been correct in her observation that Katie had whatever it was that men liked. Lord Linden controlled himself with difficulty. Dragging his sight away from Katie, he went through the opened veranda doors, dropped the comforter over the arm of a settee, and tossed off a quick glass of cognac before returning to his too tempting protegée.

Taking her bare arm, Linden led Katie down the narrow walk of crushed white stone that terminated in a trimly painted arbor. Pink climbing roses had been trained up the Chinese lattice sides and the sunlight flickered through to cast dappled shadows on Katie's fine-boned cheeks as she sat on the cool marble bench beneath. A small box elder tenanted one corner of the garden and among its glossy, dark green leaves, Katie saw a goldfinch entertaining the garden with its golden song. Lord Linden joined her on the bench.

"Laurel made me take a bath this morning," said Katie, to break the silence. "I'm afraid that I wasn't very good."

"Dear me," said Linden, smiling with lazy good humor. "I hope you struggled like an unbroken filly."

"I did. But Laurel didn't like that much. She said that I looked like something from the circus and that you'll have to buy her a tiara. Oh, and Antoinette's told Laurel's servants that I am Laurel's cousin from the country. Do you think they'll believe that?"

"Not for a minute, but don't let that trouble you; they'll pretend to. Do you like Laurel?"

"Not really," said Katie honestly. "She pinches. Hits, too!" she added, remembering her slapped cheek.

"Hit her back," he recommended without hesitation. "That's what I did."

Katie regarded Linden with awe. "Did it work?"

"She's never raised a finger to me since." Linden grinned engagingly. "You see what a black-hearted wretch I am, *petite*. And speaking of wretches, I visited our friend from the cock pit this morning to see if he was the gentleman trying to renew his acquaintance with you last night."

"Nasty Ned? Oh, you went into the Rookery? Do you think it was him?"

Linden observed his companion pensively. How much to tell her? Nasty Ned had been deferential, cowed by Linden's presence, and seemingly eager to please but not ultimately forthcoming with much information. As Linden had begun to suspect, Ned's attacks on Katie had not been accidents of an unfriendly fate. Ned had been retained to seek Katie out at *The Merry Maidenhead* and cause a fracas that should end with Katie's closing her eyes for the last time. But as for trying to break into his lordship's house, that was something he'd never do, he wasn't no bloody cracksman, beggin' his lordship's pardon, he hadn't no quarrel with no one no more, being easy to get along with. Who had paid him? "A cove," said Ned. "Jest a bloke. Oi niver seed 'im before, nor since either, for that matter."

The bluish-gray back of a nuthatch flashed in the sun as it hopped through a golden bed of dwarf chrysanthemums. Linden studied the high, fragile cheekbones of the lovely girl beside him and decided to keep the full truth from her. The load on her young shoulders was already heavy enough.

"No, it wasn't him."

"I've thought about it this morning and I haven't even a grain of insight into it," said Katie seriously. "I'm a deal of trouble to you. You can't like that."

"I don't," he said frankly. "All the same, I'll feel

guilty as hell if I don't make a push to protect you. Your defenses are about as developed as those of a newborn chick."

The blue eyes widened in protest. "Oh, no, my lord. You've gotten a bad impression because I've been in this trouble with Nasty Ned. In general I can take care of myself very well. I've always taken care of myself. I think it's only that I'm country bred and not used to the way of things in London yet. I daresay I'll find my feet soon, don't you?"

"No," said Linden bluntly. "I think that if I put you back on the streets you wouldn't last the hour. Who ever told you that you were qualified to take care of yourself?"

"Papa."

"I might have known," said Linden, with some bitterness. "Papa. I'd like to put that man on a slow boat to Babylon. If I ever find him."

Chapter Eight

Of all the hazards surrounding the sojourn of a virtuous young lady at the establishment of an infamous Cyprian, probably the least expected would be boredom. Yet it was boredom that had driven Katie into Laurel's library by the evening of her third day there.

Of Laurel, she had seen little. Her hostess went out constantly: to parties, to the opera, to ride in the park. Sometimes visitors came. Peeking between the draperies, Katie could see coaches arriving, filled with dazzlingly gowned ladies escorted by well-tailored gentlemen. Antoinette would whisk Katie into her bedroom, and the ground floor of Laurel's townhouse would be filled with malicious chatter and laughter, then the visitors would leave to flutter away like a flock of aggressive, restless starlings, leaving the house quiet except for the barely heard rattle of crockery from the kitchens.

Katie began to feel the confines of the city. In the country, she had walked and dreamed for hours, following tracks that travelled from shallow wooded valleys to meadow hilltops, carpeted in lacy veins of nodding oxlip and butterfly orchids.

Or there had been chores to do at the cottage. They had owned horses when her father's luck was good. These had to be curried and fed and their stalls cleaned. She had done the housework, too, and the cooking, with an untrained, incompetent enthusiasm, like a child playing house. In the heat of the afternoon, Katie would cover her feet to the ankles in a swift stream and then lie under a dripping willow and read novelettes from the circulating library. It had been an isolated life, at times acutely lonely, but there had been occupation. And without occupation the hours seemed to spin out dizzily before her, to be filled with worry and longing.

Katie liked Laurel's library; it was decorated in a style *la* Steele fondly called Egyptian and Lord Linden unfondly called garbage. There was a marble table with crocodile feet, gilt sphinx-shaped stools and several large statues of scantily clad women playing harps. Katie had pulled a slender, leather-bound volume from the shelves; the gold lettering on the binding read, tantalizingly, "The delightful Aspect of the Male Form." Katie was about to open to the title page when Laurel passed by the library, glanced in at Katie, and gasped.

"Oh, no you don't, Little Miss Scandal Broth!" Laurel took the book abruptly from Katie and slid it back in place. "That's no book for a baron's daughter, no matter how bad he might be."

"Is it improper?" asked Katie.

"Grossly!"

"Oh." Katie sank to a sphinx stool and ran her fingers over the lion's mane armrest. "Do you have anything I could read that's not improper?"

Laurel gave a thrill of laughter. "What? Cookery books? Bedtime tales? Gardening hints? Of course not. Can't you sew a sampler or something?"

"Antoinette gave me a pillowcase to embroider, but I can't sew without pricking my finger, so I'm afraid it got sadly bloodstained. Antoinette said only a vampire would be willing to sleep on it."

"A disgusting anecdote!" said Laurel, eyeing Katie with disfavor. "And here's Lesley gone about his merry way, leaving me to find some way to entertain you. I suppose we shall have to think of something, or it's bird lime to biscuits you'll fall into some mischief. Is there anything that you like to do that wouldn't be any trouble to me?"

Katie gazed at the ceiling and answered shyly. "Well . . . I had been thinking that if you had any horses, perhaps I could help exercise them? I'd like to do something active . . ."

"I don't have any horses," said Laurel irascibly. "I detest the creatures—nasty, sweaty brutes. I rent my coach from a livery. Could you not have picked something . . . Oh . . . wait a minute." Her face brightened. "We shall ask Linden to take you riding. Why not? 'Tis a neat way of reminding him of his responsibility for you without nagging him, eh? Oh, but it might not serve after all. Linden's horses are quite as ill-natured as he. He might not have a mount suitable for you."

"I could ride them," said Katie eagerly. "Papa's horses were all of them only half broken. But do you think he'll take me?"

"We shall see. What's the harm? If you could go early enough in the morning, you need not even worry about creating tittle-tattle for the gossip mills."

Laurel sat down at a desk ornamented with pharaoh's heads and composed a tactful note to Linden. She sent it to his rooms by footman and received a reply within the hour.

> Laurel,
> Of course the chit has ennui. Your best entertainments come with your mouth shut and your clothes off. Have her dressed to ride at six A.M. tomorrow. I won't wait for her if she's late. Yours, etc. L.

"Linden, you're a horrid distempered creature!" Laurel crumpled the note and thrust it aside.

"He said no, then," said Katie, disappointed.

"He said yes," said Laurel.

The next morning Katie was ready fifteen minutes before Linden arrived. She had been watching for him from an upstairs window and was halfway down the stairs before the butler had admitted him into the foyer.

"Lord Linden! How happy I am to see you! How fine you look!" cried Katie, who had few artifices at her command. Indeed, she needed none. The baron's daughter was the picture of glowing beauty. Laurel had regretfully allowed Katie to wear her new riding habit of royal blue velvet, which winked and gleamed with every movement. A matching, modesty-crowned hat was arranged becomingly over her rich, dancing curls and tied with a soft pink silk scarf that complimented Katie's camellia complexion. Linden resisted an unsettling impulse to catch her in his arms. Instead he raised her gloved hand quickly to his lips and said coolly, "I'm pleased to see you, brat, but I won't have my nags stand for anyone, so come along if you wish to sit a horse today."

Lord Linden's nags were among the finest blood stock in London and as renowned for their free action and proud carriage as their nasty tempers. It was a standing joke in the mews that the surest path to suicide would be to try to steal one of Linden's horses. Linden was riding his half-Arabian bay stallion, Ciaffa, who had been less affectionately but more appropriately nicknamed Death Merchant by his attendant stableboy. For Katie, Linden brought a light gray gelding with a bright, floating trot and an alarming tendency to deliver painful bites to anyone foolish enough to venture near his head. Linden tossed Katie into the saddle and warned her sternly that the gelding was fresh yet and she'd better pay attention if she didn't want to adorn the pavement. As they rode through the awakening streets to Hyde Park, Linden saw that his advice was quite unnecessary. Katie rode as though the horse were part of her.

They passed through the stone posts at the park's entrance and turned down a well-packed bridle path passing beneath the timbered intimacy of a row of hybrid limes. Looking across the park's rolling hills and spouting fountains, one could see that there were few souls who enjoyed the park at this unfashionable hour: one stout nanny with rambunctious boys in tow, a pair of sleek red squirrels bounding through the lawn's clipped grasses and, as Katie and Lord Linden passed the sunken rose garden, an elderly gardener looked up from his pruning to raise his hand in comradely salute.

Katie's lips parted in a happy smile. "I swear, my lord, 'tis a gem of a day, isn't it? Laurel should, after all, have gotten up this morning even though she doesn't like to arise betimes."

"Lord, child, never say you tried to get Laurel out of bed this morning?" asked Linden, amused.

"Well, I did, but she threw a pillow at me so I knew it was no use."

"How, er, acute of you. Does she still pinch?"

"No. But then, I haven't seen her very much—" Katie stopped and squinted across the green into the pale morning sunlight. "Look, Lord Linden. That rider coming toward us. I think that I've . . . oh, he's the young man I saw at your grandmother's house, the one you said was your brother. But . . . is he coming to talk with us? What do you think he wants?"

"I'd tell you," said Linden grimly, "but, God, would you blush."

As Linden's brother rode closer, Katie could see the resemblance to Linden that she had been too distracted to notice in the few minutes she had been in Lady Brixton's parlor. The boy's brown eyes were lighter than Linden's, though, and his hair blond.

"I don't remember inviting you. What'd you do, bribe Roger?" asked Linden when his brother was close enough to hear.

"Not him," answered the boy. "One of your stableboys. I wanted to meet the girl who leveled Grandmother at her own *soirée*. You've been smart to avoid Brixton House, Lesley. Introduce me."

"No," said Linden. "Get lost."

His brother embraced Katie in a warm, enchanting smile. "You want to meet me, don't you, sweetheart? God, what a love you are. Where did Lesley find you?"

"In a gin shop," said Katie.

"Did he? What a funny place to find an angel. I'm Andrew, and don't believe anything Lesley says about me, I'm a benign soul." He extended his hand to Katie and she responded shyly, but instead of shaking her hand, he peeled back her glove and kissed her wrist lightly.

"All this lechery," said Linden drily, "and he hasn't even breakfasted yet. Drew, watch out before Katie's gelding takes a chunk out of your animal's flank."

"Katie?" asked Andrew, backing his mount several paces. "Is that your name? I'm glad to know. In my mind I've been calling you 'the girl with the red hair.'"

Linden sighed. "Since you're so damned persistent, Drew, I suppose I'll have to let you ride along. But, for God's sake, cool your oven or I'll dump you into the next fountain."

Andrew raised his eyebrows. "Oh, morality and the virtues above all things! But tell me, Lesley, when did you take your vows?"

"Four—no, three days ago," said Linden, drawing his horse alongside Andrew, "and if you want to befriend Katie, then you'll have to take them, too."

"What!" said Andrew, turning quickly to Katie. "Are you virtuous, then? How disappointing. I'll try to keep my hands off you though, if that's what you'd like. But why are you fraternizing with Lesley, sweetheart? *That's* playing with fire with a vengeance."

Katie looked at him doubtfully. "It's a long story. I don't think you'd like . . ."

"I like long stories, Peaches," he said, gazing at Katie's lips. "Tell me about the gin shop."

Katie hesitated, looking at Lord Linden.

"Go ahead, child," said Linden. "Never pass up a sympathetic audience. Tell Andrew about your wicked friend Zack."

Since Andrew was indeed a sympathetic, not to say doting, audience, Katie soon found herself detailing far more of her life's story than she ordinarily would have. Within three-quarters of an hour, the two had become fast friends. Katie decided that Drew was a delightful companion when one grew used to the friendly familiarity of his manners and his rather disconcerting tendency to let his gaze drop from her face to wander over her graceful curves.

At length, Drew straightened in his saddle and repositioned his hat thoughtfully. "Lord, you have had the adventures, haven't you? I swear, it beats anything I've seen in the theater. And you beat anything I've seen in the theater, too. No need to be cast into the blush, Peaches," he grinned. "That was a compliment. Girls are supposed to like them, you know. How does it suit you, living with the toast of the male half of the *monde?*"

"Very comfortable," returned Katie, "but I wish there was more to occupy myself with. Laurel says I mustn't read any of her books. And I have no accomplishments like playing the piano or sewing, so—sometimes I play cards with Antoinette, she's Laurel's lady's maid, and sometimes I help her take care of Laurel's bedroom. Laurel won't let the housemaids clean in there because she says they're forever breaking her perfume bottles and the smell lingers in the carpeting for weeks." Katie turned to Linden, who had been a silent but appreciative audience to Katie's discourse with Andrew. "Do you know what Laurel has hanging over her bed?" she asked innocently.

Linden's face was carefully expressionless. "The mirror? I might have known you'd notice that."

"One can't help noticing it," said Katie. They were pacing beneath a spreading oak and Katie reached up one graceful hand to catch the low-hanging leaves. "Antoinette says that Laurel had it put there so she could apply her rice powder without getting up from the bed in the mornings but it is such an awkward angle for that and she could better use a hand mirror, couldn't she? I think it's a very odd location for a mirror."

"I daresay you do, child," said Linden, with a composed countenance, "but I'd advise you to put the whole question out of your mind. Laurel's always had more hair than wit. God knows there's no more bizarre collection of junk than she's got stuffed into her house."

Katie was aghast at this criticism. "Oh, no, my lord. Surely not! Antoinette says that Laurel's boudoir is filled with the finer things in life."

"Don't, for God's sake, believe everything Antoinette tells you. The only finer things in life in that boudoir," retorted Linden acidly, "are provided by Laurel. Between that gaudy tent bed and those damned gilt sphinx settees, the place looks like a low life kip house."

Katie's brow puckered. "Well, but don't you think that picture on her bedroom wall of that plump lady and the swan is very clever? Antoinette says that it's a Greek god named Zeus and the plump lady is called Leda. Zeus," continued Katie knowledgeably, "became a swan so that he could sneak in to make love to Leda, which seems very odd because I didn't know that swans could, with people. And, it seems to me to be a shabby way for a god to conduct himself. You know, I am fast coming to think the ancient Greeks were a very strange sort of people."

Linden met Katie's unwavering gaze. "Katie, have a care. If Drew becomes any more titillated, he'll probably fall from his saddle. And swans don't, with people. It's only an allegory."

"What's that?" asked Katie.

Linden regarded her with amused exasperation. "A symbolic representation. Lord, sweetheart, don't you know anything?"

"Not very much," she admitted. "Oh, I do know the text of the Declaration of Independence of the United States of America. Winnie, Zack's lady-friend, taught it to me when they came to stay with me in Essex one summer while Papa was off at the races. I said it for Papa once and he cried all the way through and vowed he'd go to America one day. Of course, he was in his cups at the time. Would you like me to recite it for you?"

"No, thank you," said Linden hastily. "It seems that everything your family and their associates ever taught you was either treasonous or immoral. Except your seat on a horse. You ride like Diana, little one." Katie looked puzzled, so he added, "Diana was a goddess who rode very well."

Katie went pink from pleasure at his compliment and smiled at Linden as though he had handed her the Holy Grail. "Thank you so much, my lord! No one has ever compared me to a goddess before.

How generous you are!" The blue eyes shone adoringly into Linden's. Poor infant, Linden thought, touched in spite of himself. Someone wants to kill you and no one gives a damn. Except perhaps Andrew, who is only a boy, and myself, who is within an inch of debauching you. It seemed incredible that such a lovable vital jewel as Katie could be so fatally unprotected. It was as though a serious oversight had been made in heaven on the eve they were assigning guardian angels. Linden's horse was beside Katie's and without really being aware of what he was doing, Linden reached to cradle Katie's fragile cheek in his palm.

"You burden me, child, with your trust," he said lazily. "You are far, far too lovely to be left so unshielded."

"Lovely?" whispered Katie, in a trance. "Antoinette says all the virgin's milk in the world won't get rid of my freckles. And they're all over me!" I'd like to kiss every one of them, thought Linden. "She says my nose is too little, too," continued Katie, determined to confess her weak points.

"Your nose is adorable, darling," said Linden. He dropped his hand and turned to his younger brother. "My dear Drew, there's really no need to gaze at me with that irritating expression of vacuous bewilderment." Linden touched Ciaffa's flank lightly with his heel. "Well, children, this stretch is deserted so I think it would be suitable for us to canter. Would you like that?"

Chapter Nine

Katie returned to Laurel's with her cheeks flushed from the exercise and attention. It was the last of both she would receive for several days. Linden did not come again, and Laurel was mostly out. As before, Katie had nowhere to direct her thoughts other than toward her own problems, which seemed curiously unsolvable. A worrisome idea occurred to Katie: that her father might contact Zack and Zack might fail to relay the message to her. After all, Zack didn't know where she was now and it was hardly likely that he would send her word through Lord Linden, considering the deception he'd practiced on him. This idea took hold of Katie's mind and she began to brood on all kinds of fanciful contingencies. She imagined that her father had given Zack a ticket for her to travel to meet him in America; or perhaps a message that he had fled to the Continent and she was to come to him at a certain fashionable address in Paris. She became so agitated by these thoughts that she was moved to interrupt Laurel during her preparations for a ball to ask her if she would invite Linden to come so Katie could discuss these fears with him.

"Is this some kind of a jest?" demanded *la* Steele,

leaning into the mirror to spread the rouge artistically over her wide cheekbones. "If you have forgotten the perverse reply I received the last time I sent Linden a message on your behalf, I have not! And if you think I'll do it again," she snapped, "you're out of your mind. Linden will come in his own good time."

Katie's strategy in life had heretofore been defensive; her rearing had taught her to float astride the wave of events rather than shape them herself, but she was beginning to realize the pitfalls of allowing her life to drift, rudderless. She was imposing on Laurel, who owed her nothing, and on Linden, to whom she herself owed much. She would never be able to repay either of them now or in any foreseeable future, and this thought gnawed uneasily at the corners of her consciousness. If only she could find her father.

It was on the fourth morning after the day she had ridden with Linden and met Andrew that Katie resolved to visit Zack at *The Merry Maidenhead.* Even if Zack was ignorant of her father's whereabouts, she could inform him of her new domicile, so he could contact her if the need arose. Any bitterness she felt toward Zack for his infamous plans for her was overshadowed, though not erased, by her need to locate her father. Katie had no confidence that the Bow Street Runners would find him. Zack was right; if her father was so much in debt, it was unlikely that he would let himself be found.

Katie donned a willow green walking dress, a dashing chip straw bonnet and a pair of kid boots, and left a note saying that no one was to worry, but she was off to *The Merry Maidenhead* to talk to Zack. Laurel was still abed and the servants were occupied with their morning tasks, so there was no one to see her as she slipped out the fan-lit doorway into the street. She could have taken a hack, as she had the fifty pounds that Zack had given her on the night he had taken her to Linden's, but she had a strong repugnance toward the idea of spending it, as she had a very firm suspicion as to its source. She had never quite nerved herself enough to ask Linden if he had indeed paid Zack fifty pounds for her, though she decided rue-fully that it was only too likely.

A tight, puffy fog groped through the streets, disguising the thoroughfares and lanes that were not very familiar to her in clear weather, so Katie was forced to stop often to squint at street signs and strain to make out landmarks that rose hollow and featureless from the fog. It was far to the Maidenhead, but not outrageously so to someone who was used to tramping mile after mile through the country—the gray billows kept Katie feeling hidden and protected until at last she arrived, damp but exhilarated, at *The Merry Maidenhead*.

The door to the Maidenhead was closed. Katie looked through the window, past the film of greasy dust and the streaking water droplets, to see Zack sitting inside, his elbows leaning on a rickety oak table. He was engaged in a lethargic conversation with Winnie and a husky young man with untidy, shortish hair and wire-rimmed glasses. Katie pushed open the door and went in.

Zack's chair gave a sharp, rending squeak as it was pushed back hurriedly and then he was stand-

117

ing before Katie, taking her tiny chin into his hands and studying her face intently. "Katie?" he asked, his voice quiet.

Katie took a quick back step and pushed his hands away. "Yes, it's me, you arch-traitor! I may as well tell you that I've come on a matter that's strictly business and from now on you can call me Miss Kendricks and desist from any kind of touching."

"Ho ho!" said Zack, with a credible expression of outraged integrity. "Is that so, Miss Kendricks?" Zack laid heavy emphasis on the Miss. "You come here, spruced up like St. Jacob's goose and looking for all the world like you've landed in clover and then get mad at me for arranging it for you! Little ingrate! I suppose it would have suited your maidenly imagination better if I'd left you to Nasty Ned—you could have died martyred and pure and then maybe in three hundred years the church would have made a saint of you. You can't humbug me into thinking you'd have liked that arrangement better than where you are now, Mousemeat, no matter how many saucy names you call me!"

"You," said Katie, simply and with a great deal of dignity, "don't understand me."

Zack rolled his eyes and tipped his head to the left. "That, at least, is God's own truth! What did you come here for?"

"I wanted to see if you'd heard anything from Papa," said Katie.

"Well, I ain't," he replied. "But since you've come, you might as well sit and take a glass of stingo with us. Winnie here's been worried about you. Oh, this," Zack gestured toward the young man with the wire-rimmed glasses, "is Patrick—Pat's a damned radical crony of Winnie's—they've been kidnapping together."

"Kidnapping?" gasped Katie, her mind fastening on the word. She sank into a low bench that Zack had tugged forward for her. "I'm glad to see you, Winnie, but oh, never say you've kidnapped somebody?"

"Well, oi 'ave," confirmed Winnie stoutly. "Or, leastwise me radical cell 'as. We've taken one o' 'is majesty's admirals as a political 'ostage 'n we don't mean ta give 'im up 'til our demands is met!"

Katie took a modest gulp of the strong beer Zack had slid onto the table before her. "What kinds of demands are they?" asked Katie, torn between sympathy for the unfortunate victim and an abounding curiosity.

Winnie shrugged. "Usual sorts o' demands. Loike Westminster Abbey oughta be split into apartments fer war widows."

"Oh," said Katie, her face awash with doubt. "That sounds like a good thing, though I should think the widows would find it a trifle drafty. Has the government responded to your demands yet?"

"Na, they's been ignorin' 'em," admitted Patrick, entering the conversation. "But they's bound ta cave in. Oi means, an admiral ain't nobody."

Katie had to admit this was true but could not forbear to ask anxiously what they intended to do with the admiral if the government remained adamant.

"Don't be bird-witted, Kate," recommended Winnie, "we'll let th' fellow go, o' course. We can't spend th' rest o' our lives guarding some rascally admiral. Couldn't afford it neither. The fellow drinks loike a German 'n it's costing us a fortune ta keep 'im in grog."

"He must be a queer sort of admiral," said Katie, disconcerted. "What's his name?"

"Um . . ." said Winnie, "oi forgets. Calls 'im 'The Admiral' mostly. 'E's Admiral . . . Entail . . . Entangle . . . no, I mean Enfield. Admiral Enfield."

Zack shook his head derisively. "War widows, indeed! Bugger 'em! The two of you will be lucky if you don't end up adorning Tyburn Tree. You're an odd pair of dogs." He turned to Katie and looked her over closely, as if performing mental calculations as to the cost of her costume. "Linden's got you decked out fine as a heifer on fair day. I'll say one thing. The man ain't pinchfisted."

"He's not," said Katie, regarding Zack with dislike. "But it's not he that has the dressing of me." She leaned forward with the air of one who was about to make a momentous announcement, the trace of a small expectant smile beginning on her lips. "You're the one who's been dished, Zack. Because Linden didn't seduce me, I haven't become his mistress, and these aren't his clothes. I'm living with a friend of his, Miss Laurel Steele, and these are her clothes."

Zack stared at her for a moment, speechless. Then the blank look left his eyes and one side of his lip curved into a wry smile. "Dished, ditched and dinged! Laurel Steele? Queen of the Fashionable Impures? Are you going to tell me the tale or should I let my imagination fill in the details?"

She hastily sketched a picture of what had happened since Zack had left her on Linden's doorstep.

Zack looked skeptical. "Well, I'll never be moved from the opinion that you've made a rare muddle of a golden opportunity. And why Linden is helping you now is more than I can figure out; there's nothing in it for him." A light dawned in his eyes. "I suppose he's decided to take his time with you. A slow seduction is more amusing for him than a quick rape."

Katie flushed and jumped to her feet, upsetting the tarnished tankard she had been resting on her knees. A golden shower of frothy beer spread in all directions. "Zack, are you incapable of understanding that someone might do something out of kind motives?" she asked angrily. "Lord Linden isn't like that. He's . . ."

"They're all like that," interrupted Zack. "Don't deceive yourself, darling. You don't like what I'm saying, but I'm being honest with you."

"Like you were being honest with me when you took me to Linden's house and said he was a friend of yours? And said I would be safe there?" exclaimed Katie wrathfully. "Zack, I've trusted you since I was a baby and you turn around and sell me like a slave at auction! I can't hate you for it because I understand you; I'll probably even be able to forgive you someday. But not," said Katie, jerking open the door, "for a while."

She hunched against the penetrating damp, her running footsteps smacking the pavement. *The Merry Maidenhead* disappeared into the fog, but she heard Zack calling behind her. It was the closest she had come in her life to having a fight with someone, and she was shaken. Her shoulders ached and her stomach felt cold. Irregular shapes of passersby materialized and disappeared in the fog: a pieman, a group led by a link-boy carrying a flambeau. She hurried on and had nearly reached a cross avenue when a gruff voice hailed her.

"'Ey, where ya goin' in sech a 'urry, missie?"

Katie hoped the voice was not directed at her and quickened her step.

"Say, wot's th' matter wi' ya? 'Avent ya got time fer a poor sailor 'ome from servin' 'is country?"

Katie turned. Bearing down on her with some speed was a jolly old tar dressed in a seacape and pegging agilely along on one good leg and one wooden. Sailors and admirals, thought Katie, feeling that her day had been cruelly overset by the navy.

"Can I help you with something?" she asked, trying to recall her best gin shop form when dealing with querulous customers.

"Can she 'elp me wi' somethin'," growled the tar, not unfriendly. "Methinks when she sees th' color o' me money, mebbe she can 'elp me wi' somethin'." He walked up beside Katie, flashing a fistful of pound notes. "Mebbe she'll 'elp a lonely old sailor ta find a little 'appiness in this cold world, I says. 'Ow about duckin' into one o' these establishments along in 'ere, lassie? Mebbe we both be thirsty fer some Blue Ruin . . . or somethin' else." He wiggled his eyebrows expressively.

Katie groaned inwardly. "Oh, dear, I'm afraid not, sir. You see I have to get home now or they'll be getting worried."

"Well, them at 'ome will be right 'appy when ya bring 'ome one o' these, won't they?" snickered the sailor, trying to push a pound note into Katie's palm. "'Ey, come on 'n take it now, wench. Ya'll be earnin' it from me soon, won't ya?" The man chuckled, made a suggestive gesture with his fingers, and clutched Katie tightly by the arm.

"No! Sir, you quite mistake things, I assure you. I don't want your money and there is no one who would be the least happy if I brought it home," said Katie, trying resolutely to disengage her arm from his clinging fingers.

"Well, ain't we th' fine talkin' little chippy!" gasped the sailor indignantly, his good nature vanishing. "Wot's yer problem, eh? Not enough money fer ya? Ya can name yer price then."

Katie was becoming alarmed by the strength in the sailor's grip. "F-fifty pounds," she stuttered, hoping fervently that she had named a figure beyond the sailor's resources.

Traffic on the through street moved carefully in the fog; the approach of a vehicle could be heard before seen and now the smart trot of a high-stepping thoroughbred heralded the arrival of a sleek high-perch phaeton. Katie's eyes dilated in amazement as she saw the rakish driver, who was accompanied by a slender youth with peach-blond hair and lively pale brown eyes who clung easily to the stepping-board behind. The phaeton pulled to a sharp halt beside Katie and her would-be cavalier. Its driver set his bicorne to the back of his head, pushed his fog-dampened ebony hair away from his eyes, and looked down at the sailor.

"Has this young lady been accosting you, my good fellow?" inquired the driver, in a tone that might have been civil.

"Lord Linden! Andrew!" cried Katie. "Oh, how glad I am to see you!"

The sailor seemed to wax increasingly offended. "Oh, it's 'lord' is it, now. Do ya mean ta tell me, my fine buck, that ya know this 'ere piece o' goods?"

"Never seen her before in my life," said Lord Linden ignobly. "What's she done?"

The sailor perceived at once that he had captured a sympathetic masculine audience. "Why, oi offer this article 'ere a decent bit o' business 'n she tells me she's not ta be 'ad fer less 'n fifty pounds! Fifty pounds!" The poor old salt was fairly staggered by the enormity of Katie's demand. He waggled his finger emphatically at Lord Linden. "By all that's 'oly, it's a crime, that's wot it is. 'Ow's an 'onest workin' man like meself ta 'ave a little tumble 'n tickle if that's th' way prices is? Seems ta me that th' London bawds 'as gotten right out o' 'and, so it does."

"Very true, my good man. Parliament should look to it," agreed Linden readily. "But perhaps if we bargain with her, we could persuade her to accept a more reasonable offer. What do you say to thirty pounds, wench?"

"Not enough," said Katie, wishing that the street would open and swallow her.

"Well, I niver 'eard th' like," exclaimed the sailor, "not in all me born days. Not ta say she ain't no prime armful, but ain't no woman worth no fifty pounds."

"You are a sage, sir," said Linden, regarding Katie smolderingly. "And I am fully in agreement. Yet . . ." He ran his gaze slowly down the length of Katie's slender frame. "As you say, she's a prime armful." He drew a fifty-pound note from his coat and leaned over to tuck it into the bosom of Katie's gown. "I think I am compelled to experiment with your theory. Come, wench, up with you. Let's see just how far short of your price you fall." He put out an imperious hand and pulled Katie up to sit beside him on the phaeton with a force that nearly wrenched her arm from its socket.

"That's th' wicket, guvnor," cheered the grizzled sailor. "Show th' uppity jade wot it's for!"

"That," said Linden grimly as he snapped the reins, "you may be sure of."

They rode without speaking for a few minutes before Katie turned to Lord Linden and said contritely, "You're mad at me, aren't you?"

"Yes."

Linden had a certain genius for injecting mountains of meaning into a monosyllable. Katie subsided into a snubbed silence. She twisted her head to look at Andrew, who signaled his sympathy and grimaced at Linden behind his back. "Courage, Peaches," he mouthed.

When they arrived at Laurel's house, Andrew ran up to take charge of the horses.

"Walk 'em, Drew," Linden ordered, and assisted Katie into Laurel's library with a roughness quite in keeping with his callous reputation. Once there, he took Katie's shoulders, thrust her into one of the despised sphinx settees and stood regarding her as though she were a particularly obnoxious bug that he would enjoy swatting.

"Do you know," he asked conversationally, "what I would like to do to you?"

"Something painful?" suggested Katie in a small voice.

"Something very painful," agreed Lord Linden.

"Did you not like it that I went out by myself?"

"No. I did not." Those crushing monosyllables again.

"I'm sorry."

Lord Linden dropped beside Katie on the settee and ran one finger slowly across the bridge of her nose. "I would like to make you much, much sorrier but, unfortunately, this country has a legal system that refuses to smile upon the horsewhipping of girls in their teens, no matter how justified. A pity."

Katie's shoulders sagged and she leaned her head back against the tapestry-worked upholstery. It was hard to settle comfortably with the straw bonnet on, so Linden untied the wide satin ribbon and pulled off the bonnet. Katie's hair tumbled to her shoulders.

"I wanted to go to *The Merry Maidenhead* to ask Zack if Papa had sent him a message for me yet. But he hasn't," said Katie, trying to keep the hurt from her voice. "Laurel said that I shouldn't bother you about it and besides, it gave me the feeling that I was doing *something* toward finding my father. But I wouldn't have gone if I'd known that you wouldn't like it. I owe you so much; I would never wish to distress you." It was an artless speech uttered in a pitifully conciliatory voice that might have wrung tears from a stump. On Lord Linden's handsome countenance it had no softening effect.

"Katie. You grow tiresome," he said coldly. "There is a man somewhere in this city who would like very much to free you from your rather unhappy mortal existence. If you wander about the city alone, then you may be sure that he will do so. Furthermore, this is London, not Essex, and young women do not traverse the streets without some kind of attendant unless they wish to be mistaken for members of the muslin company. Nor do they pass their time in earnest chats with every chance-met male who feels inclined to accost them. What would you have done if he had *had* fifty pounds?"

Katie remembered then that she still had Lord Linden's fifty-pound note stuck into her bodice so she drew it out and handed it back to her benefactor. "I don't know," she said sheepishly, "but it wouldn't have mattered, would it? The sailor thought fifty pounds exorbitant—I don't think anything could have induced him to part with that sum. Besides," she added, a flash of spirit animating her lustrous blue eyes, "if I ignored *all* chance-met males, I should never have become acquainted with you."

"A fine example," said Linden sarcastically. "I almost raped you. Doesn't that tell you anything?"

" 'Twas only because you were quite drunk at the time," said Katie, looking up at him placatingly.

"Of all the obtuse . . . is that really what you think? Is that why you've stayed within my protection, because you thought I was safe when sober?" Involuntarily, Linden's hands rose to Katie's shoulders and he pulled her close against his chest. "Little idiot. Don't you realize that when men look at you, they feel like the prize stallion on a stud farm?" He let his hand glide deliberately from Katie's shoulder down the soft cup of her breast until it rested on her curving hip. He heard a tiny, startled gasp in her throat as though she had suddenly needed to fill her lungs with air; her breathing changed its pace, quickening imperceptibly. Her clear, jewel-like eyes were as readable as any child's, emotions filtering through them like bright water sparkling over stones in a stream. She was struggling with herself. He could see she wanted to push his hand away, and it was so hard for her to do, hypnotized as she was by the pleasure his touch fed her.

The cold highlights in Linden's eyes seemed to dim, then glow.

"Katie," he said softly. "My quaint, silly darling. You're sorry; you hope I don't mind; you don't want to distress me. Look up at me, little virgin. That's right, my dear. Hush, I won't hurt you." Carefully, carefully, he pressed a light, lazy kiss on Katie's trembling lips. His fingers played slowly with a red-gold lock of hair which curled over the rise of her cheek. A shiver of fear and longing disturbed her sweet, high cheekbone; he brushed it away with his searching lips. She felt a warm relaxing sensation flooding over her, as if she had been brought from a cold winter storm and set in front of a roaring fire. Her lips parted softly, and were covered by his in a long, caressing kiss. Now she was floating, out of her body, and reached an arm around his shoulder as if to anchor herself safely in this sweep of passion. He fit her closer to his hard body, savoring her yielding softness, her stunned surrender; his lips moved hungrily over the fragrant curve of her neck, whispering her name over and over as if it were a magic charm that would increase his power over her until, finally, she would be his. He told her that he wanted her, that she shouldn't be afraid, that he would help her, please her. One of his hands pressed firmly on her back, his facile fingers opening first one and then another of the buttons that bound her inside her dress, and his lips moved up to her ear, murmuring reassurances.

But the library's japanned rosewood door swung open on its well-oiled hinges, banging into the wall with a crack that caused Katie to jump nearly out of her half-buttoned dress. It was, in Linden's opinion, at least, a bad moment for Laurel to enter the library. In fact, one might shy from so mild an expression as "enter" because Laurel's advent was more in the nature of an invasion. She whirled angrily into the room, her silk skirts flushed and scolding, her hands clenched into fists. A bad moment indeed.

"Don't disengage on my account. *I've* no objection to the public celebration of fertility rites," she said snappishly.

"Plague take you, Laurel, don't you know how to knock?" There was a range of emotions in Lord Linden's voice. Regretfully, shame was not among them.

"Why, Lesley, this is *my* house. But you misinterpret, my dear. I merely came to ask if you might like to use my bed upstairs? Perhaps little Katie would care to borrow one of my negligees?" asked Laurel, all civil sarcasm.

Linden smiled. It was that particularly unpleasant, one-sided smile that made *la* Steele long to scratch it from his face. "I don't need a bed or a negligee, sweet; I'm not so fastidious."

"No, you aren't, are you?" snarled Laurel. "You're a vicious, self-indulgent rakeshame and well I know it! How you screamed at me an hour past for letting your precious Katie go out in London unattended and then stamped off to find her without so much as a by your leave. And now, after all your damned lies that the wench is purer than the untrodden snow . . ." She came to a choking halt, overcome by temper.

"She is *still* pure as the untrodden snow," snapped Linden, his voice taut with exasperation. "I knew I should have locked the door."

"And I suppose you brought the chit to my library intending to seduce her? Lesley," said Laurel, turning purple under her rouge, "how could you?"

"How could I? Well, you jealous bitch, it's not easy, with people bursting into the room like Roman candles and Katie gazing up at me as though I were the archangel Gabriel. Damnation, I brought the chit to your house precisely because I didn't intend to seduce her. But I'm not a damned gelding. Oh, Jesus, why couldn't I have been born eighty and impotent?" said Linden acidly to the room at large. "No, here, Katie, you've put the wrong button in that hole. Put your hands in your lap, I'll do it. Damn you, child, if you shrink away from me like that I swear I'll box your ears; it's obvious that I'm not going to do anything with Laurel whining at me. That fastidious, I am . . . sneck up Laurel, I know you think I'm incorrigible, you've told me so enough times in the past; but I'll be damned if I'm going to apologize to you for my morals. Katie, if ever I attempt you again, I want you to lay hands on the nearest blunt object and fetch me a good, swift blow in the head. Without a doubt, little one, you must be penance on me for the sins of a past life."

"Penance for a past life?" interrupted Laurel

waspishly. "You have more than enough to answer for in this life, I assure you!"

"Go to the devil," retorted Linden, and strode from the room.

For the second time that day, the door to the library was banged with a savage energy that could be felt even on the upper floor, where, in Laurel's sumptuous bedroom, the shock sent the ostrich plumes of the enormous tent bed into wild swooping waves.

Chapter Ten

It had been fortunate for Katie that Lord Linden had behaved with such unrepentant rudeness to Laurel; thus he drew the greatest portion of that affronted lady's wrath on his own graceless head and so saved Katie all but an absent-minded scold. Katie could understand Linden no better now: the restless, uncertain temper that could change in one devastating second to a sweet seductive tenderness that made her feel as though she were swimming in volcanic honey. Part of her saw him as the knight in armor who had saved her life twice, but the clear-headed voice of her conscience told her that his actions in the library lent color to Zack's unsavory accusations that Linden had only saved her so that he might use her himself. Dear, dangerous Lord Linden. Katie knew that she must somehow remove herself from his tempting vicinity soon or decide that virtue was well lost for love. No! It wouldn't be, couldn't be, because tomorrow always comes, and Lord, Lord, what would life be like when he tired of her?

But she knew now, as she had always known, that her halcyon days as Linden's *cygne noir* were a transitory arrangement. Already, it seemed he had tired of playing King Cophetua to her beggar-maid, because on the morning after the scene in the library, which Antoinette referred to as the Battle of the Titans, Linden sent Laurel a curt note informing her that he had to go to Dorset for a few days and that if she threw Katie out, he wouldn't pay the tab on her diamonds.

"The wretch," Laurel said, after reading the note. "I suppose he's gone to some horrid sparring match. Was there ever a more cynical, irresponsible scoundrel? He's supposed to be looking for your father. What's to be done with the man?"

What indeed? If anyone had told Laurel, or even the reverential Katie, that Linden was engaged in that very quest, they would have been incredulous.

Some four afternoons later, Katie and Antoinette sat opposite each other at an inlaid game table, playing *Piquet au Cent* for *la* Steele's hairpins. Antoinette had decided that the blond salon on the upper floor would be the most comfortable place to play. There was a fine framed window there that let in the drowsy late afternoon sunlight and this was the first day in many without the dismal fog. Antoinette soon discovered that this idyllic spot had its disadvantages; this same fine window directly overlooked the small scoop of carriageway, and each time a vehicle passed beneath, Katie jumped up and ran to the window. This became a major irritant to Antoinette, especially since she was losing. When, for the third time within a quarter hour, the snap-rumble of cart wheels came down the street, Antoinette checked Katie before she could rise.

"*Eh bien, petite,* enough! Anyone with ears can tell that is not a carriage of fashion. Do you think my Lord Linden will arrive in a farm wagon pulled by a fat dobbin? Have done, and lead your last card, *s'il vous plaît*."

"As you will, Antoinette, here. The nine of clubs. Oh, can you not take it? You should have retained your diamond jack, you see?"

"*Vraiment?* Do you think that I am a stupid that you must tell me that? It is the height of discourtesy to criticize the play of another. How many points have you? Seventy? And the capot as well!" Antoinette flung up her hands. "That's it then, you take this rubber. And may I say that it is not at all comfortable that a child your age should play the *piquet* so well, like the Greek *banditti*. This lose, lose, lose, it puts me off!"

"Would you like me to let you win for a while?" asked Katie, the soul of amiability.

"Mon Dieu, the things you say! *Mais, non,* the only thing flatter than losing is to be allowed to win."

Katie leaned back in her chair. "I wouldn't know about that. No one's ever allowed me to win like that. Papa taught me, but when I got good enough to beat him, he marked the cards so he would always win. He said it was bad luck for a gambler to get beat by his daughter, but Zack says he just enjoyed cheating. Oh, listen, Antoinette, a smart trot." Katie flew to the window as an ungainly traveling carriage pulled up below. "Oh, but the wheels are picked out in chartreuse, which Linden told me he abominates, so . . . Well. What an odd man, do look, Antoinette, it must be a friend of Laurel's. No, never mind, he's come into the house now, you can't see him anymore." Katie turned back from the window. "Ah, well, where were we? Would you like a new cut for the deal?"

They played for another quarter hour. As Antoinette was about to claim *carte blanche,* a lackey came to the door and informed them that Miss Steele had requested Katie to come to the library.

"Me? Isn't there a gentleman with her? There is? Oh, but . . ."

"How you chatter, Katie," admonished Antoinette. "These dreadful but-buts. Go, then, you find out why she wants you. No, not with ribbon falling like a hoyden; let me fix. Ah, there. Off with you now, but remind yourself to act like a young lady of breeding, if you please."

Katie made a shy entrance into the library, with an inquiring glance toward Laurel and a curious one toward her visitor. The gentleman appeared to have been stuffed into his clothing rather in the manner that ground meat is stuffed into its sheath in homemade sausage. His waist, surely nipped in by a corset, proclaimed the dandy, but he was a large man so the effect was absurd. On one ruddy hand, he wore a large diamond solitaire that cried out for a cleaning.

"Katie," said Laurel slowly. "What do you remember about your mother?"

Katie was quiet, surprised by the question, and then replied, "Nothing. All I know about her are things my father has told me."

"Which are?" Laurel prompted.

"Umm, Papa said that she was so beetle-witted that she could hardly set one word next to another in a sentence, but she was so pretty no one ever

135

noticed." And that was one of her father's more repeatable comments. Katie wondered why Laurel didn't introduce the gentleman, who had risen politely on Katie's entrance, and now stood shifting uneasily from one boot to the other as though he wasn't sure whether to sit again or wait for an introduction.

"She died when you were a baby, didn't she?" asked Laurel. "And her family, why did you never stay with them? After all, your father was not out of the teens then. Weren't any of your mother's relations able to help the youthful widower with his infant?"

"No," said Katie, interpreting the question literally. "Papa said that the rest of Mama's family were not like Mama at all; he said they were full of juice, ugly as slugs and nastier than molting weasels. Papa said his father-in-law was a damned lionizing mushroom who made his money exploiting a lot of starving miners, then got socially ambitious and bullied Mama into marrying my father because he thought it would be a great thing to have a baron in the family. When he found out that poor Papa was quite, quite *déclassé*, he cut them off without a groat. That's what Papa says, *I* don't know; but when Papa disappeared, I wrote my mother's father telling him about it. I said that he could find me at *The Merry Maidenhead* if he wished, but I've heard nothing from him, so that speaks for itself, I think."

Laurel threw a smug, happy look at the man and waved one dismissive hand in his direction. "This . . . creature," she said, "is Ivo Guy, and he claims to be your mother's blood cousin."

"Dearest little Katie," said the man, coming to-

ward Katie with his arms outstretched in an offered embrace. Even a child could have seen how
forced was his smile. Either Laurel had set up his
back before Katie had entered or he wasn't happy
with Katie's highly unflattering description of his
family.

Katie submitted stiffly to his hug, which consisted of his pulling Katie's face abruptly into his
soiled muslin cravat, and then releasing her to
arm's length while he looked her up and down in
a self-consciously paternal manner. Katie rarely
held anyone in dislike, but already she was in a
fair way to cordially detesting Ivo Guy. Every
inch of the man bespoke the hypocrite.

"How do you do, sir?" asked Katie, tucking her
hands behind her back. She had more than done
her duty with the hug; shaking hands would have
been too much of a bad thing.

"Very well, very well," said Mr. Guy. "It's a joyous meeting for us, is it not? So affecting for me.
Why, you're the very replica of your beloved
mama!" Which could hardly be said to be a compliment following hard on the heels of Katie's description of her mother as a beetle wit.

"Papa says that I am nothing like my mother,"
protested Katie. "He said that I am a typical Kendricks with a puny nose, carrot locks, and freckles.
Did you know my mother well?"

Laurel interrupted. "He's been telling me what
great confidence your mother reposed in him and
how he got along so famously with your maternal
grandfather. He seems, in fact, to be the sticking
plaster which held your family together." She sent
a darting glance of dislike at him, which elicited
a queasy smile.

Katie regarded Guy with new interest. "Could it be that you have come from my grandfather?" she asked.

"Ah," said Guy, his pudgy face acquiring a lugubrious pose. "From your grandfather. No, indeed, my little cousin, because you see, your grandfather has gone to a better land."

Katie bore this announcement prosaically. "Oh," she remarked, sagely, "America. Papa says that it's the most up and coming part of the world right now."

Laurel gave a choke of laughter. "Try to be a little less blockish, Katie, the foolish creature is merely trying to say that your grandfather is dead. And we'll have no maudlin nonsense about it, Guy. Even the most cringing sentimentalist could not expect Katie to mourn the death of a relative she has never met and what's more, who treated her with callous disregard the whole of her life."

Ivo Guy coughed, looked at the ceiling, and ran a mottled hand over the flabby surface of his unshaven chin. "Most, most unfortunate. But you see, Katie, your grandfather was . . . shall we say, an eccentric."

"We shall if you like," said Katie, "but Papa said he was a drunkard."

"Your papa ought to know!" snapped Guy. "That's a subject upon which he can speak with authority!" He controlled himself then, apparently remembering that this was supposed to be a joyous meeting. "But let us not quarrel, my dear. Don't be hurt that your mother's family made no attempt to claim you earlier in your life; it was your father's doing. He wouldn't let you come to us. Understandably, I feel, as you were his only consolation after your dear mama went to a better . . . er, died."

"Well," returned Katie disconcertingly, "if you think I was my father's only consolation after my mother died, then you don't know my father. Zack said Mama was hardly cold in her casket before Papa began a liaison with one of the housemaids."

Guy regarded Katie with pained distaste. "I can see that your unfortunate rearing has left its mark upon you. You stand in need of a firm and loving guidance that has been denied you in these long years, which I am prepared, on behalf of your mother's family, to supply. It was hard indeed to keep track of you while you were growing up; you moved so often, and your father was so hostile to his in-laws. But your letter to your grandfather finally came into my hands—I was the manager of his business, you see, and his correspondence is now turned over to me."

"Come to the point, Guy," demanded Laurel impatiently. "How do you propose to supply 'dear little Katie' with this firm and loving guidance?"

Ivo Guy supplied a smile that his eyes did not share and a tiny wrinkle appeared on the veiny flesh of his shiny, balding pate. "Ahem. It would seem as though you have appointed yourself guardian of this poor, displaced girl. You are to be commended for this, indeed. May I say that a woman of your, uh, posture in life is not usually expected to have concern for the homeless?" He raised his skimpy brows sarcastically and bowed stiffly to Laurel. She looked back at him as if he were a large frog flattened under a carriage wheel and tossed in her path. Guy smirked and continued, "It is not necessary for you to burden your-

self any longer. Our family will care for its own."
Guy fished in the pocket of his dusty suit for several seconds, finally producing a large, official-looking piece of parchment. "I have here a legally notarized document appointing me the guardian of this unfortunate girl, so irresponsibly abandoned by her father. In short, we of your mother's family receive you with open arms."

"What do you mean, receive me?" asked Katie, with some misgiving.

"Why, what but give you a home? To protect and guide you as one must a young girl. It is my intention that you immediately accompany me to my home outside London, where I will place you in the tender nurturing care of my mother. Now, now, my dear, I can see you are confused, but it need not be so. We will do all within our power to make you comfortable. What could be deeper than the blood bond?"

"Mawkish ass," snapped Laurel derisively. "There'll be no more talk of 'immediately.' Katie was placed in my care by Lord Linden and here she'll stay until he says otherwise."

Waiting for Lord Linden's say-so in no way figured into Ivo Guy's plans. "I wonder, Madame, that you have the gall to admit Linden's connection with the girl! Be blunt, if you will. What has Lord Linden to say in this matter, may I ask?"

"You may ask all you like," said Laurel with mock cordiality, "but it remains not your affair."

"That's where you are wrong, Miss Steele," hissed Guy. "As the child's guardian, it is very much my affair. If you will have it out in the open, then I will admit that rumors have reached me that Linden has formed an . . . unfortunate connection with a young lady of Katie's description. I think it would be better for Katie if we could forget and put behind us this regrettable episode in her life but I warn you if either he or you tries to stand in the way of my custody of Katie, I will not hesitate to approach the law! The courts will not be generous with a man trifling with a minor."

Laurel snorted derisively. "Linden's earldom is related to half of England. The half that counts! Try taking this issue to court and he'll smash you like an ant!" She laughed. "If Lesley were brought to book every time he trifled, they would have to extend their hours to Sundays to handle the case load."

Guy ground his teeth. "This is no subject for mirth, Miss Steele. We are speaking of a young girl's purity."

"If we are, then I wish we weren't," said Katie, mortified by the channels the conversation had begun to explore. "If you wish me to come with you, Mr. Guy, I will. And thank you very much." This last was said with difficulty and an almost heroic determination. It was a favorite saying of the baron's that "God will provide—if only God would provide *until* he provides." Katie could only wish that God had provided someone other than Ivo Guy. But it was not her custom to question the inscrutable workings of divinity and in this case it appeared she had very little choice. She had exploited Lord Linden's not very good nature too long already. She had been nothing but an unmitigated nuisance to Laurel. She was not so stripped of all pride as to go on and on indefinitely dependent upon their generosity. Ivo Guy at least had the virtue of being Katie's cousin, or so he said, and Katie was sure it was true. He fit her father's description of her maternal relatives to an inch. And to give the man credit, which Katie found herself strangely disinclined to do, he said that he wanted her. It was the first time anyone had ever told Katie they wanted her, if she discounted Lord Linden, and since the way he wanted her was the way he had wanted scores of other women, it could hardly be said to count.

Katie's life, for the most part, had been filled with exhausting self-sufficiency. Her nature was warm and loving, and she had valued even a table-scrap of affection far more than guidance or support. These were things she had learned to function without. Katie's greatest fear had always been that she would alienate the fondness of those she loved by becoming an unwanted burden. It had ruled much of her relationship with her self-centered, blithesome father, and now it would bear upon her relationship with Lord Linden. "Katie, you grow tiresome," he had told her on the afternoon of her recent trip to *The Merry Maidenhead.* He could not have known it, but there was no more potent weapon to use on Katie. She had felt as though a cold metal hand had squeezed her throat. Surely it would be better to throw herself into a well than to be "tiresome" to Lord Linden.

Ivo Guy might not be a well, but he was, in Laurel's opinion, a pit. Katie's decision to go with him had taken Laurel by surprise. It was clear as distilled water that Katie was in love with Linden. That she would trade his protection for that of this cloddish cousin was beyond Laurel's comprehension. She wondered briefly what motives prompted the chit. Should she let Katie go with him or not? How would Linden react if he returned and found her gone? He'd said that he wouldn't pay for her diamonds if she threw Katie out; but releasing her to her lawful guardian was hardly throwing her out. If Katie were, in truth, not his mistress, then perhaps he would be glad to see the end of a care for which he could have little relish. On the other hand, Laurel thought irritably, it would be just like Lesley to object to any arrangements that were not of his own making. Still, if Katie had made up her mind to leave, then she would probably raise a squawk if Laurel tried to detain her, and Guy looked like he might be peasant enough to call in the courts to support his claim. Laurel had known Linden long enough to learn that there was one curious flicker of kindness in him that might lead him to take temporary responsibility for a waif such as Katie, if there was no one else to do it. Still, it was obvious what construction anyone else would place on Linden's interest in a beautiful young woman. Laurel decided for caution and put herself on record as opposing the plan by raising numerous objections to their immediate departure.

Ivo Guy answered Laurel's objections with a certain oily persistence. It was clear that he meant to have the chit with no further delay.

"Very well then, Guy," said Laurel, leaning back in her chair and gesturing his dismissal, "you may wait outside. We shall see to Katie's packing and then send her out to you."

Ivo Guy thankfully made his escape. Katie and Laurel could hear the overburdened legs of his tightly fitting suit whistling against each other down the corridor.

"I don't have anything to pack," said Katie, feeling that it ought to be mentioned.

Laurel tugged the braided gold call bell.

"No matter. Antoinette will pack the clothes you've been wearing. I've an old valise you can use. We can hardly send you out in the world naked, even though you arrived here that way," said Laurel sourly.

"I wasn't naked. I had on my nightclothes," corrected Katie. "Please, I cannot take your beautiful dresses. If perhaps one of the servants has an old . . ."

"Really, Katie," interrupted Laurel, "you're too gauche for words. Every one of my staff has seen you in those dresses. Do you think that I'd wear them secondhand, like an old peddler's wife? Besides, they've been altered for you, since you insist on remaining so odiously slim, through no fault of mine; God knows I've fed you well enough!" continued Laurel, in a tone that suggested Katie had retained her graceful curves for the express purpose of vexing her hostess. "You may as well take the dresses. They won't do me any good, though I do regret that heavenly riding habit. But nothing," she added with a shudder, "could induce me to wear it since you've worn it to Hyde Park. Lord, if anyone should notice!"

"But, Miss Steele, your clothes must have cost hundreds of pounds."

Laurel drew herself into a haughty composure. "There is nothing more detestably vulgar than a discussion of the monetary value of one's wardrobe. But if it gives you any comfort, then you may as well know that Linden will very likely pay me for them."

Why the knowledge that Linden would pay for her clothing could be of any comfort was more than Katie could see and she pointed this out to Laurel. "Besides, isn't it so that no lady with even a thimbleful of self-respect could allow a gentleman to purchase her anything as intimate as clothing?"

"Well, Linden pays for mine, and I," said Laurel baldly, "have plenty of self-respect."

There was no answer for this that would not have been appallingly uncivil, so there was no more for Katie to do but express her gratitude to her benefactress. "You've been very good to me and you can't have liked it much," she said, "because really, there wasn't the least reason for you to let me stay here."

"Well, if you think there wasn't the least reason, then you haven't yet learned the futility of placing your will in opposition to Lesley's, because he's never hesitated to tread over anyone's wishes," said Laurel tartly. Then she remembered the lovely diamond set now snugly reposed in her velvet-lined jewel case upstairs. "Besides, there are other . . . oh, never mind. I hope you know what you're doing. That cousin of yours is a muckworm—I know his type. It's fawning and humbug and 'dear little Katie' but no one could maintain that posture for long. I'll wager his real nature is quite the opposite. And this mother of his, what kind of mother would have produced such a locust?"

Since much the same thought had already occurred to Katie, there was not much of a reply to make, except that when she found out, she would write to Laurel and tell her. And with that, Laurel had to be satisfied.

Chapter Eleven

The battered traveling coach thundered west, carrying Katie past the stately homes of Mayfair, past a corner of Hyde Park, then through the cozy suburbs. The carriage had been rented, that much was obvious from the small brass plaque on the door informing the rider that he was privileged to enjoy a sound equipage from the livery of Bentworth and Bentworth. That these worthies had never traveled in their own carriage was evident; otherwise, they would not have categorized its ride as a privilege. The thing rolled like a rock. There was nothing served, either, by trying to lean back against the seats to relax; the musty sawdust cushions had all the comforts of a Calvinist church pew. At one particularly hard lurch, one of the bolsters rolled to the floor and Katie could see, on the now uncovered wooden side of the carriage, where some previous disgruntled traveler had scrawled an obscenity with the tip of a penknife.

Farms rolled by Katie's window in a glumping shaken procession, then a dainty whitewashed hamlet with windowboxes bright with calliopsis and baskets o' gold. From time to time Katie caught a glimpse of her cousin as he rode beside the coach on his goose-rumped mare, his heavy features settled in a sullen frown.

The afternoon's pleasant sunlight had faded into a damp dusk and a frisky draft swirled around the carriage floor, nipping casually at Katie's ankles. She fastened her sable-collared cloak more tightly against the chill.

After perhaps another mile, they turned onto a rutty dirt road and Katie was attacked by a cloud of dust. The dull orange of the setting sun flickered intermittently in and out through the trunks of the tangled copse through which they passed. The unhappy combination of the coach's jostling and an acute melancholia that Katie couldn't seem to shake off had produced an uneasy throb in her interior that she recognized as nausea. It was with gratitude that she felt the carriage take a last turn and stop its swaying. Katie roused to see a barren yard, and a long low flintstone hunting lodge with a red-tiled roof, surrounded by a border of half-hearted violets. A dead elm loomed over the house from the rear, framing the scene with twisted, shadow-casting limbs.

There was a decrepit hitching rack near the lodge's door where a pinch-kneed piebald gelding stood cropping dispassionately at a tuft of dry hay. Guy secured his mare beside the gelding and Katie heard the jiggling of coin as Guy paid the coachman. The door opened and Guy handed Katie down. An owl hooted in the copse while the turning of the carriage wheels faded in the distance.

A leonine door knocker garnished the lodge's front door, but rust had transformed its snarl into a rather disappointing grimace. Guy smacked the knocker impatiently, muttering to himself. The door opened and a dark frame appeared silently, silhouetted against the flickering candlelight from a wax-fouled candelabrum projecting from the inside wall.

"Ah, good evening, Chilworthy," said Ivo Guy in a satisfied tone. "We have a female guest, as we anticipated."

Chilworthy made no audible reply, but stepped inside to let them enter the lodge. Crossed on the wall was a dark pair of double-headed axes which apparently belonged to the days of thumbscrews and racks. The dead yellow light from the candelabrum streaked across Chilworthy's face. Katie stopped in her tracks and brought a hand inadvertently to her mouth, staring at the visage that resembled all too closely the villains that haunted some of the more improbable romances she had read. Chilworthy's head was flat as a tabletop, adorned by spikes of gray hair, and his forehead might have been modeled after a paving brick. His almost lipless mouth was a blank rictus in the wavering light and his eyes were dark craters under his beetle brows. Most harrowing of all was the livid scar which coursed across his neck from one ear to the other.

Guy smiled at Katie's fear. "Don't let Chilworthy startle you, my dear," he said blandly. "He is quite competent in spite of his odd appearance. Chilworthy, take Miss Kendricks's valise to the room we've prepared for her. Katie, you may follow Chilworthy. I'm sure you would like to freshen for dinner; I will do the same and you may join me in the dining room at your leisure. How pleasant it is to have you with me," he finished. "I believe we have a promising future reunited as one family."

Katie could not agree. Nor were her spirits improved by a trek down the long hall in Chilworthy's wake. The occasional candle burning on the wall cast an orange square of light into the stale rooms they passed, and Katie caught ghostly glimpses of bulky furniture slumbering under Holland covers.

When they had reached the end of the hall, Chilworthy set down her valise and fumbled for a few seconds with a large key dangling from a ring at his belt. The key scraped inside the lock with a rusted, hollow whine, and Chilworthy pushed open the narrow door to reveal a small stuffy bedroom. The fidgeting candle flame trembled over the looming shapes of a heavy cabinet, washstand, and bed —nothing more. The scene was strongly reminiscent of several passages from an ancient tome Katie had examined once in a bookstore, "An Educative Research Upon Atmospheres Amenable to Ghastly Occurrences or Scenes Where Murders Have Been Committed." Katie looked up at Chilworthy and made a poor attempt at a smile.

"Thank you," she said, trying fervently and without much success to put all the "Educative Research" firmly from her mind. "I can find my own way back to the dining parlor when I'm ready."

Chilworthy clicked his heels together and bowed from the waist. "Very good, Miss." His voice was hoarse and papery. Perhaps resulting from the throat injury? Chilworthy lit a chimneyed candle on the washstand corner and left the room.

Alone, Katie walked slowly across the carpetless room to the window and gazed out. The moon had half risen now, bestowing its stark blue-white smile on the rustling landscape. Timid moonbeams hovered doubtfully among a gossamer mist that had begun to seep upward from the spongy floor of the surrounding woods. From one corner of the desolate yard came the low, slinking form of a hunting fox. "Watch out, little birds," whispered Katie.

The sour stink of dust and disuse permeated the bedroom, so Katie tried to pull open the window. It stuck. She tried again, this time putting the full strength of her arms into it. Nothing. She brought the candle closer and examined the peeling white-wash of the sill and found that the window had been nailed shut, and recently, too, for the metal heads of the nails gleamed brightly under the supple flame. Then, for no particular reason, Katie recalled where she had heard Chilworthy's deep, grating whisper.

She whirled around and raced down the dim hallway until she came before an open doorway that blazed with light from a triple set of many-cupped candelabra. Ivo Guy looked up from behind a newspaper as Katie came into the room.

"This isn't your country home, is it?" she asked breathlessly. "And your mother isn't here."

Guy set down the paper and rose to his feet. "Well, no, my dear," said Guy, slyly apologetic. "You see, it couldn't be because I don't have a country house and my mother's been dead these twenty years. You recognized Chilworthy's voice, didn't you? I thought you might. No matter. Of course, at the time I was rather perturbed with him for whispering your name through Linden's door. True, it might have panicked you into doing something foolish, but as it didn't work, its only observable effect was to put Linden on his guard —which didn't make our task any easier, I promise. Still, all's right that ends right."

The nausea that had begun to attack Katie in the rocking carriage now took a firmer grip. "Are you really my cousin?" she asked tightly.

"Oh, yes, that much is certainly true. Of course, your 'dear' Mama never wasted ten minutes of her giddy time on my family. We were always the 'improvident' Guys, the 'spend-thrift' Guys, the 'not quite clever enough' Guys. And your mother's family—filthy, reeking rich. How I had to beg your grandfather for a job! And how he made me slave for him, the old bastard, made me gallop under his goad, made me work a dozen times over for every wretched penny of my beggarly salary. And then when the old devil finally slipped his wind, do you know what he left me? Do you?" he demanded sharply. "He left me his sprung pocket watch . . ." Guy's voice dulled, ". . . and second in line to his estate."

Katie gazed in disbelief at Guy's florid, popeyed features. Oh, my, she thought, when's the next stage back to London? Aloud she said, "Why did you bring me here?"

Guy's eyes narrowed into a hot sneer. "Why, my dear, because I'm going to marry you."

"M-marry me?" said Katie, totally blank.

"Yes, indeed," chuckled Guy, rubbing his palms together. "Dear little cousin, it is my honor to make up for the long years of my family's neglect of you by offering you the protection of my name."

"No, no," said Katie, more quickly than the rules

of social usage would have allowed. "Thank you. But no. Really!"

Guy took a few steps forward, reached out one obese arm and clasped Katie to his food-specked shirt. "You are shy, my Venus. It is not surprising. But you see, I am not unskilled in the manly arts." Forcing up Katie's chin with a stained, pudgy finger, he pressed his greasy bulbous lips on hers.

Katie's queasy stomach contracted into a tough, throbbing knot. When at last her lips were freed, she gasped, "Sir, I warn you that if you repeat your action, I will probably retch." She was hastily released.

Guy turned his back and walked to the other side of an inlaid Sycamore writing table. When he turned back toward Katie, his eyes had shrunk to cruel, raging slits.

"So . . . that is how you wish to play, eh, my ignorant little chippy?" he whispered, his throat rattling with suppressed rage. "You are young. I was willing to make concessions for that, I was willing to be gentle with you. But, believe me, little cousin, the game can be played much more roughly." Guy opened a narrow drawer in the writing table and withdrew a short-barreled pistol. He cocked it and pointed the muzzle at Katie's chest.

"Sit."

Katie lowered herself slowly into a carved mahogany armchair, regarding Guy with a wary, unwavering stare. "I think," she suggested, in a measured tone, "that I might play the game better if I knew what the rules are."

"Ah, the rules! The rules, Katie, were set up by your so-loved maternal grandfather. I've already told you that I am second in line to inherit his estate. Perhaps you can guess now who stands first in line?"

"N-not I?"

"Oh, yes, you! For years the old man claimed nary a penny of his would go toward feeding any misbegotten Kendricks brats, but then, almost upon his deathbed, he changed his will to give everything to you. Unless," he paused, waving the pistol slightly, "you should die without issue. The old vandal claimed he had a visitation from his dead daughter begging him to provide for her poor, orphaned Katie." Guy laughed unpleasantly. "What he had was too many visitations with a wine bottle, the damned old sot."

Katie folded her hands in her lap and looked down at her pale knuckles. "So," she said, "what do you want me to do? Die?"

Guy walked to Katie, his lips parted in a feverish leer. "I must confess, my Venus, that when I got your letter and found that you were coming to London to work in a gin shop, it did cross my mind that it might be . . . convenient if you met with an accident there . . . perhaps an altercation with an irate customer? These things are so common in those low slums, aren't they? So I had Chilworthy slip a few coins to, let me see, what was the fellow's name . . . ?"

"Nasty Ned," said Katie, her voice strained.

"Thank you, cousin. Nasty Ned, it was. Of course, you know that story. Really, my dear, it's not as though you've lead such a merry life that you would wish to hang onto it so. As long as your death was accomplished quickly and without a great deal of pain, what could it possibly matter, hmmm?" Guy rubbed Katie's silky cheek lightly with the nose-cap of his pistol. "But that's all past, my heart. You see," he breathed, leaning closer to Katie, "that was before I had seen you."

Katie grit her teeth. "Don't tell me," she said tersely, "I make you feel like a stallion on a stud farm. Well, I'll tell you something, cousin, I'd rather be had by a stallion on a stud farm than by you! Don't waste your time trying to make love to me; frankly, I mislike it worse than your threats."

It was not, perhaps, the most tactful thing to have said under the circumstances. Guy's nostrils flared with fury and he grasped Katie's slender throat between his angry palms. "Bitch!" he shouted. "By God, you ought to thank God fasting that you can find anyone to marry you. Linden's whore, weren't you? Before you're much older you'll find yourself strapped in my saddle or nobody's!"

Katie sat deathly still under Guy's crushing grasp. She raised her frightened blue eyes to look at him. "How can you expect me to marry a man who's been trying to kill me? I don't think that foreshadows a happy married life." Guy's fingers tightened perceptibly. "B-but we could compromise, couldn't we? If you let me go, I'll sign a paper saying you can have Grandpa's money. After the things he said about me, I wouldn't have it on a platinum calabash."

Guy gave a faint, wheezy snicker. "No, no, Katie. No compromises. I'm not such a fool as to chance your escaping me now." He released her and called down the hallway, "Chilworthy! A task for you!" Guy's lips pressed into a loose gloating pout as he walked back to the library table and thrust the pistol back into its drawer. "Yes, my sweet little cousin, we shall have our accounting! If you choose not to marry me, why then," he shrugged moodily, "I'll kill you. But first, little rabbit, I'll have you! And Chilworthy, too, would you like that? I know Chilworthy would. I'll give you one hour to think things out. Perhaps on reflection you'll become more reasonable, eh? Ah, Chilworthy, bind her wrists, will you? Yes, the drapery cord will do nicely, just make sure it's plenty tight." Guy pulled Katie's wrists in front of her while Chilworthy wrapped them. "There. Now come with us." Guy pulled Katie violently down the long, tunneling hall and threw her into the bare bedchamber. "One hour, Katie," he snarled after her. "Either put yourself in the mood for wedlock or so help me, God, I'll splice you without it!"

"Do as you like," responded Katie wearily through the door, "but I can't promise that I won't get sick."

Chapter Twelve

Lord Linden had cast his long body into one of Laurel's Nile green side chairs. He stroked the gilt gesso acanthus carving on one arm absently with his graceful fingers as he listened to Laurel's account of Ivo Guy's visit. Laurel observed with asperity the slow frown gathering in his sable eyes.

"Ha! You don't think I should have let her go with him this afternoon, do you? I knew it!" said Laurel, eyes flashing. "If you intend to reproach me, then pray remove your boots from that klismos. The maids forever complain that you muddy the seat covers and I won't have myself and my furniture abused at the same time."

"What the hell is a klismos?" asked Linden, momentarily diverted. "Oh, you mean this chair? You're mispronouncing it, you know."

"No, I didn't know, but thank you for correcting me," said Laurel sweetly, wishing that she could slap the smirk from his face. "Would it be your pleasure to enumerate your objections to my allowing Katie to leave my house in the care of her legal guardian?"

"All right. One, how do you know he was really her guardian? Two, how do you know that he could be trusted with her? And three, doesn't it strike you as a little odd that he knew she was here?"

A neat deck of cards lay on a short saber-legged table beside Laurel. She picked them up and began to shuffle them idly from hand to hand. "Very well. One, I knew he was really her guardian because he had papers to prove it. Two, I don't know for certain that he can be trusted with her, but then, I do know for certain that you can't. And three . . . what was three? Oh, yes. I suppose it was odd that he should know she was here. Perhaps there was some gossip that she was here? Well, all right, I know what you want me to say. You think he paid someone to trace her whereabouts. So what? You might have done the same if you heard your cousin was lodged under the wing of a notorious libertine. You still haven't taken your feet from my klis . . . my chair."

Linden dropped his head backward over his chair's twisted floral backing. "Libertine? I've always thought of you as a woman of the world, Laurel, but would you go so far as to call yourself a libertine?"

"Stupid!" she snapped. "I meant you. Go ahead, then. Storm after the chit and demand her back from her legal guardian on the vaguest grounds. Lord, and with your reputation, too! A pretty fool you'll look." Laurel leaned to one side and began to lay the cards one by one on a spindly rosewood side table. She watched Linden from the corner of her eye. "You know, Lesley," she said calmly, "if you really care about the girl, you ought to be grateful that she's in the hands of her family at last."

Linden lifted his head and massaged the back of

his neck. "Oh, Laurel, you are so clever, so canny. 'God grant me to contend with those that understand me.' What makes you think I care about the chit?"

"Oh, I'm a fey creature, my dear," she said with an airiness that she didn't feel. "If you want to know where she's gone, it would be easy enough to find out, in all faith. Guy took her in a rented carriage. Antoinette said the wheels were trimmed in chartreuse. That would be Bentworth, would it not? These livery stables keep a record of their transactions, don't they? By greasing the right palms . . ." Her voice trailed to a halt. "Well, Lancelot, will you chase about the countryside to assure yourself of the well-being of your lady?"

Linden rose from his chair and stretched. "Laurel, I've spent six hours in the saddle already today riding in from Dorset and I'm promised to Sefton for cards at eight. Do you really think that my care for the chit is strong enough to have me set out after her like a hound trailing a lame jackrabbit?"

Alone in the darkened bedroom, Katie stood gazing from the window, her shoulders slumped under the folds of the traveling cape. The cape had belonged to Laurel and was lined with sumptuous, frothy sable. Katie was glad that she hadn't removed it before Chilworthy tied her hands; the scratchy damp of the fog had crept silently into the house, and Katie could feel its bleak whip on her bare ankles. She saw the fox again, its lithe body stretched and taut as it crept across the yard.

For a time, Katie had tried to loosen her bound wrists, sawing her arms back and forth, hoping to loosen the rigid knots. She had succeeded in shaving off the top layer of her skin, nothing more. She was no more successful when she tried to twist her fingers to pick at the knot. It wouldn't budge.

The clouds sneaked across the sky, sometimes cloaking the moon in their stealthy folds and throwing dodging shadows at the earth below. Several times in Katie's hour she had heard the distant pounding of hooves on the road. The ragged ears of the two horses tethered outside would lift with interest as the hoofbeats drew closer and then grew fainter until they passed into the night's silence. She could not see the road, concealed as it was by that evil copse of twisted trees. He's going to kill me, thought Katie. He's going to kill me.

A virile, rhythmic canter cut across the hollow wail of the perching owl. Katie wondered what rider would be reckless enough to canter his mount in this dense fog bank. She waited for the hoofbeats to die in the distance and was amazed when they didn't. They slowed to a walk and grew more audible yet. Through the thin wedge of land clipped through the rotted woods came a shadowy form that blended and condensed into a single rider and horse, the mist curling around the horse's powerful hocks. Katie recognized the horse almost before she knew the rider. Ciaffa. And Lord Linden.

Katie drew in a shaken breath and watched without moving as Linden dismounted and rapped abruptly on the lodge door. Fearful that he would vanish into the dense, lonely night, she wanted to call out, scream his name. The lodge door opened cautiously and Chilworthy walked out a pace, bathed in the rich candlelight. She could see them exchange words. Sweet Jesus, thought Katie, Chilworthy will tell him some lie and he'll go away. It was some forty yards from her window to where the two stood talking and the glass was thick. If she cried out would he hear her? Or would Guy run back to silence her before she could attract Linden's attention? Then, as though her thoughts had materialized him by some malevolent power, Katie heard Guy's heavy tread snapping quickly up the corridor toward the bedchamber.

There was an old cotton towel on the washstand rung and Katie dove her hands into it in feverish, unthinking haste. Do this right, she told herself fervently, you may get only one chance. Katie lifted her bound hands over her head and brought them down against the window with one stunning blow. The window exploded as though cannon shot had been pumped through it.

Protecting her face with her cloak, Katie hurled her body over the sill and onto the ground, landing in several hard, tumbling somersaults. Clumsy with terror, she pushed up to her knees and then to her feet, stumbling over the awkward confining skirts of her gown and cape. Glass had swirled and splintered everywhere. It glinted in Katie's hair like well-cut diamonds as she ran jerkily toward Lord Linden at last, calling his name, over and over and over.

Linden had turned toward the sound of glass rending in time to see Katie fling herself from the shattered window. He reached her before she had time to cover half the distance between them.

"Katie," he said, steadying her shoulders in a careful grip. "Katie, what in God's name . . . ?"

She spoke in a tumbled rush, her blue eyes wild.

"He wants to kill me, my cousin wants to kill me because my grandfather left me his money. He paid Nasty Ned to kill me and . . . and Chilworthy came to your house that night." She was shaking and Linden released her shoulders to cup her bound wrists firmly between his hands. "He said he'd marry me, my lord, and he said if I wouldn't, if I wouldn't . . ."

"What the devil's going on out here?" came the stentorian tones of Ivo Guy. Chilworthy moved back a step and the misty rectangle of light was blocked by Katie's puffing cousin. He took a few lumbering steps from the doorway. "So you're the famous Linden, eh? I'm not surprised to see you're pursuing your illicit passions with this helpless young waif here. It must shake you to the depths of your carnal soul to have my innocent cousin snatched out of the reach of your filthy desires." Behind him, Chilworthy vanished into the house.

"Life is a continuing surprise," said Linden softly. He drew Katie into the shelter of his arm and carefully picked a few shards of glass from her hair. "My poor little Katie," he murmured. "Would you like me to crush this vermin or simply get you out of here?"

"You're not taking her anywhere! I have legal custody of her and you've no authority to remove her, my fine lord." Guy's eyes narrowed into porcine slits. "What lies has the little witch been telling you? Heed her not. She has a hoaxing tongue. It's her rearing; she's wild to a fault."

Linden raised a gentle eyebrow. "In fact, so wild that you found it necessary to bind her wrists," he said quietly.

Guy looked flustered. "I was disciplining her."

"In the style of de Sade?" sneered Linden. "Does your legal authority include physical abuse?"

Chilworthy had reappeared silently from the house, creeping up to the scene shielded by Ivo Guy's bulk, and carrying one of the long-handled double-bladed axes from the set in the hallway. Accordingly, Ivo Guy suddenly found himself in possession of the heavy weapon, and Chilworthy went rapidly around him toward the hitching post.

"Ha!" ejaculated Ivo Guy triumphantly. He whistled the wicked blade in a giant arc through the fog. "Now the shoe is on the other foot, my fine blueblood! I'll chop you down like a tree!"

Linden thrust Katie behind him. "In the fiend's name, Guy. Put that thing down before you hurt yourself," he said irritably.

"I'm not the one who needs to worry about that, my friend." The blade sliced the miasma again and Ivo Guy advanced a few steps. "You think to interfere with my plans for the wench? I think you will not!"

Linden pushed Katie back against the side of the house before walking back to stand not quite four feet from Guy. There was light enough from the window for Katie to see the subtly insolent grin that sparkled in Linden's coffee eyes as he stood, one hand resting carelessly on his hip, facing Guy's naked blade.

"No!" cried Katie. "My lord, you don't have a weapon! He'll . . ." Her voice trailed off as she suddenly remembered the pistol Guy had drawn from the library table inside the house. "Oh, Lord Linden, he has a pistol. And I know where it is! Please, wait. I'll run and bring it!"

"Katie, no, damn it. I don't need a pistol. Come

back here." But she was already gone. "Damnation!" he swore and jumped back lightly as Guy reared the mammoth axe and swung it toward Linden mightily.

"Swine!" said Linden, and the smile vanished. He shifted his weight quickly to his left leg, then braced, balanced, and flowing like whitewater over rapids, he threw Guy a kick that caught the big man squarely below the jaw and sent him flying heavily onto his back on the driveway. A fine powder spray of dirt rose and blended into the silvery moonlit mist. Then two things happened at the same time; Chilworthy came out of the dark leading the pair of saddled hacks, and from somewhere inside the lodge came the muffled crack of pistol fire.

Lord Linden had no wish to let Chilworthy dump Guy on one of those saddles and escape into the night, but there was no hesitation in his step as he turned from Guy and strode through the lodge's open door into the shadowed interior. "Katie?" he called.

"In here, my lord. The dining parlor," came Katie's voice.

Linden followed the voice and found himself inside the overlit, muggy room where Katie was standing alone beside a small table. Her body was completely covered by the cloak. He could see only her face which bore a rather startled expression.

"My lord," she said, not moving, "the pistol went off."

"I heard."

"Yes. I drew it from the drawer. And I held it under my cape." She seemed confused. "Then . . .

then I tripped on the edge of my cape and the pistol went off. Where are they?"

"Your attractive cousin and his *âme damnée* are on their way back to town presumably. Can't you hear their horses? Gone, Katie, don't worry about them. Katie, where was the barrel of the pistol facing when it fired?"

"Toward . . . my shoulder." Katie heard Linden draw in his breath sharply. "You see, at first it felt like a punch and I thought, well, I thought that the pistol had jumped as it fired and hit against my shoulder. B-but I feel hot now, hot inside my chest. Lord Linden," she said, at once sheepish and stunned, "I'm sorry, but I'm very much afraid that I've shot myself." She drew her hands from her cloak, still clutching the short-barreled pistol, and stared at them. Her small fists were blotched with blood.

She didn't look up as she heard Linden cross the room and felt herself lifted and then laid on a homely couch. The harsh bonds fell from her wrists as he produced a small knife and parted the cords with one hurried slash.

"Lay still," he commanded, and then was gone.

Katie peered glassily at the far-off ceiling and began to sing a low, atonal melody, trying to concentrate on each note in sequence.

"O, Glor-i-ous Home-land just o-ver the line, Pre-pared for the wea-ry by Christ the di-vine . . . Oh, Lord Linden, are you back? Where did you find all those towels? Oh, no, please don't open my dress!"

"Struggle," he said harshly, "and I'll knock you out. Christsake, child, you haven't got anything I've never seen before. About a thousand times."

"A thousand times? Really? Why is my dress blackened?"

"Powder burns. Point blank range. This will hurt you but I can't help it. Take a deep breath, sweetheart, and close your eyes."

Katie's universe spun and pitched for a moment, then dipped back to dully painful comprehension. She opened her eyes again to find the strained face above her.

"What happens when you press like that?" she asked, her voice a thread.

"Slows the bleeding."

"Oh. Isn't it funny?"

"Hmm? What's funny?"

"My cousin wanted to kill me but . . . oh, that feels so . . . my lord?"

Katie felt his hand cool against her cheek. "I'm here, Katie."

"Yes. Yes. Well, my cousin wanted to kill me but I saved him the trouble by shooting myself. Don't you think that's funny? Why did you come? I didn't think that there was any help for me."

She felt the steady, efficient hands change position. "Because I knew I wouldn't sleep tonight unless I was sure you were all right. No, be still, child. Lay quietly."

"Am I going to die?"

"No. God, no." It was as though he made her a promise. "You aimed well, little innocence, missed all the arteries. But the bullet didn't travel through so it must be lodged against bone. You'll have to have it out, Katie, but not until I get you to a doctor. First, though, the bleeding must slow down. Tell me about your cousin Ivo." Linden changed towels over the wound, this time applying pressure with one hand while the other tucked the cape firmly around Katie's shivering limbs. Gently, he stroked the hair from her pale forehead, and then touched her dry, bluish lips.

"Ivo?" she said hazily. "Ivo would inherit my mother's father's estate if I died. Mother's father's, does that make sense? But then he said that he would as soon marry me, because then he'd have control of the money, anyway, wouldn't he? I didn't handle things well and I made him angry. Oh, and he said he was skilled in the manly arts."

"A gentleman of rare finesse," said Linden. "Your knees must have grown weak from such an excess of gallantry."

Katie gave him a quick feeble smile that went straight to his heart. "Weak knees and weak stomach. I told him if he tried to make love to me, I'd be sick."

"No one will ever be able to accuse you of coquetry. Having failed at claiming French pox with me, no doubt you dared not try it again?" His attentive fingers had been softly massaging Katie's finely drawn cheeks but now they slid down to rest briefly over her heart, feeling its too rapid, fluttering pulse. "And then?"

Katie laid her tongue tiredly over her upper lip. "Then, I think that's when he said that I was your, well, your woman. But he used another word for it."

"Oh? Then I'm doubly glad that you didn't tell him you had the French pox. Only conceive the reflection that would have been on me." He watched her face closely. "Did he make you bed him, my dear?"

"No. Only kissed me, and that was distasteful

enough, not at all like when you do it. I don't think that he could have been speaking the truth when he claimed to know about the manly arts, do you?"

Linden shifted the cloth and was relieved to see the bleeding had diminished. "Oh, a *blanc-bec* of the first water. Now, Katie, I'm going to bandage your shoulder and then we'll go for a short ride on Ciaffa." Katie watched the practiced hands as they packed and bound her shoulder. She could tell he was taking great care not to hurt her but still she had to take her lips between her teeth to keep from crying out. His sober brown eyes scanned her blanched countenance. "Here, stay a moment, Katie. I'll be right back. Sing again." He left her side and she tried to sing, though it was harder now to concentrate on the words.

"A-sleep in Je-sus! Bless-ed sleep! From which none . . . none ev-er wake to weep." How thin her voice had become. "A calm and un-dis-turbed re-pose, Un-broken by the last of foes."

"Cheerful," observed Lord Linden, as he reentered the room carrying a silver flask. He sat beside her on the couch. "Katie, I'm going to lift you some. No, don't try to help me, let your body relax. That's right. So. I think you'll stand the ride better if I make you a little drunk first. Can you sip from this if I hold it for you? Try now. Dieu, what a face, child. And this my best cognac! A palate that can tolerate sour milk has no business rejecting vintage brandy. Come, Katie, again."

"Very well, my lord . . . but it tasted like you filled your flask from the ditch."

Chapter Thirteen

Perhaps imbibing a liberal amount of Linden's
brandy had something to do with it, but Katie
found no extraordinary discomfort attended the
transition from the couch to Ciaffa's well-muscled
back. Lord Linden had arranged her before him
on the saddle to give her the greatest support.
There could be no joy in holding her thus; in feeling the vital child reduced to this pathetically limp
creature whose head fell so heavily against his
chest. Katie unconsciously clasped and unclasped
her cold, benumbed hands, and on her wrists he
could see the flayed skin where Guy had bound
her. The flesh had contracted over her cheekbones
until they stood out in drawn and rigid bas-relief.
There was no key in Linden's hard young face to
the emotions that moved him, nor did he permit
any uncertainty to flaw the rocklike steadiness of
his hold on the wounded girl.

Ciaffa's slow, musical canter flew across the earth
like the free wingbeats of a blue heron in flight.
Katie could see the sparkling milky paradise of the
night sky; it seemed as though she were floating
through the stars, a lonely, wandering comet. But
not alone.

"Still with me, little one?" said Linden.

Katie stirred in his arms. "Yes . . . my lord? I don't remember—did I thank you for coming? Have I thanked you for all the times you've saved me? I would have been killed many times if you hadn't saved me." She giggled weakly. "Although you'll probably tell me that it is an anatomical impossibility, for a person to be killed more than once. Anyway, I wanted to say thank you."

"Forget it, child. How's the pain? Do you think you could sleep?"

"The pain is better than it was, but I don't want to sleep. I want to enjoy being awake and safe."

The moonlight lent a silvery cap to a nearby stand of European larches rising in narrow pewter towers from the corner of a hop field. She was lying very still, and he had begun to wonder if she had fainted when she spoke again.

"There is something—I wish I could stop thinking about."

"What?"

She looked up at him with dazed misery. "Ivo Guy said that he was going to—going to take me beneath him, and he would give me to Chilworthy too. It makes me afraid when I think of it."

"Don't think of it."

"I can't help it. What would have become of me if that had happened? My cousin said it would be better if I died. Do you think so?"

He was shocked by his own reaction to the horror in her voice. "No. No matter how they had hurt you, Katie, I would have found you and taken care of you." He stopped, silenced by an awareness of the inadequacy of his comfort. To his amazement, though, some of the tension seemed to leave her body, and she said with something close to contentment, "Oh, yes."

Involuntarily, his arms tightened their hold. They rode on in silence, Katie lying quietly against him. The houses were becoming closer together, and the traffic was increasing to a regular rush, until the passing of a vehicle was no longer as remarkable as a clear space in the road. They were coming into Mayfair now; passing to their left a palatial mansion lined with glimmering windows and crowned by an array of improbable pinnacles. Linden kept Ciaffa to a steady pace, riding through pools of amber streetlight, finally turning onto a beautiful square. Katie saw across the square a giant abode, fourteen windows wide, with a gray stone front and unadorned portico and pediment, set within a graveled courtyard.

"My lord, that house . . ." said Katie, struggling to sit up.

"Carefully!" said Linden sharply. "Katie, you mustn't move, or the bleeding will increase."

"But, my lord, this is your grandmother's house, isn't it? Lady Brixton? I thought you were going to take me to a doctor." He heard real fear in her voice.

"S'death, child, will you be still? There's a doctor only down the street; he will be fetched."

Katie turned her head to stare at the crenelated outline of the mighty house. "Take me to him at his home. Please."

"So haughty, My Lady Disdain? You lived above *The Merry Maidenhead*, you lived with Laurel," he said quizzically. "Won't you try living with a duchess? It's uphill all the way."

"I didn't *want* to live with Laurel," pointed out

171

Katie. "You made me. That was one thing, but this," she faltered, "is quite another."

"I've never heard it so well put," he said with mock admiration. "Stop squirming."

"Well," said Katie, "I'm not very articulate but I do know that duchesses don't entertain nobodies. And I'm worse than nobody. I'm . . . I'm an ivory-turner's daughter! And your grandmother is, oh, the elite of the elite! And that kind of people despise me, my lord. Please, you can't know. The squire near my home in Essex had three daughters, all respectable, and once when they were out riding they found me playing with one of their father's lambs and they said . . ."

"Hell and damnation, Katie, will you spare me any more of your pitiful scenarios? Bon Dieu, they're enough to harrow Attila the Hun! I'm willing to believe you've been insulted and mercilessly mistreated on any number of occasions, but you have a bullet lodged in your shoulder that will kill you if it doesn't come out and I'll be damned if I'll take you to a place where you won't get proper care. If it's any consolation to you, my grandmother was one of the town's most notable fallen angels in her youth. Age may have lent her the cachet of moral rectitude, but believe me, fifty years ago no one would have called her respectable. Our family is noted for wild youth and pompous old age."

They reached the stone steps of the portico and the tune of Ciaffa's even pace faded.

"Even so," said Katie, her frigid hands clutching at the neck of her cape in agitation, "she won't like me to come into her house."

"Of course she won't like it. So what? She'll calm

down after I explain. Besides, when I think of it, this is a damn good time to take you into her house. She can't throw out a wounded juvenile," he said callously. He slid lightly from the saddle, leaving one sustaining arm around Katie. "Relax your body and fall toward me. Don't worry, I won't let you drop. There. Katie, what the . . . stop! Saints save you, you'll kill yourself."

"I don't care," said Katie, squirming desperately in his arms. "At least let me walk. That's all I ask —not to be carried in like a hunk of mutton. Let me stand. Please!"

Linden bent one arm to set her feet on the top stair. "You'll collapse before you go two steps, little tiger. And I'll have to carry you anyway." He saw the hysterical shock bright in her pained eyes. He didn't dare try to collect her in his arms against her will. The Lord only knew what kind of damage she might do to herself with a struggle.

"I won't faint," she said shakily, "I never faint and I never cry and I never get sick. Except that I almost got sick when Ivo Guy kissed me." She gave Linden a wavering smile. "I'm not off my head, really I'm not. Only I feel enough of a spectacle without being carried. Can you understand that?"

"No," he said uncompromisingly. "You're out of your mind. I think it would be in your best interest if I slapped you insensible, and I'd do it, too, if you weren't staring at me like a lost dove. Come on, then. Step." He urged her forward, keeping a firm hold of her shoulders. It amazed him that Katie could even stand in her condition. When they reached the door, Linden banged the knocker with his free hand.

The door was opened by an imposing white-haired butler whose salt-and-pepper eyebrows levitated at the sight of the surprise visitors.

Linden returned his stare with annoyance and said, "Don't stand there gawking like an under-footman, Fawnmore. Find a groom for Ciaffa. Where's Lady Brixton?"

"Here's Lady Brixton," came a strong female voice from the vestibule. "Linden, is that you? You have deigned to answer my summons at last? Come in!"

Linden drew the shrinking Katie beside him through the massive stone threshold to stand before Lady Brixton, the Perfect Duchess. She was a ramrod straight woman with an air that was almost martial. Her three score and ten years had added wrinkles and an uncrossable dignity to what once had been great beauty; her skin was translucent white as though to hint at the blue blood which ran beneath, and her hair was the palest mix of silver and gold. When she saw the red-haired sylph at Linden's side, her expression became one of incredulous consternation.

"Grandson! Have you taken leave of your senses?" demanded Lady Brixton, nearly shouting.

Katie huddled closer to Linden.

"Don't be a fool, *Grandmère*," snapped Linden. "She's an unplowed field. Do you think I'd ask you to play pimp to one of my pigeons?"

"Linden! Would you try to cultivate a less ribald tongue? And lower your voice," said Lady Brixton in a furious tone. "This has got to be the most far-fetched stunt you've deeded yet. Pigeon, canary, or game pullet, she's not going to be plunked under my roof! Get her out before I have her thrown out!"

"Do," invited Linden with a snarl, "and she'll die. Look." He loosened Katie's cloak and let it slide to the floor, revealing her trembling, blood-drenched frame. Lady Brixton slapped her palm to her forehead, clenching her teeth.

"Of all the stupid, overdramatic . . . Am I to suppose it was beyond the scope of your imagination to walk into the house and say, see here, Grandmother, I have a wounded girl, could you render me assistance? Someday, Lesley," said Lady Brixton with conviction, "you're going to give me an apoplexy. Fawnmore, for God's sake, send for the doctor. Well, Linden, pick your victim up and follow me upstairs. Unless it would amuse you to watch her bleed to death in my foyer?"

When Linden lifted her, Katie made no move to resist him. The slender reserves of strength that had held her on her feet had fled, leaving her alone to face this spinning world. Linden felt her nerveless fingers pluck spasmodically at the collar of his riding coat as he mounted the colossal stairway.

"In here, Linden, it's the closest," said Lady Brixton, leading him into a lovely blue bedchamber. Linden eased Katie onto the japanned four-poster, noting with concern that the frost-blue tinge in her lips had deepened and all pigment had faded from her skin.

Light footfalls sounded on the carpeted hall outside, and Lady Suzanne McDonald fluttered into the room. She was a diminutive lady in sober black, the plainest, least clever, and sweetest natured of all the Brixton grandchildren, a group of cousins noted for their intelligence and good looks. Her own parents had been staid and provincial; in the worldly, sophisticated Brixton household she'd always felt like the cricket who came inside for the winter. She looked at her grandmother, at the tall, rather frightening cousin she'd always secretly admired, and then at the injured girl on the bed. Her eyes grew wide as dinner plates, and she clasped her hands over her round cheeks.

"Linden!" she said. "You've shot someone!" She stumbled back against the door frame with whitened cheeks. "My smelling salts! Hartshorn!"

Linden swore and grabbed her upper arm with a grip that would leave her bruised for a week. "A crack in the mouth would work faster than smelling salts," he hissed. "Do you still feel faint?"

"N-not at all," she replied limply. "Please, my arm."

He released her. "Sorry," he said shortly. "But, Jesus, it's outside of enough for you to pull vapors on me right now, especially since I need you. This child's got a bullet in her shoulder."

"Oh, the poor, poor little girl," said Suzanne, pulling herself together. She hurried across the room to lay a hand on Katie's brow. "How terrible! Has Dr. Carr been summoned? I'll call for Nurse. We'll have her put to bed and made ready for the doctor." She pulled the bell rope and looked toward her cousin. "Never fear, Lesley, I shall take the greatest care of her, I promise. And, of course, Nurse will know just what ought to be done. You must take yourself below, however, so she can be undressed and made comfortable before the doctor comes."

Katie had slipped behind a spinning screen of

fatigue, but Suzanne's words swung her back into reality.

"No," cried Katie, nearly flinging herself from the bed in alarm. She clung to Linden's arm in a sick, childlike plea. "Don't leave me. I need you, I need you." She stopped then, horrified that those frantic, mewling words were her own. She raised a dazed hand to her lips and whispered, "Help me. What's happening?"

"Nothing, *chérie*, it doesn't matter. Here, softly now, easy. It's only shock from the wound," said Linden, pushing her gently down. "I won't leave you. I'll only be downstairs, I promise."

"Stay," begged Katie. She gave Linden a tiny, sweet smile. "It won't be anything you haven't seen a thousand times before, my lord."

"Oh, dear," said Suzanne, seeing Lady Brixton puff like a steaming teapot.

"My lord," said Lady Brixton, "ought to be ashamed of himself." She draped an arm around her grandson's taut shoulders and said dulcetly, "If it's a thousand times, then I'm afraid the field's been plowed, mulched, cultivated and very likely seeded as well. You might as well stay."

He did stay. And neither Lady Brixton nor Suzanne, or even Nurse, who had known Linden since his cradle, could recognize the harsh, cynical rake in this tender man who sat beside the ailing child, teasing, distracting, and talking inventive nonsense to her while they bathed her in warm water, laid her under smooth sheets, and tucked heated bricks at her cold feet.

He stayed, too, while Dr. Carr made his careful examination of Katie's wound and announced with finality that the bullet must come out. Katie's eyes dilated as Carr laid out the shiny surgical implements.

"No, Katie, look at me," said Linden, taking her cheeks inside his palms.

Dr. Carr regarded Katie with a frown. "I've given the child all the laudanum I can. I think we might proceed. It's taken what hold it will."

Which is not a great deal, thought Suzanne worriedly. Katie was certainly confused, both from blood loss and the judiciously administered drugs, but she was still very much awake. Suzanne watched Lord Linden's face spark with feeling as Dr. Carr began to probe the injured shoulder. She sensed rather than saw Linden's anguished pity, and thought that never had she seen the warm sable eyes so vulnerable.

"*Doucement*, little one," he was saying, stroking the wisps of hair from Katie's cool, sweaty brow, "breathe deeply. Poor butterfly. Hold me. Katie. Katie."

Katie saw him through a shimmering net of chiffon. "Would you . . . like," she gasped, "to hear the Declaration of Ind . . . Independence?"

"Yes, say it," said Linden. Dear God, he thought, why doesn't she faint?

"When in the course . . . of human events . . . my lord?"

"I'm here, little star. What comes next?"

"Next. It becomes . . . it becomes necessary for one people . . . one people. . . ." Katie could hear her lips repeating the words after she could no longer understand them. It was as though her mind had sent one final meaningless message before dropping a heavy film between herself and all outside. Four giant eclipsing suns covered the corners of Katie's vision; in a single, concise, mercy-serving explosion they bloated until merging. She jerked one hand over her eyes and fainted.

It was sometime later that Lady Suzanne made her way into the evening room where she found her cousin Andrew, still wearing his evening formals. He had been sitting in one of the elegant Hepplewhite armchairs, his head thrown against its concave oval back panel while he made an absentminded study of the ornate plaster ceiling.

She blinked with suppressed agitation. "Oh, Drew, is it you, back from Almack's?"

"Of course it's me," he said with some impatience. "Who did you think it was?"

"Why . . . you, of course," she said, blinking her eyes again, with surprise.

Drew looked pained. "Stupid. And there's no need to act like you're guarding the Secret of Life. I've had the whole story of Linden's precipitous arrival this quarter hour from Fawnmore. But you look like you've swallowed a grapefruit. Come." He drew his cousin down beside him on a cream and floral settee, laying an arm across its serpentine back. "Was it dreadful when the sawbones came?"

"Yes," she said, shuddering with remembrance. "Poor girl. The laudanum hardly helped and she suffered and suffered and finally blacked out as Dr. Carr was removing the bullet. Horrible. And the girl bore it like an Amazon. Why, she's valiant to the heart."

Drew frowned. "Do you know how she came to be shot? Did Lesley tell you?"

"Not a word. His attention was only for the girl.

When the surgeon was done, Nurse shooed us out, Lesley and me, that is, so the poor child could sleep. She'll recover safely with proper nursing, Dr. Carr says." She looked sideways at her handsome young cousin and said, rather shyly, "Nurse thinks Katie (I believe that's her name) can't be a day over eighteen. Such a baby. She's . . . she's not in Linden's usual style, is she?"

"Ho," said Drew, with a censoriousness reserved for young female relatives. "And what do you know of Linden's usual style, may I ask?"

"One hears things, Drew. Now that I've been a married lady, people don't scruple to repeat the most scandalous things to me," she said, intimidated by his tone. " 'Twas Lady Jersey, you see, when I rode in the park with her and *Grandmère* a few weeks ago. We passed Linden in his phaeton, looking, oh, dashing, as he does, and he tipped his hat to us."

Drew resumed his study of the ceiling. "Such adventures you have, Suzanne," he drawled.

"You don't need to sneer, because I *was* coming to the point, which was that Linden was accompanied by . . . by a lady, though *Grandmère* would only call her a creature, with the most lustrous long blonde hair which she wore right down her back, not styled. Lady Jersey said that Linden favors ladies who are quite up to snuff, which I don't think Katie is at all. *Grandmère* says that he should never have acknowledged us when he's accompanied by one of his, I believe you'd call them, Lights of Love?"

"What I'd call 'em ain't in the least germane, Suzanne," he said with youthfully pompous disapproval. "You can't call 'em that. Can't call 'em anything, not even supposed to know about 'em. I think you've gotten devilish loose at the aft."

They were interrupted by Linden, who let himself into the room and dropped into a heart-backed armchair.

"Has she?" he said with a sarcastic assumption of interest. "I was wondering when she was going to drop to the standard of the rest of the family."

Drew strolled to the demilune sideboard. "You've had a difficult day, Lesley. Please," he said, "don't bother to maintain that benign façade on our account."

"Go to hell. But first, give me the brandy. Not in that damned glass, either. I want the bottle."

Drew handed it to him. "Guzzle to your heart's content, my dear."

Lord Linden had just lifted the slender bottle to his lips when Fawnmore appeared at the door to announce Her Grace, Lady Brixton. Her Grace wasted not a glance on Drew or Suzanne, but crossed directly to her least tamed grandson. It was a pity, in Drew's opinion, that the duchess had entered in time to see Linden drinking straight from the bottle.

"His Grace, my late husband," the duchess majestically informed her erring grandson, "had a prize boar who used to swill at the trough looking exactly like you, Lesley."

"You do me too much honor, *Grandmère,* I don't aspire to such heights," said Linden, rising to place a frugal kiss on his grandmother's blue-veined wrist.

"Sarcasm," said Her Grace, "is a moron's lance. Do you know what we did with prostitutes in your grandfather's time?"

Lesley fell back into the chair and took another swig of the brandy. "Whipped them behind cart tails?"

"On the contrary! No vulgar public displays. We kept them removed from the sight of decent citizens! I have never objected to a gentleman's discreet amusements, but I cannot countenance my own grandson flashing his strumpets in the face of polite society—and you ought to be sick with shame to have brought your mistress under the same roof as Lady Suzanne! As for the wench pursuing you naked into this house during my *soirée,* I will say nothing."

"So I see," said Lesley, drily. "She wasn't naked."

"What was she then?" demanded the duchess.

"She was . . . oh, damn, she was wearing a nightdress."

"And today," said the duchess, continuing her list of incidents in which Linden's moral shortcomings were brought to the fore, "you remained in the bedroom with her while poor Suzanne undressed her for Dr. Carr."

Linden's eyes held flame. "Yes, I did. I thought, Jesus, why not initiate a little bacchanale? Why should a petty thing like a bullet wound interfere with my pleasures? And it would be more piquant with Suzanne looking on . . ."

"Lesley, pity me," cried Suzanne, hands over her ears. "I cannot bear it when you are so nasty."

Before Suzanne knew what was happening, Linden had hauled her from the sofa and pinned her against the wall. "You have no idea," he said, his voice slow and soft, "just how nasty I can be. But Katie does. And do you know, she faced me with less fear than you show when I tell you 'good morning.' "

"Hotter than a penny pepper tonight, aren't you?" observed the duchess. "Let your cousin go before you give her the sobs. It isn't Suzanne's fault that someone's shot your *chère amie.*"

Drew watched this family quarrel with the air of one accustomed. He plucked Suzanne from his brother's grasp, patted her shoulder reassuringly, and pushed her down on the settee. "Well, Suzanne, you might have known how it would be; you ought to know better than to draw Linden's attention to you when he's in one of his moods." He turned to Lady Brixton. "*Grandmère,* I think you ought to know that I've met Katie before, last week when she was riding in the park with Linden. And she's not his mistress. Believe me, *Grandmère,* Linden's behaved to Katie like a dashed saint, damme if he hasn't. After hearing her story, I can tell you that Linden used a hell of a lot more restraint than I would have. You can see he's half out of his mind worrying about her. This is no time for you to be raking him over the coals."

Linden walked slowly across the room to set the brandy bottle on the chimneypiece of Siena marble. With one knee bent, he folded his arms across the mantel and buried his face inside them. "No, Drew, I've ruined her," he said. "I never laid with her, but no one will believe that, will they?"

Drew and Suzanne exchanged glances. The Duchess hesitated, then moved forward to lay a hand bracingly on her grandson's shoulder.

"I'm a wicked old woman, boy," she said briskly. "Forgive me. God knows, though, you hide your feelings so well that no one ever knows you have any. Whatever your sins may be, Lesley, you've never been a liar. Who is she?"

Linden turned, allowed his grandmother a brief embrace, and lowered himself onto the settee beside Suzanne. He slumped, crossing his long legs at the ankles, looking very young and more than half exhausted. Drew's heart went out to him; he poured brandy into a crystal tumbler and slid it between Linden's slack fingers.

"Thanks," said Linden. "Katie's Baron Kendricks's daughter."

"What! The Bad Baron's daughter?" said his grandmother. "She's of gentle blood then! You shock me, grandson. Tell me everything," commanded Her Grace with relish.

Linden shrugged wearily. "There's not a lot. When I met her, she was waiting table at a gin shop in the Rookery. *The Merry Maidenhead.* I know, *Grandmère*, you wonder what the hell I was doing there. Pursuing my, what did you call them? My discreet amusements." The faint trace of defiance in his voice brought a smile to Lady Brixton's lips. Linden answered it with a rueful smile of his own.

"There, *Grandmère*, how quickly you can reduce me to a schoolboy. Feels like the time Drew and I put a dead rat down Suzanne's gown."

"Those were easy old days. Before you and Drew were interested in what girls had *under* their gowns," said the duchess with a twinkle. "Proceed, lad. I perceive you weave me a romance."

Linden sipped the brandy thoughtfully. "Well, it's a devilish baroque one then. I took her back to my apartments."

"To rescue her from the horrible gin shop," exclaimed Suzanne, clapping her hands together. "How fine!"

Drew patted her head kindly. "Dense," he said.

"Suzanne," murmured Linden, his lips twisted into a half-smile, "you know me better than that. I took her there to seduce her."

"Oh, horrid! How frightened she must have been," said Suzanne, in quick sympathy.

"Don't be such a pea-goose," admonished Her Grace with a derisive sniff. "The chit should have been flattered! Besides, she must have been willing or she wouldn't have gone back to his rooms with him, would she? Or do you think he forced her at gunpoint?"

Suzanne looked at Linden's sensual, rakish countenance, and reflected that such a lawless act would be quite in harmony with numerous other incidents that spotted his infamous career. But those past scandals belonged to another man than the one who had been so kind to the injured red-haired girl. Suzanne saw Linden scan her face. His smile grew more cruel, as though he had guessed her thoughts.

"Gunpoint, of course," said Linden cordially. "Then I took off my belt and strapped her down . . ."

"I beg you to have done with your nettling," gasped Suzanne. She moved down the settee closer, and nudged his shoulder pleadingly with her small fist. "You think I'm foolish, don't you? I've noticed often that when you think someone is foolish you take a great deal of trouble to make them feel you are worse than you really are. Quite cross-grained! It may divert you to satirize people so, but indeed,

I find your profanity very wearing. I know that you use it like armor to deflect questions you don't wish to answer or to waylay the conversation, but I wish that you will not be so very . . . dexterous. Continue, please, but talk nicely."

The anger melted from Linden's eyes and his smile grew more friendly. "Very well, ferocious. I'll blunt my fangs if you'll remove your paw." He grinned down at Suzanne's small fist, and watched as she whipped it quickly away.

"Enough flirtation, children. We stray from the point. Once you had the wench in your clutches, Lesley, why not take her virtue?" asked Her Grace, who was every bit as plain a speaker as her grandson.

"Oh, 'pour not water on a drowning mouse,'" quoted Linden, shrugging. "She's as stupid as Suzanne—didn't understand that I was only interested in . . . oh, aye, Suzanne, I'm mute. Anyway, she didn't want it and I decided, in a burst of damned maudlin sentimentality, not to force her. Besides, I don't doubt I was too drunk anyway."

The duchess nodded approvingly. "A good thing, then. I'm surprised to find you so nice in your notions, grandson. Nothing," added Her Grace with a shudder of conviction, "can be more unpleasant than the performance of one's duty under a gentleman in his cups."

Drew leaned over and ran a finger down Suzanne's crimson cheeks. "Shame on you, *Grand-mère*, behold poor Suzanne's blushes. I swear you're worse than Linden. But he's looking more acerbic than usual, so I suppose he's tired of our interruptions. I'll keep my potato trap shut, brother dear. Go on . . ."

Chapter Fourteen

Katie lay snugly inside an opium-spun cocoon the next morning when Lord Linden came to see her. He stood beside the bed for a long time watching the fine-boned features, so woefully drawn. The freckles dappled her face like spots on a newborn fawn nestled in a forest thicket. She wore a thin flannel nightgown produced by the capable Suzanne; it was chastely high-necked and long-sleeved, with delicate ribboned lace patterned across the bodice, which rose and fell gently with the rhythm of Katie's sleep-breaths. Linden lifted one of the hands that lay slack with palm up outside the bedclothes. It was cool to the touch. There was no fever then, no life-threatening infection. He stroked the velvet surface of her fingernails, seeing that the skin beneath was still bluish from shock and blood loss.

It was becoming more familiar to him, this aching tenderness that he had never thought to feel toward another human being. At first he had refused to recognize it or to acknowledge its power over him; Katie would be one more incidental object to be used and discarded. And now he wanted to do neither. It had been hard for him to accept this budding affection. He had distrusted its permanence and disliked the vulnerability it seemed to press on him. Linden's defenses were strong; he had not welcomed this innocent invasion of them and yet . . . Carefully, he bent over to rest her hand on the quilted silk bedspread and touched one curl.

"My poor lamb," he murmured, but so softly that Nurse, standing across the room stowing fresh linen in a cedar chest, could not hear him. Linden turned and left, closing the door quietly.

Downstairs, Lord Linden found Drew and the duchess serving themselves from steaming serving dishes along an ancient oak sideboard in the informal breakfast room. One wall was dominated by a large window with gothic tracery. Before it sat a tier table bearing a *vase à sirènes* filled with long-stemmed violet iris. Linden growled a good morning and went over to gaze out the window, stroking an iris petal with a moody finger.

Such cavalier treatment in no way pleased Her Grace. "Vandal!" she snapped. "Do you think your pretty face will excuse your bad manners? If this is an exhibition of your social graces, then little wonder you've reached the estate of eight and twenty still bachelored! Greet me properly, if you please."

"Pardon, *Grandmère*," said Linden in an indifferent apology. He made her a graceful bow and placed a perfunctory kiss on her cheek. "It's true. I'm a surly fellow."

"We're accustomed," said Drew, stirring his tea with a silver spoon. "Eat, Lesley. You look as though you've been awake all night."

"Thank you." Linden scattered a ladleful of scrambled eggs on a floral-embossed china plate and carried it to the table, folding himself into a hoop-backed chair beside his brother. He made no move to eat; instead he sat flipping the eggs distractedly with his fork. After a moment he rose again and returned to stare out the window. A pair of expensive Brussels lace curtains framed the window and Linden tapped thoughtlessly at them, setting the starched folds into swinging motion.

"Stop worrying those draperies, boy!" barked Her Grace. "Resty, testy, fretsome stallion! Many's the time I've told your mama to take a firmer hand with you but she would always let you have your head. Drove your tutors into Bedlam with your brusque ways, never could sit still for a quarter hour running. I knew how it would be on the day you were christened—howled through the whole thing and kicked so hard the vicar nearly dropped you into the font. Irreligious even then! Have you looked in on your chit? How does she?"

Linden went to the sideboard and poured himself a glass of brandy. "Sleeping. Full of laudanum."

The duchess nodded. "That's as it should be, needs all the rest she can get." She worriedly regarded her grandson's slim tense form. "Taking this hard, aren't you? Don't fret yourself to Flanders, boy, we won't leave your Katie to perish in the gutter. And sloshing down brandy before noon like a heathen won't help you either. You'll put on flesh if you don't have a care."

"Do you think to take me in hand, *Grandmère*? God save me!" Lesley tossed off the brandy. "I'm going into the city. I want to see what can be learned about Ivo Guy."

"Will you inform the Runners on the fellow?" asked Her Grace, lightly spreading marmalade on a breakfast roll. "I think you had better not. The thing will spill into the newspapers and your Katie has dispensed enough scandal-soup. Best you find this Ivo yourself and deal with him quietly. Mind you, though, not dueling. Even the prince will not be able to protect you this time—the gossip over your last duel has barely begun to quiet."

"I know, *Grandmère*. I won't honor the *canaille* with my sword," said Linden. His lips relaxed into a smile. "I should have brought Katie to you earlier, you know, but I thought you might not have her. *Tiens*, I did you an injustice. Thank you." Linden gave her a swift kiss and was gone.

The duchess watched Linden go out, and then turned to her younger grandson, who sat dreamily chewing a piece of bacon.

"Your brother," the duchess informed Andrew, "is a willful rascal. I make no doubt that I shall be said to be opening an asylum for his used Paphians."

"Not you," said Andrew, smiling, "you'll outwit the gossips." He was silent for a moment and then said, "Do you know, *Grandmère*, it's Suzanne's opinion that Linden's in love with Katie."

"Ridiculous!" snapped the duchess, her body suddenly rigid. "Suzanne's opinion, indeed!" She glared at her grandson. "Do you mean to tell me that you think Lesley would try to seduce a gently born girl that he's placed under my roof?"

"No," said Drew calmly. "I think he might try to marry her."

Words failed the duchess. She regarded her

grandson with impotent fury, her face becoming suffused with purple.

"Lesley's altered when he's with Katie," continued Drew imperturbably. "He has a gentleness that's . . . well, you saw him with Katie last night, didn't you notice it?"

"No, I did not!" returned the duchess, snipping off each syllable with awful emphasis. "Chatterhead! Atlantis dreamer! Would you idealize your brother? In love? Ha! He uses women like an opiate, out of need, not affection. He shows a little kindness to a miserably used, orphaned child and you and Suzanne feel you must manufacture silly tales about the business. Frankly, Drew, I wonder at you!"

Andrew steadily met his grandmother's fierce stare. "Oh, very well, *Grandmère,* if you will have it so. . . . But if," he said, slyly, "Linden wished to marry Katie, hypothetically speaking, mind you, would you oppose the match?"

"Oppose the match? I should say so!" said Her Grace, her voice raised alarmingly. "A Byrne of Linden wed to a chit of disgraced name, impoverished, untitled, ill-reared? Unthinkable!"

"Her father's barony is old and respected, even if her father is a scamp," Drew reminded her.

"And her mother's family? Merchants!" said Her Grace with loathing. "Do you think I want my grandson to be related by marriage to such as Ivo Guy?"

"Lesley will deal with Ivo Guy," said Drew confidently. "*Grandmère,* do you remember last year when you and Mama had your heads together to find Lesley a wife?"

191

"Yes, but the wretched boy would have none of them," remembered Her Grace bitterly.

"I recollect at the time Mama said that she didn't think that Lesley would ever be forced into matrimony unless he fell in love. Then you said that if only Linden would choose someone and wed her, you would accept the girl, even if she were a barmaid. *Grandmère*, I think Lesley may have found his barmaid." Drew smiled seraphically at his grandmother, blew her a quick, saucy kiss and made a hasty retreat from the breakfast parlor.

Day had barely peaked into evening when Katie finally struggled from the laudanum-induced net that had enveloped her. A heavy soreness had settled into the wounded shoulder that sent stinging tendrils throughout her body. She hadn't moved much in her drugged slumbers; a dull, gnawing stiffness added to her misery.

She was aware of a mobcapped motherly lady uttering soothing monosyllables and spooning something into her mouth—a warm, tasty liquid that she swallowed instinctively.

The bedroom in which she lay, Katie had seen last night, though she had been too pained and frightened to appreciate its panelled walls of carved oak, painted white and pale blue. Clear dusk light sank into the room from windows hung in blue camlet, and lit upon delicate furnishings upholstered in striped silk. Katie saw a chandelier of gilt bronze and enameled metal above her, its design based on the Montgolfier air balloon that she had seen pictured in periodicals. By the time the mobcapped lady had washed Katie's face and brushed the red curls into smooth clusters, Katie was well on the way to full consciousness.

A short girl in a well-cut black mourning gown entered the room and Katie recognized her as Linden's cousin, Lady Suzanne. Katie shrank back against the pillows, fearful that this exalted young woman had come to berate her for her unwelcome intrusion to Lady Brixton's august mansion.

Suzanne came to stand right by Katie's bedside and lifted one of Katie's trembling hands, patting it kindly.

"There, there, Katie, you mustn't be shy of me," said Lady Suzanne, with one of her tender smiles. "I'm the most humdrum of creatures, I promise you. You must feel quite in the doleful dumps; I know I should if I were ill and placed among a motley group of strangers. How awful it's been for you! You have my every sympathy! I should tell you at once that Lord Linden has confided the whole of your trials to us—you needn't be afraid a single word of it will be repeated, of course. How vexed I was with Lesley for not bringing you to us at once, instead of lodging you with one of his horrid . . . well, I'll say no more on that head. Only that you have borne a great deal! Please don't hesitate to tell me if there is any way that I can be of service to you."

"No, no," protested Katie feebly, almost undone by so much benevolence. "I stand greatly in your debt already."

"What nonsense is this? It's my pleasure to have you here—though I'm sorry that it took such a dreadful accident to accomplish it. You must know that—ah, well, that I am most eager to meet you. Linden's never had the least love for women, you know."

"Oh, no," said Katie, surprised that Lady Suzanne should have such a mistaken idea of Linden's character, "he loves women all the time. In fact, Laurel told me that he can love . . ."

"Katie! Uh, perhaps I could fluff your pillow for you?" interrupted Lady Suzanne, readily able to perceive the rather alarming trend of these naive confidences. "There, that's better, isn't it? I must tell you that I was referring to another sort of love."

"Another sort of love?"

"Yes. But you've taken me quite off the subject. What I had begun to say was that Lord Linden seems very fond of you, which is the oddest thing in him. Oh, dear, not that I mean to imply that it's odd that he's fond of *you*. I mean it's odd that he's fond of *anyone*. A very self-contained man, you know, and not at all given to philanthropy."

"Well," said Katie, "Lord Linden's been very kind to me, but he's not in the least fond of me. To give you the truth without honey on it, he says that I'm a great trouble to him, that I'm an idiot, and that I make him wish he'd been born eighty and impotent."

"Those things," said Suzanne wisely, "you needn't regard. Lesley has said far worse things to me in a temper. In fact, when I think it over, I recall that he's said far worse things to me, even when he's not in a temper. Ours is a very . . . fiery family, you see, except for me, and perhaps Drew, though sometimes even he can be . . . ah, well, that's neither here nor there. But there's so much kindness in Lesley, I know. Why, animals always love him—that shows!" Suzanne refrained from adding that Lady Brixton had always ascribed this particular trait of his to what she described as the ability of animals to recognize one of their own.

Katie wriggled her toes, watching the bedclothes wrinkle slightly above them. "You see," she said, looking down at her hands, "he pities me."

Suzanne was daunted but pursued gamely, "Katie, recall the words of John Dryden: 'pity melts the mind to love.'"

Katie digested the quote. "I don't think Mr. Dryden could have been referring to Lord Linden, do you?"

"Of course he wasn't! He's been dead for more than a hundred years," Suzanne giggled.

"I thought so!" said Katie triumphantly, "A dead person! The vicar back in Essex was forever quoting them—and they say the queerest things, too. I never place too much credence in dead people. Pity, in Lord Linden's case, is more likely to move his mind to irritation. However much I wish it might be otherwise," she added wistfully.

Suzanne sighed and looked cast down. "I fear you are right. How melancholy." She thought a moment and then brightened. "But Drew thinks as I do. We talked about it last night. And in general, Drew knows Lesley better than anyone. We shall see! Anyway, I should not exhaust you with my bibble-babble. Let me give you another draught of sleeping powder—a lighter one, though. Dr. Carr was in to see you this afternoon while you were still asleep; he says that you'll do very well but you must have mounds of rest before you're fit for fishing. And no visitors, either, until you've got more of your strength back." Suzanne measured out a spoonful of the syrup and carried it to Katie with one hand cupped below to catch any wayward drops. "Nasty, is it? Have some lemonade? It will take away the bad taste, I think. Oh, I forgot to tell you—we've had your clothes brought from that horrible house that your cousin took you to. Lesley thought they might be there so we dispatched the coachman this morning and sure enough, he found your valise."

"Did you—did you look in the valise? I'm afraid you must have been shocked. Those dresses have not, I think, been conceived to benefit female virtue."

"No," admitted Suzanne, "they were perhaps a thought dashing, but Katie, I'm coming to the opinion that modest females would do more to prevent vice if they dressed themselves more like ladies of questionable morals. Then the gentlemen would be happy without visiting their light ladies and that would benefit female virtue!"

Katie slept most of the next two days. Each time she awoke, she could feel herself gaining in strength; but after her hair had been brushed and she was bathed and fed by Lady Suzanne or Nurse, she felt drained and ready to sleep once more. For the first time in her life, Katie had every comfort, every kindness, and the problems and worries of the past and future receded to some distant gray area behind Lady Suzanne's warm smile and Nurse's gentle touch.

On her third afternoon at Brixton House, Katie woke from a nap feeling hot under her blankets, and kicked them away fretfully. Then, delighted with the vigor of her legs, which had felt leaden that morning, she pummeled the covers repeatedly with her small feet until they were a tangled lump at the footboard. Dr. Carr had set tomorrow as the first day Katie might rise from her sickbed, but Katie felt ready now. Heartened by her defeat of the bedcovers, she pulled herself to her feet with the help of one carved bedpost, and made her way to the window. Katie pulled back the curtain to get a long deferred glimpse of the yew trees and trimmed shrubbery on this side of the mansion when she heard a door open behind her, and the airy murmur of skirts. A woman had entered the room.

"So," came that woman's voice. "You took a bullet in your breast three days past and now you're up on your feet like a peasant after childbirth. It isn't decent, girl, get back to bed!" Katie turned to see a striking elderly woman dressed in a modish gown of regal red. "Ha! I can see you know who I am! Linden's grandma. No, don't try to curtsey to me, you nitwit. Are you trying to give yourself the faints? Come, let me take your arm. Back to your rest . . . That's the trick! Wait, I'll punch up your pillow so you can sit up to talk to me instead of lying flat as a friar. There. Comfortable, are you?"

"Y-yes, Madame," said Katie.

Lady Brixton regarded Katie with irritation. "You needn't go calling me 'Madame' as though I was some damned procuress. 'Your Grace' will do. Well. Linden says you're an innocent. I'm not saying the boy's a liar, but it doesn't seem so damned innocent to me to stride through the capital in breeches and hobnob with young *roués* like my grandson."

"He only says I'm innocent because I wouldn't let him make love to me," said Katie, determined not to present herself to the duchess in a false light. "I . . . I'm sorry if you don't like my being here, though I like it very much. I never imagined that Lord Linden would impose on you so."

"Humph! Then you haven't got much imagination. Linden would impose on me up Mount Vesuvius and down again if it suited him, and don't you forget it! Selfish as a spinning spider, always has been and always will be. Spoiled by that mother of his. French, she is," said *Grandmère* darkly. She pulled forward a small chair, its back carved in lions' masks, and sat down close to Katie.

"Yes," said Katie. "Lord Linden talks French a lot; at least I think it's French, because I don't understand it."

Grandmother looked at her with approval. "I don't either. Don't know why the young people these days have to blather along in a foreign tongue when they've got a perfectly good language of their own. Damned unpatriotic. But that's neither here nor there. Fact is, I've got something I want to discuss with you."

"You don't like me?" said Katie meekly.

"Well," said the duchess, taken aback. "No call for you to look so crushed, girl. Thing is, don't know you. But Drew likes you. Nurse likes you. Suzanne likes you. And Linden must like you, because he never walked across the street to help anyone he didn't like. So I daresay I'll like you well enough when I get to know you. But that isn't what I wanted to say to you. It's this; that giddy Suzanne and little Drew are whispering of bridals—take my advice and don't gild your dreams with that illusion, my girl. Anyone with eyes can see why Linden would want you, but my warning is that you'll get any ring you want out of him but not a wedding band. His warmer feelings might lead you to a pretty peppy evening, but they won't lead him down the aisle."

The skin over Katie's cheekbones grew taut, and the slight shadows under her eyes deepened as though the light in the room had suddenly dimmed. "I never thought so," said Katie in utter sincerity. "Never."

Lady Brixton began to understand the spell Katie had cast over the household. She found herself leaning over to pat Katie's cold cheek. "There, there. No need to sink your boat. Only meant to warn you. That grandson of mine's broken more hearts than I'm able to count. If it's any comfort to you though, if you ever did bring the thing off, you won't find me raising objections. Linden's been indulged since the day he was born; the family's always given him everything he wants, and if he decided he wanted you, so be it. In any case, you'll find I'll stand your friend." Which was the last thing that Lady Brixton had expected to say when she walked into the room.

Next afternoon, when Lady Suzanne came in to arrange an oversized bouquet of sunny pompon dahlias in a crystal urn by Katie's bedside, she found her young guest awake. She stayed on to help Katie into a becoming bedjacket of crocus gold Thai silk and arranged a white rose with thick, satiny petals over Katie's ear.

"Would you like me to read to you for a while, Katie?" she asked. "Nothing heavy, mind you, merely entertaining. Where do your tastes in literature run?"

"I'm not terribly particular, so long as it's lurid. Do you have a story with a dragon in it? I'm partial to those. Also, I like . . . I can't remember their names, but they have a woman's head and all the rest is lion. That's what Laurel has, but Lord Linden doesn't like it."

"I should think not!" Suzanne giggled. "You mean sphinxes, don't you? And I collect they are motifs in her furniture? 'Tis very fashionable, you know, but Lesley is rather a connoisseur of such things, so I daresay he finds imitations sadly bloodless. I'll tell you what, though. I have a story with both dragons *and* sphinxes, or at least one sphinx, and I shall bring it directly."

Happily the story proved eerie enough to satisfy the most jaded palate and Suzanne read for over an hour as the shadows lengthened and the day crept warily into dusk. Lady Suzanne had opened the windows to admit the furtive evening breezes, which stole around the room like sullen gypsies, fingering the frilly table scarves and their tasseled fringes. At infrequent intervals the air currents would change direction and the crisp camlet drapes would be sucked outward, hitting the window's edge with a decisive smack, startling the ladies. They would look at each other, smile nervously, and plunge blissfully into the penny dreadful once more. A chorus of summer frogs began a rhythmic, sinister chanting in the reaches of the night.

Finally, Lady Suzanne looked over, found Katie had fallen asleep, and with a smile, closed and marked the book. Then she departed, leaving the door partly open.

Which was why half an hour later, Drew was able to glance in, in passing, to see Katie deep in sleep, the fantastic auburn beauty of her hair stark against the pillows. She looked like something in a fantasy, a dream. He was drawn further into the blue bedroom. Drew studied the thick, downy eyelashes, the plush cream of her skin, and the ruby velvet lips. On impulse, he rested his hands on the pillow beside her shoulders, and leaned forward to brush the lips with his own. It stirred him more than he had thought possible, and he continued the kiss until he felt her lips parting sweetly under his, and heard her soft moan.

"Lord Linden?" she breathed, opening her eyes to focus on Drew who was gazing at her, enchanted. Her lovely eyes widened with confused astonishment.

"Don't be afraid," said Drew, his voice very gentle. "I was playing Sleeping Beauty."

"Oh. Was it you that kissed me?"

"Yes." He smiled. "Poor Peaches, how disappointed you look. I'm sorry that I'm not Lesley. Wish I were." Drew sat on the bed beside her. "Suzanne says you are stronger today?"

"Yes. I was up most of the morning, walking steadily. Lady Brixton says that it's most unladylike of me to recover so quickly. She told me that if she's ever had the good fortune to get shot, she'd have made capital off it for a month."

"That's nothing on m'mother," said Drew. "She turned her ankle ten years ago and still thinks she must have someone to support her up the steps. What else do you and *Grandmère* talk about when she visits you?"

Katie wrapped an auburn curl thoughtfully around one finger. "Well . . . we talked about Laurel a bit. And about what her house looks like inside. Lady Brixton has never been there, you know."

"I should hope not! What else?"

"Freckles," responded Katie promptly. "This morning Her Grace said that I might have been a pretty girl but it was a shame about the freckles. I told her that Lord Linden said he liked them, but your grandmother said, 'That's just the kind of thing a man will say when he wants up your skirts, my girl. Men would admire your bunions if they thought it'd get 'em anywhere.'"

Drew gave a gasp of laughter. "Oh, dear. Were you very shocked?"

"Not at all," replied Katie candidly. "In fact, it sounded very much like something that my father would have said."

"As well for you that you weren't," said Drew. "*Grandmère* always holds anyone in contempt that she can shock. Lesley's the same. He's coming to talk to you tonight, did Suzanne tell you?"

"No!" Katie hadn't seen Linden since the night he had brought her here and the thought of seeing him again sent the petal lips curling into an excited smile. She tried to jerk herself into a sitting position, but as she did, her vision began to narrow until the room about her seemed to be at the far end of a long, dimming tunnel. She could hear Drew's sharp exclamation through the crackling hum that overlaid her hearing. A moment passed and then a second male voice filtered through to her.

"You're all right, little one. Rest now."

"My lord?" said Katie fuzzily. She sensed rather than felt the comfort of his arms.

"Yes," came Linden's calm voice. "Don't panic,

Drew. She's only lightheaded from trying to sit up too fast. She'll find herself again in a minute."

Katie shook her head slightly to focus her washed-out field of vision. "Yes, I will. I'm sorry to make such an exhibition of myself." She tilted her head back until she was able to smile welcomingly into Linden's eyes. "I was just so happy to hear you were coming to see me. It's been three days." Her voice made it sound like an eternity.

Keeping one arm around her shoulders, Linden stacked the pillows into a smooth heap and laid her back against them; his fingers rehooked her bedjacket's top button, which had slid out of its silk buttonhole.

"I can see," drawled Linden, "that you haven't lost your delightful knack of tumbling out of your clothing. How's the shoulder?"

"Like new," lied Katie.

A frown came into Linden's coffee eyes. "Like hell," he said. "Little liar." He caressed her curving cheekbone lightly with his thumb; the pale skin deepened in color under his hand and grew warm. Abruptly, he removed his hand and rose from the bed. He hesitated a moment, then dragged forward an armchair and sat down. Drew looked at him questioningly and perched on the chair's arm.

"Do you feel well enough to talk, Katie?" asked Linden, his gaze intent on her face. She nodded, looking a little scared by his cool tone.

He studied her and then said, "I've been to see your grandfather's lawyers. He had a law firm in London, very respectable. It seems that everything Guy said was true—you stand to inherit some twenty thousand pounds from your grandfather. Unfortunately, sweetheart, that's not the good news that it sounds to be." He saw her clench one small hand into a fist and bent forward to straighten her curling fingers and stroke the back of her hand. "Your grandfather, it appears, was something of a misogynist; he left you the money in your father's name and the way the will stands, if your father is your legal guardian, then the money can go to meet his debts."

"But you said *if* my father is my legal guardian!" said Katie, her hand tensing again under Linden's. "He is. Of course, he is."

Linden tucked her hand against the warmth of her hip. "I'm sorry, Katie, but that's not so. Ivo Guy's gotten legal custody of you by claiming you've been deserted by your father. He's got a weasel of a solicitor starting a suit against me to demand you be returned to him. Where Guy himself is, nobody's been able to discover."

Katie twisted the back of her hands to her cheeks in agitation. "I shall have to go back to him," she said, her voice weak with horror. "No one will believe that he threatened me. They'll think I'm lying. Lord Linden! Lord Linden!"

Linden moved swiftly to the bed and caught her trembling wrists with one hand. His other hand flew to her chin and held it, forcing her to look up into his cold eyes.

"Enough!" he said sharply. "You'll work yourself into a fever. Do you think that I'd go to all this trouble to save your pretty body and then turn you over to tease Guy's manhood? I won't let Guy take you. I'm fully aware of what that would mean to you. Damn you, Katie, breathe deeply or you'll grow faint again! Easy, child. . . . Better. Listen to me. If I have to, I'll kill him. But I doubt it'll come to that. We're going to court to get a temporary order placing you in my grandmother's custody. In the meantime, though, we look for your father . . . and watch out for Ivo Guy."

Chapter Fifteen

The May rain clattered in cold pellets against the pavement outside, but Fawnmore had caused a fire to be lit in Lady Brixton's green drawing room so no unpleasant consequences of the elements need disturb its noble occupants. Lord Linden had just, under Andrew's encouraging gaze, finished telling his grandmother the same story that he had told Katie earlier this evening, only this time he spared nothing of its grimmer details.

Lady Brixton had listened without comment, her face serious. Finally she said, "You think the girl's in danger then."

Linden crossed his legs at the ankles, his teak eyes remote. "Guy's only choice now is to kill her before we can win custody in your name," said Linden, his voice without emotion. "Or before we find her father and his credit-sharks can claim the money."

"He's a madman!" declared Lady Brixton. She cast an impatient glance at Linden. "Why can you not find him first? Lord knows, boy, you've enough connections with low life men from your work spying for the War Department, of which I will never approve, not if I live to be a hundred. Ahem.

Point is, why can't you hire one of those wretched fellows to locate Guy?"

"I have," said Linden calmly. "But, *Grandmère*, do you have any idea how many places there are to hide in a city the size of London? Of course, we'll find him eventually, but . . . damn, I wish I knew where her father was!"

"Perhaps it wouldn't hurt to contact Katie's pal, Zack, again?" ventured Drew, who was sitting on a wool carpet in front of the fire, his arms resting on knees that he had drawn up to his chest. "Katie went there once to see if Zack'd heard from her father. Might be worth one more try."

Linden nodded. "All right, Drew. But that boy's tough as timber. I have a feeling that he wouldn't tell me anything for money, love, or fear. But if I brought him here to see Katie . . . I will."

Lady Brixton's gaze riveted indignantly on Linden. "Oh, you will, will you! You're taking a lot on yourself, aren't you, boy? First I'm to adopt the Bad Baron's daughter and then you expect me to entertain some rascally scum of a pandering gin-shop owner at tea! You brided your jezebel Laurel with jewels; what blandishments do you offer me?"

Lord Linden offered her his most Elysian smile. "You've got more jewels than a sultan's harem. Would you do it for my eternal gratitude?"

"Conceited calf! Bamboozler!" said Her Grace. "I'm not doing it for you, anyway, I'm doing it for Katie. Nice little gal, sort of chit I like. Got a way about her . . . and she's not stuffed full of fuss and affectation like most modern misses. And I'll say this for your little Kendricks, she could have made life easier for herself by serving gentlemen's conveniences. She didn't choose to, which says a good thing for her morals, if not for her brains." The duchess regarded the shaded brown eyes of her grandson. "As you say, she's an innocent."

Linden set down the wine glass that he had recently emptied, leaned back into his chair, and spoke coldly. "*Comment cela, Grandmère?* What convinced you? Beside, of course, my word."

The duchess chuckled. "Well, I didn't harass the chit with an interrogation so you needn't glare at me as if I were poisoned porridge. It's obvious the chit has her virtue—when she told me about Laurel's bedroom—oh, aye, frown your head off, boy, I don't care! If you don't like it, you oughtn't to have taken her there! Anyway, Katie didn't know why Laurel had a mirror hanging over her bed. That's innocence."

"Didn't know?" asked Linden. "Past tense?"

"Past tense," agreed the duchess, mischievously. "She knows now. I told her."

The duchess had taken a strong liking to Katie but if this was any comfort to Linden, it didn't show. Her Grace had invited him to take a late dinner with his family but she soon saw she had made a mistake. Before the meal was over Linden had drunk enough to have laid any other man under the table several times over. Something, it appeared, was worrying his lordship. He had gone from wine to cognac to a tankard of dark ale. Every so often Lady Suzanne, who was quite unused to heavy drinking, would pause in her discourse on the day's activities (just now she was confiding to a politely glazed-over Andrew the finer points of pruning the garden rosebushes) to glance uneasily in Linden's direction. When she had directed her fourth nervous peek at her inebriated cousin, Linden slammed his tankard onto the dinner table's mahogany surface in a blow that was to forever mar its satiny finish.

"Hell and damnation, Suzanne!" lashed Linden. "Must you cutty-eye me as if I were a vampire from hell? God knows, I'm only swilling at the trough . . . in the great family tradition of *Grandpère's* prize sow. No, boar. Damn. Do you know what you can do with your rosebushes? I can see by your face that you do. Good." Linden lurched to his feet, sending his chair flying into the wall behind him and oversetting a silver fruit dish. He swore, snatched a bottle of port from the sideboard and grabbed the hapless Suzanne, twisting his hands into her hair and kissing her full on the mouth. Then, not opposed to adding insult to injury, he released the bewildered girl roughly and remarked, most unfairly, that if that was all the better she could kiss, it was no wonder her late husband had seen fit to break his neck.

"Lesley," observed the duchess, "is not behaving well."

She found her elder grandson in the library some ten minutes later. Linden had pulled off his jacket and flung himself into an oversized armchair. One long booted leg was cast carelessly over the chair's molded arm and he swung it idly to and fro while perusing a short sheet of gilt-edged note paper. Lady Brixton came into the room, closing the door quietly behind her. Linden looked up.

"There are times," said the duchess tranquilly, "that you are inconsiderate and thoughtless, Lesley, but I have never known you to be a bully."

"You're right. I drink too much," he answered her, his voice without expression.

Lady Brixton sat on the edge of his chair and tenderly brushed the dark curls back from his forehead. "That's all right, then. You can drink too much as long as you know you're drinking too much."

"Christ," he said irascibly, "living with Suzanne has turned you into a damned petty philosophizer."

Her Grace received this criticism with equanimity. "I thought so. Suzanne's done something to anger you, hasn't she? Interfered with your business? How you hate anyone to do that! The chit's a born meddler. What's she done? Aside, I presume, from the lamentable lapse in manners that led her to discuss her rosebushes at the dinner table?"

"She's taken to sending me instructive dispatches. I found this note pinned to a pillow cover in the bedroom." Linden handed the note to his grandmother between two fingers. "Remark, if you will, that it bears the heading 'Axioms for Lord Linden.'"

"It's Suzanne's hand, all right," said Lady Brixton, scanning the small sheet. "Dear me. It says, 'Whoso findeth a wife findeth a good thing. Proverbs 18:22." Her Grace laughed softly. "Oh, Suzanne, you brat."

Linden waved one hand and raised the wine bottle to his lips with the other. "Continue, *Grandmère*. You will see, we progress through history."

" 'Man's best possession is a sympathetic wife. Euripedes. 5th c. B.C.,' " read Lady Brixton, "and it continues, 'There is no more lovely, friendly and charming relationship, communion, or company than a good marriage. Martin Luther. 1569.' Poor Lesley, how galling to have your deepest concerns guessed and reduced to a series of obscure platitudes."

"*Voilà*," snarled Linden, "she's as subtle as a cocked musket, your Suzanne. And too damned well-read." He closed his eyes for a long time and sat without moving. The duchess was quiet beside him, looking away from him so as not to disturb his thoughts by the intensity of her gaze. At length, he opened his eyes and said, "Katie has enough problems without trying to flow in my harness. I've done her too much harm already."

Lady Brixton regarded her attractive grandson curiously. "And you think it would harm her more if you married her?"

"Without a doubt. I'd make a devil of a husband."

Lady Brixton dropped a loving hand on Linden's shoulder. "Lesley. You're too hard on yourself. You always are, you know. But, of course, we both know that this is nothing I can help you with. What I can do is to cease my petty philosophizing and go beat Suzanne for you. Good night."

Much later that evening, when Lady Suzanne came into her dressing room to prepare for bed, she found a scrap of note paper addressed to her standing in a folded pyramid on her dressing table. She opened it and recognized Lord Linden's impatient scrawl. At the head of the note was one word, 'Sorry.' And below it read 'A saying for Suzanne—More belongs to marriage than four legs in a bed. Thomas Fuller. 1732.'

* * *

The rain stopped an hour before sunrise and the passive night breezes brought London a comfortable daybreak. It was the last comfort the city was to feel that day. As quickly as the new, angled sunlight hit the still damp pavement, thin, wet noodles of steam rose upward in sun worship. This was to be the day of the sun, the most unseasonably hot, humid day that London had suffered in twenty-five years. It was hot as blazes, hot as hell. The heat rebaked the bricks of the National Trust, broiled the broken eggs of pigeons nesting on St. Paul's dome and roasted fishermen casting their nets on the Thames. Ladies sacked their wardrobes for their lightest garments, gentlemen discarded jackets and cravats and Lady Brixton ordered the housemaids to forbear their dusting and the chef to prepare no meals that didn't come out of the cool cellar and needed no heating.

At nine o'clock, Katie took her promised walk in the Brixton gardens, sharing a parasol with Lady Suzanne. By nine-thirty, both ladies were forced to admit it would be madness to go on. Though Katie felt the strongest she had since her injury, in fact, almost well, a faint pink heat flush had crept under her skin and the humidity had attacked Lady Suzanne's curling-ironed coiffure and what had been ringlets an hour ago had become straight mousy-brown hanks. The ladies repaired to the Lady Suzanne's boudoir where they shed as much clothing as modesty would permit, fanned themselves vigorously with large palm-leaf fans and drank unladylike quantities of lemonade. Conversation, when it existed at all, was desultory and concerned mostly with the cruel and unpredictable nature of the elements.

Sometime during the afternoon, Lady Suzanne stretched out on her daybed and fell asleep, her arms outflung, her petticoats riding up to her knees. Katie was tired, too, but also a little restless, so she sponged herself with cool rose-scented water from Suzanne's porcelain ewer and struggled into an eau-de-Nil green gown of silk gauze. The sleeves were small and puffed, the waist cut high under her breasts, and there were twelve tiny buttons inconveniently set down the back seam that caused Katie a fair amount of grief to fasten. It took five minutes of painful effort and much backwards consultation with a full-length mirror before each button was in place.

"Thank God," she said and started from the room, only to be stopped by the sight of the hairbrush staring reproachfully at her from the sycamore-stained vanity. Katie returned guiltily to run it through her hair and thread a dark green ribbon through the peaking curls in the way that Antoinette had taught her, except that it didn't look quite the same as when Antoinette had done it herself.

Katie wandered fascinated through the long, carpeted halls and Italianate marble anterooms of the great house, a diffident, respectful tourist among the refined opulence. At length she came to the billiard room where she found Drew, who had most improperly engaged a young underfootman in a game. They stopped when Katie came in and at length Drew bore her off to the orangery, which, he claimed, was the only room in the house with a temperature below roasting.

The orangery proved to be a large, delightfully exotic room closed in by shaded glass, and thick with a velvet jungle of bushes, vines, ferns, and timidly blooming bulbs. Drew led Katie to the center of the room where a hissing fountain sent out a perpetual spray of crystal vapor. She sat on the cool granite floor beneath a spreading umbrella plant and began to question Drew about the plants. What were their names? Did they come from Brazil? Were they poisonous? Did Lady Brixton have a bush with fruit that could make you drunk? Drew had been about to indignantly refute any suggestion that he knew anything about a bunch of damned plants but Katie's last question and the credulous expression on her pretty features spurred his sense of the ridiculous. Grinning, he began to weave Katie several long and totally imaginary tales about the monstrous botanical rarities of Brazil. He achieved a considerable success with a plant that drugged its human victims with an irresistibly intoxicating fragrance, then drew them inside their leaves and digested them while the unfortunate victims had visions of Utopia. Katie began to look nervously at a lazily curling frond which was nodding seductively over her shoulder.

Lord Linden had been to visit *The Merry Maidenhead* that afternoon and had just returned to Brixton House accompanied by Zack. The two men entered the orangery in time to hear Drew's last mare's nest. Linden came to the fountain, brushing aside a few boldly straying branches and tousled his younger brother's hair.

"I ought to throw you in that fountain," Linden said pleasantly. "The poor child probably believes every word of your Irish bull." He bent to touch

Katie's cheek and ran a quick searching gaze over her face.

"If I'm ever to be thrown into the fountain, I'd as lief it be today as any. Sounds devilish refreshing." Drew studied the thinnish youth with shoulder-length straggling hair and tight breeches who had followed Linden into the room, and nodded, keeping his hands at his sides. "You must be Zack. I know you from Katie's description."

"If it was from Katie's description, then you must be expecting the Demon King," said Zack matter of factly. He dropped to sit on his heels in front of Katie. "How are you, Katie, pet? Christ, you're pale. Linden's been telling me about your escapades! Seems like I no sooner let you out of my sight but you embroil yourself in a set of madhat shenanigans."

"Of all the unkind, unfair . . ." said Katie, setting her hand on the fountain's edge to pull herself upright. She was still angry about his attempt to force her into elegant prostitution. "It was a shame that you didn't know about Ivo Guy before you *sold* me to Lord Linden. My cousin might have paid you more than fifty pounds for me."

Katie turned her back and would have marched from the room, but Zack stood and caught her around the waist, pulling her back against his body.

"Whist, Mousemeat. Will you listen a minute? There's nothing that could ever make me sell you to anyone who'd hurt you. I think you know that." He ran a tender hand through her curls. "Dammit, are you going to hate me forever? As it turns out, if this Ivo Guy was going to come after you, then

215

you were a hell of a lot better off under Linden's protection than mine."

"I'd have been better off under the protection of a cannibal tribe than yours!" said Katie wrathfully, but weakening. "Why did you come? To see if anyone's bought me a Viennese villa? Well, they haven't. Good-bye."

Zack laughed, planted a friendly kiss on her cheek and released her. "Saucy chit," he said indulgently, "I came to see you in your hour of illness, of course. Lord Linden came to the Maidenhead and told me you'd been shot. Behold me here, to see for myself that you were all right. Even though it wasn't any picnic going through the streets in this heat. I worry about you, y'know."

"Do you really, Zack?" asked Katie, half skeptical, half sincere. She sighed and sank down on the fountain's variegated Carrara marble edge. "I'm glad that you do because Papa certainly seems to have forgotten about me."

It would have been nice to be able to comfort her, but her words so nearly echoed the sentiments of the three gentlemen present that none of them felt able to do so. Drew sat down beside Katie and looked at Zack.

"Unless Zack has gotten a message . . . ?" he said.

"Well, I haven't," returned Zack testily. "As I've been telling Linden here a good half-dozen times. I'm as stymied as you are. The last I heard, the baron was nosing after some married woman in Dorset, whose name I don't know. I suggest you check that."

Linden's only concession to the heat was a half-open lawn shirt. He had been leaning against a tubbed palm tree, his arms crossed in front of him, the onyx hair curled only slightly more than usual against his chiselled cheekbones.

"I've checked there," said Linden blandly. "He went to Dorset, yes. And visited his ladyfriend. After that, he disappeared. She has no idea where he went."

"The lady told you that?" questioned Zack. "My compliments on your powers of persuasion."

"A persuadable lady," replied Linden with a noncommittal shrug. "She's twenty-two, her husband's sixty-eight. She's lonely and bored in the country."

Drew's interest was drawn away from the subject previously under discussion at the reception of the latter intelligence. "Twenty-two, eh?" he said. "What's her name? I'll keep it to myself," he added as an afterthought.

"She's Maria Enfield. It won't do you much good, though," said Linden. "Her husband is recently retired from the Admiralty. He's very doting on his beautiful wife and in constant attendance. It took me some time to get her alone to query her on this . . . subject."

"Enfield," said Katie thoughtfully. "I've heard that name before. Why, Zack, how queer you're looking. Are you getting heat sick?"

Zack was indeed looking singularly scarlet. "Her husband, the admiral, couldn't have been there," he said flatly. "You must be mistaken, my lord." He stared at Katie for a few long seconds, until suddenly she covered her mouth with her hand, the pastel blue eyes widening into sugar biscuits.

"You're right, Zack," said Katie with a gasp. "He couldn't have been there because Winnie and

Patrick and their friends kidnapped him! Enfield was his name, wasn't it?"

"It was Enfield all right," said Zack glumly. "But it couldn't be . . . I mean, Jesus . . . there couldn't be two Admiral Enfields, could there be? Brothers, perhaps? No, I didn't think so. When did you go to Dorset, my lord?"

"Wednesday last, before Ivo Guy came for Katie."

"And you're sure this Admiral Enfield was there?" asked Zack.

"Yes, of course I'm sure," said Linden with a snap. "I know I'll regret asking this, but what kidnapping are we talking about?"

Zack pulled a gray handkerchief from his pocket and pushed back his hair with it, obliterating a miniature tidal wave of sweat. "Has Katie talked about Winnie at all?"

Linden glanced at Katie. "Yes. The Declaration of Independence."

"Exactly," continued Zack. "Winnie's the queen of London's 'Give Me Liberty or Give Me Death' set. Nothing her and her half-witted cohorts like better than to cause some disturbance or engage in a petty intrigue. They decided that kidnapping an admiral would be an effective way of gaining some attention. They thought they'd have the government in the palm of their hands, but the government has been paying them no attention at all. And now we know why. The brainless wonders got the wrong man!"

"The wrong man," said Linden thoughtfully. He walked to Katie and pulled her to her feet. "Go fetch your bonnet, sweetheart. We're going for a ride."

Lady Brixton's town carriage was upholstered in titian blue velvet with gold frogging, which made elegant contrast with the high polish of the mahogany fittings. The carpeting was etched with the Brixton ducal crest, and was so clean and bright that it looked as though it had never known a shoe print. Katie could hear, from inside this plush cradle, the conversation between Lord Linden and Zack, who, with Andrew, were mounting horses to accompany the carriage.

She heard Linden's voice. "You say he's being held in a warehouse? Have you ever been to this place?"

"Yes, but not since the kidnapping. Very atmospheric. You'll like it."

"God," said Linden.

The team moved sluggishly in the heat, their hooves in slow walking rhythm. Katie leaned back against the cushions Drew had arranged for her. Traffic moved imperceptibly on the London streets. No dogs barked, they panted instead. The pigeons on Bennett Street didn't fly, but flocked, complaining about the reeking incandescence. Katie was excited and her wounds ached, but the heat was weakening her and, coupled with the carriage's pacific sway, it soon slipped her into sleep.

She did not awaken even after they had reached their destination and the carriage had halted. It took a gentle hand on her good shoulder to rouse her. Katie tried to sit up, but was prevented by the pressure of that hand.

"Wait. Wake up a bit first." Katie looked up into Linden's impassive face. He was stroking her cheek with the back of his hand. "We're now at the radical redoubt, about to make contact with an organized threat to the security of the Crown." He helped her to her feet and, going before her to street level, turned and lifted her down. She leaned against him unsteadily, flinching against the harsh white light. They were stopped in a warehouse district, in the rotting heart of London; red-shingled warehouse roofs were being beaten under the hammer of the sun upon the anvil of the hard-packed, deserted dirt streets. The reek of decomposing rope and the stench of the Thames were suspended in the air. Above them stretched the cream and yellow rough bricks of their destination. From close by came the deep, hollow slap-slap of sluggish river water on the side of a tethered barge. Zack had dismounted and was standing near them, shifting his feet. Drew was still on horseback, standing in his stirrups to get a better look at the building.

"Well, now what happens, Zack?" asked Linden. "Do we make our way through a subterranean tunnel littered with the rotting bones of their previous victims?"

"No," said Zack, grinning. "We're not quite *that* atmospheric. This warehouse has a door. Follow me." The foursome made their way along the edge of the building until they came to a large double door set off the ground by about three feet. There was a scuffling movement from behind the door, and a gun barrel slid out of a knothole, nearly colliding with Zack's nose.

"Watch it with that thing, would you?" said Zack. "It's Zack, you booby."

"That's not th' password," came Winnie's muffled voice, with the tremor of a laugh in it.

"Devil take the password, you paper-skulled

puzzletext. Open up this door!" Zack commanded.

There was the raw sound of a deadbolt being removed and the double doors swung outward, revealing a smirking Winnie, leaning seductively on an ancient musket, dressed in a long, flowing red frock, barefoot, with large brass hoops in her ears.

" 'Ello, Zackie," she said. " 'Ow's me better 'alf?" Winnie stopped, looking over Zack's head to see Zack's companions. "Glory be, is this a raid?"

"Pretty close to," said Zack. "Where's that admiral you're holding? Haven't let him go, have you? No? Good. Because we want to see him."

Winnie's jaw dropped. "Want to see 'im?" she repeated stupidly. "Why?"

"Because, Win, the fellow ain't Admiral Enfield. Lord Linden here's come from Dorset this past week and seen your admiral there frolicking in his garden without the cares of a bachelor bunny. Your admiral upstairs is a fake!"

" 'E ain't a fake, neither!" said Winnie, angry and a little frightened. " 'E says 'e's th' admiral!"

Zack gave a snort of disgust. "He did, did he? The old . . . Winnie, if I was to tell you I was an admiral, it wouldn't make me one, would it? Best thing for you to do is to take us up and see."

Winnie ran her tongue worriedly around the toothed-sized gap in her mouth. "Ya kin if ya like but this lift 'ere ain't never carried no earls before. God strike me blind, but this 'ere's a 'andsome crowd. 'N why a war 'ero like yerself, Lord Linden, 'd want to 'elp a band o' cadge-paws like us is more than oi kin figger out."

"Disabuse your mind of the illusion that I'm doing anything to help you," said Linden acidly. Zack had hopped onto the ledge beside Winnie and he reached out for Katie. Linden handed her up to him, two hands about her waist. "What does your kidnappee look like?"

Winnie tugged one brass earring. "Dunno if oi could say, really. Only seen 'im oncet, an' it was fair dark at th' time. Th' fellow tried to give me a slip on th' shoulder! So oi stays away from 'im, see, 'n mostly watches th' door while oi'm 'ere."

Zack pulled the door shut; Winnie laid her musket on the floor, and began a hand-over-hand motion on a pair of ropes stretched between two pulleys in the corner. The floor lurched and Winnie cast a sapient look toward Katie, and advised, "Someone best watch over th' little mort there, looks like she's fixin' to flash her hash."

Drew went quickly to thread a sustaining arm over Katie's shoulder, and Zack frowned at her threateningly. "That's all that's needed, Katie, for you to get sick in this sweatbox! Look, this is only an old lift. See, we work the ropes and soon we've pulled ourselves up to the second floor! We'll be there in a minute, so hang onto your insides."

A gray light filtered in from above and Katie could feel the shudder and pull as the floor tugged upward beneath them. She could see grafitti scratched on the walls by young revolutionists of diverse interests and read them to herself, "Impoverish the Rich," "Hazel of Gump Street likes it with her shoes on," and in runny whitewash letters, "Give me chastity and give me continence but not just now!" signed by an individual who styled himself "The Scarlet Tiger."

"That's new since I've been here," said Zack, pointing to this last motto. "Who's the Scarlet Tiger, Winnie?"

"At's wot th' boys call th' admiral, fer a joke, like," she replied, between long pulls on the ropes. "Th' admiral 'n some o' th' blokes got a little lushy one night, then came down 'ere 'n th' admiral wrote that."

"Ho!" said Zack. "If your Scarlet Tiger is really an admiral, I'll eat my feet unsalted. Winnie, you've never met Katie's father, have you?"

"Nah, 'e was away from Essex th' time we stayed there, at th' 'orse races, ya remember. Why're ya askin' me?"

"You'll see," said Zack. "Holy Mother, will you see."

The lift came to a creaking halt. Zack helped Winnie secure the pull ropes and slid up a wooden seven-barred gate that led into an expansive storage room, with a high unplastered ceiling supported by great raw oak pillars. Dusty silver light sank in from the high-set windows to spot the room in sober smoky shadows. Across the long tar-coated hardwood floor was a partitioned corner that had been a shipping office before the building had been abandoned to the rats and the rascals.

Zack strode purposefully toward this room, his worn boots making soft sucking squeaks as each step cleared the hot tar. Katie looked uncertainly toward Lord Linden, received an encouraging smile in return, and followed Zack.

Zack was the first to reach the scarred pine door that led to the receiving office; he gripped the handle and flung it open to expose a small stuffy room, the floor littered with ancient shipping manifests; and over a ropespring cot that sagged against one wall, there hung a four-year-old calendar advertising the Universal Pill. But it was the center of the room that drew Zack's attention. Here sat three men at their leisure around an overturned barrel topped with a warped board. That these worthies had been drinking and playing cards was obvious; evidence attesting to both these activities was strewn over the makeshift table. All three seated gentlemen had discarded their shirts in deference to the heat, but one it was seen, had retained his hat. It was a forlorn affair, with tarnished nautical insignia that sat askew on the wearer's red, red curls. Beneath the flaccid brim, one found a pair of limpid robin's egg blue eyes which had opened in surprise at Zack's arrival, and a very freckled nose.

Zack was, for that moment, speechless but Katie cried, "Papa!" and flew into the hatted gentleman's open arms.

Lord Linden leaned against the door's unfinished frame, tipped his hat to the back of his head, and said, "Kendricks. I thought so."

Chapter Sixteen

One of the three cardplayers seated around the table was a husky youth of medium height wearing a pair of loose trousers, with a black handkerchief knotted around his neck. Zack hooked his fingers through this neck cloth and dragged the youth to his feet, backing him against the wall.

"Patrick, you idiot," said Zack furiously. "That's not Admiral Enfield. You've kidnapped Baron Kendricks!"

"'Ave ya cracked yer bughouse, Zackie?" said Patrick, disentangling himself from Zack's grip.

"No! Watch this." Zack walked around the table to stand before the red-haired cardplayer. "Sir! Is this your daughter?" he declaimed dramatically, gesturing at Katie.

The baron had pulled Katie onto his lap, tugged the pretty bonnet from her strawberry hair and kissed her soundly. They made an attractive pair that might have been more easily viewed as sister and brother than father and daughter. The baron was still four years short of forty and he looked more like four years short of thirty, with his slender graceful limbs and unlined boyish face. He set Katie back a bit and subjected her to a careful scrutiny.

"Think so," he said, with a grin that Linden had seen before on Katie's delicate lips. "Her mother always claimed she was and God knows she's the living spit o' me." Kendricks gestured toward an empty chair. "Anchor your arse, boy, and tell me what's toward. But first make me known to your handsome friends by the door there."

"Oi'll be damned!" cried Winnie. "That's 'ow ya pass it off, wantin' th' bloody introductions ta be made 'ere? 'N all th' time pretendin' ta be somebody ya ain't? Ya should 'ave tole us right away!"

"That's bloody telling him, Win," snapped Zack with approval. "Damn you, Morin, sitting up here on your bumfuddle for weeks on end wearing that quiz of a hat, corrupting these boobies with your cardshark trickery, leaving me to set Katie's feet on the ground in The Sisterhood. Which, let me tell you, she didn't like, and called me a damn Judas for it!"

"Strike me blind if I've ever seen you in such a peeve, Zack," observed the baron. "Truth is, it suited me fine to play least in sight for a while. In fact, it saved my bacon. The constables are on me for my defaults, y'know. It's to be debtor's prison if I'm caught."

Patrick returned to his seat by the table, gathered his disordered cards, and exchanged glances with his cardplaying cohort, a lanky, towheaded lad who was half drunk judging by the state of his bloodshot eyes and the loosely gripped, half-empty rum bottle he had in one hand.

"Damned if oi knows wot ta think," said Patrick, shaking his head severely at the baron. "It's th' surprise o' me life. Still, the government might care as much 'bout a baron as 'n admiral."

"Not this baron, ya jackanapes," said Winnie. She turned on the baron. "Ya know, it's a very serious offense impersonatin' 'n admiral. Ya could get in a lot o' trouble fer this!"

A sharp chortle came from Drew's corner, but by the time Winnie turned to glare at him, he was innocently expressionless.

"There's a good side ta this. Win-nie," said the towheaded cardplayer with drunken optimism. "Oi was worried 'ere 'at we'd end up wearin' th' sheriff's picture frame fer this caper, but if th' Scarlet Tiger 'ere is wot they're sayin' 'e is, 'e ain't likely ta infect us wi' 'emp fever." He frowned blurrily at his cards. "Dash it all, Zack, ya've messed up Patrick's 'and there 'n now th' thing's got ta be redealt. 'N oi was sittin on two aces!"

"Ah, cork yer bottle, Whit," said Winnie. "Yer drunk as a priest. As fer you, Baron Whoe'er-ya-are, 'ow come ya was sneakin' out o' th' admiral's 'ouse wearin' th' admiral's clothes in th' dark o' night?"

Kendricks collected the discarded hands and began shuffling them with a gambler's grace. "You wouldn't ask how come if you'd ever seen Maria Enfield. Why, she's the sweetest armful this side of the Atlantic. Save the one I've got here," he said, tickling Katie's cheek with his finger. "But her husband, the old admiral, is cram full of bourgeois jealousy and got his head full of nasty notions. But like I said, I was paying Maria a friendly visit one evening. I was upstairs showing her a few card tricks . . ." he winked, ". . . a little sleight-

227

o-hand, you might say, when the admiral arrives. We heard the old fool bellowing belowstairs so she sent me out through the dressing room. I had to give the servants the go-by, so I borrowed one of the admiral's topcoats, and this hat. I'm sneakin' around the corner outside, almost in the clear, when there comes a snaky blow from behind and I wake up here. Whose deal?"

"Mine," said Whit on his left, who took the deck and began to deal, slapping the cards down with boozy deliberation. "Oi 'ave ta say oi couldn'ta liked ya better if ya was an admiral, Scarlet Tiger. Ya brought more'na touch o' th' good life ta th' place. It was a good move winnin' our wages off us 'n then usin' 'em ta send out fer some 'igh quality moonshine. Taught our palates a lesson they won't ferget." He turned a lamb-like gaze on Zack. "Let me pour ya some, Zackie? Looks like ya could use it. Drive off th' 'eat."

Zack snarled a demur.

The baron fanned his cards. "Ah, keep your breath to cool your porridge, Zack. Too damn hot for emotion, boy. No doubt you'll introduce me to your friends by the door there in your own good time."

"This," said Zack grimly, "is Lord Linden. Yes, *that* Lord Linden. And I might as well tell you that he's a very particular friend of Katie's."

The baron sent a friendly smile toward Linden. "Ho ho! Sits the cock on that fence?" He patted his daughter's cheek. "It seems like yesterday you were playing jackstraws on the front steps."

Katie seized the opening. "Papa, I must tell you I've gotten myself into the most awkward situation. . . ."

"Sprained your ankle, have you?" guessed the baron. "Well, I suppose it had to come to that someday. I comprehend Linden here is your fellow? Well, I wouldn't worry about the thing too much, puss, he ain't the man to leave his bastards starving in a garret. Rich as a rent lord, they say."

"Bastards, Papa?" asked Katie, confused.

"Your father," explained Linden kindly, "has arrived at the conclusion that you are about to make him a grandfather."

Katie gasped. "Papa! I am not going to have a child!"

Whit studied Katie's trim form with polite lust. "Course yer not, sweet'eart. Lead, Scarlet Tiger."

"Papa," said Katie, with an urgency brought about by fear of a long series of card-game interruptions. "This may surprise you, but I'm being pursued by a man who means to kill me if he can."

"Oh, that's the tale, is it?" said the baron, capturing the first trick. "Sounds like the devil of the thing! Best tell me about it. Come to think, your shoulder has a bandage on it. You haven't hurt yourself, have you?"

"I have," said Katie, "but that doesn't matter. Papa, do you know Ivo Guy?"

"What? A rum-phyzed, pig-eyed cove that was your mother's cousin? I remember him. We used to call him Garbage Guts. What's the fellow to do with you?"

"He's the one that wants to kill me," explained Katie patiently. "He took me to a house in the country and tried to make me marry him."

"Were you kidnapped too? Damme if it doesn't run in the family. But what's this you say? Marry you or kill you? The fellow will have to make up his mind for one tack or the other, can't have the thing both ways."

"No, Papa, I know," said Katie, tolerantly inured to the difficulties of explaining anything to her father. "That's why it was so important that I find you because Ivo Guy is claiming to be my guardian."

The baron flipped another card to the table. "Looniest thing that's ever come to my hearing! Now you're telling me the fellow wants to be your guardian. Damned confusing. Tell you what, though. Settle the thing easy—stick with your Lord Linden here, that's the ticket. He's the fellow to set you up in style. Tell you what, let's take a glass of cognac on it. What do you say, Linden, can I fetch you a snort o' this eyewater?"

Linden left his position by the door and came to rest the heels of his hands on the table near the baron. "Kendricks," he said softly, "if you think I've compromised your daughter, you ought to be calling me out instead of offering me your damned cognac."

The baron looked hurt. "Not damned cognac, rather good cognac," he corrected. "And I'd have to be crazy to call you out—everyone knows you for a dead shot and I'm no more than average myself. 'Sides, you don't find me worrying about my little Kate." The Baron gave his daughter a hug with his encircling arm. "She can take care of herself. Lands on her feet like a cat."

"I know that you've successfully instilled in Katie the false notion that she can take care of herself," said Linden, in unloving accents. "But a more apt comparison would be to a kitten stranded on the highest limb of an oak tree. Never have I met a girl more in need of a father's protection and getting it less!" And then Lord Linden treated himself to the blistering denunciation of the quality of the baron's parenthood that he had been longing to deliver ever since he had learned Katie's identity. When finally he finished, Kendricks, who had been surveying him blandly through the whole, blinked like a badger, played his queen of hearts, stared straight at Linden and said, "If you don't like the way I've done with the chit, then you'd better protect her yourself."

"I intend to," snapped Linden.

"Good. You've got my permission, not that I think you give a damn." The baron pulled a jack from his hand and tossed it on the table. "My trick, Patrick. And give me thirty points for the pic."

Katie had listened to the last exchange with her alarm rippling like water in the rain. She wriggled to her feet and laid an unsteady hand on her father's shoulder. "Papa," she whispered in a stricken voice, "is that . . . how do you mean that? Don't you want me anymore?"

The baron drew Katie back onto his lap. "Poor old Katie," he said, laying her head against his chest and lacing his fingers gently through her satin curls. "God knows how a sweet little sprout like you pulled such a damme boy as m'self for a father. I'm sorry about a lot of things but sorry won't get the horse back in the stall, will it? It's too late, honey, there's nothing I can do for you. No money, no house, the law on my scent . . ." He rested his cheek on her head. "Take Linden, won't you, princess? You could do a whole world of worse. Katie, Katie, I'd be doing you more harm than good if I didn't tell you that there's no chance anyone but a no-noodle like Guy'll want to marry you, not with me posed as your pa. You're the pick of the litter, but ain't no decent man's ever going to like the look of your kennels."

Katie's shoulders drooped in despair, causing her small puffed sleeve to slide down her arm. There was a gasp of startled pleasure from Whit who was moved to exclaim, "I'll marry her!"

Patrick roused himself from the scoring sheet. "Aye, half-Whit, and yer wife'd love that!"

Katie heard Linden say something under his breath about "idiocy." He plucked her from the baron's arms and handed her to his brother, saying sharply, "Get her out of here, Drew. I'll meet you at home."

Winnie accompanied Drew and Katie to the lift shaft and worked the ropes that lowered them back to street level, letting them out into what was now the warm dusty evening light and closed the door behind them. Katie heard the scrape of the lock and then the subdued rumble of the lift returning to the second floor. She felt Drew's hand on her elbow and turned to look at him questioningly.

"Do you need to cry?" he asked.

Katie shook her head. "No. But I almost feel like I could. Do I look weepy?"

"Devil a bit, Peaches. Come on, let's get you home."

They walked together around the corner of the building. The air was oppressive and clammy, and there was no sound but the soft whisper of the Thames slapping against the wharf. The carriage was already losing distinction in the dusk, and the grooms had neglected to light the flambeaus. The unattended horses were somberly cropping on a few forlorn tufts of scrub grass which had worked their way defiantly out of the hard-packed earth.

The unlit flambeaus. The deserted horses. The absence of Lady Brixton's reliable coachman and two grooms. It took Drew no more than a few seconds to assimilate and interpret these facts. Suddenly he cursed under his breath and propelled Katie back toward the lift.

But it was too late. Two shadowed forms coalesced from behind a stack of kegs. The wider figure was carrying a brace of pistols; the barrels protruded from the rolled-up sleeves of an old frock coat. The taller figure hefted a truncheon.

"Ivo Guy," breathed Katie.

"Yes, my little chicken. But don't move or you will say good-bye to life a little sooner than you might," said Guy, grinning evilly. "And don't bother to look around for your servants, we have them bound where they will stay safely until we need them." He walked closer, followed by Chilworthy. A suggestive leer was on the obese lips as, keeping one barrel steadily at Drew, he ran the tip of the other barrel over the bare white flesh above the bodice of Katie's gown, and said, "But why are you strolling with this young milord here, cousin? Perhaps you're not as tasty as you look? Has your noble stallion, Linden, grown tired of your little freckled body?"

Drew's white linen shirt glowed pale blue in the fading light and Katie clutched it with both hands. "What are you going to do with us?" she asked, her musical voice unsteady.

His hot round eyes stared up and down her body. "Oh, are you trembling, now, my pretty slut? With fear? You could have trembled for me in another way. I offered you marriage!" He laughed harshly. "More fool I. You went back to take your love on an illicit bed. That's how you prefer it, isn't it? Too often carnal beauty is the mask for a lewd spirit. You're a wicked little creature and you're better off dead." He nudged the hard pistol barrel gently against her lips.

Drew pulled Katie's face into his chest, away from Guy. "Do you know who I am, Guy? Yes? You must have taken into consideration that if you kill Katie to claim your money in court, you'll have to also kill me." Drew's tone was remarkably cool. "And if you kill me, my family will hunt you down even if you crawl into the deepest rathole in England."

Guy shifted his weight irritably. "Fine talk, my young bravo, but the man who holds the weapons is the man who gives the insults. There will be no hunting down because Chilworthy and I are going to arrange a carriage accident. A turn taken too sharp across the narrow bridge, a broken axle, a plunge into the Thames, a mass drowning and the thing is done."

"And no one will ever suspect," said Drew sarcastically, thinking rapidly. "You've outgeneralled us all, haven't you? Have you had Brixton House watched?"

"Yes," said Guy, with relish, almost laughing. "And I've been bidding for this moment. But now, get into that carriage."

"All right," said Drew, making his voice very soft, "but Guy, think. I have an idea that would make this moment even . . . sweeter for you. If you'll listen only for a second. You want Katie, don't you?" Katie jerked in his arms but he ignored her.

"Want her?" said Guy. "What do you mean?"

"Desire her," said Drew ruthlessly, calmly. "So do I. She's always been Linden's and I've always wanted her but I've never had the chance. We could share her, Guy, first me and then you. In that warehouse across the yard." Drew heard Katie gasp his name. He slid his hand to cover her mouth. "Why not, Guy? As a last request, you might say."

Guy's eyes narrowed with suspicion, but his breath came faster. "It's a trick."

"How could it be a trick? You keep the pistols."

Guy laughed nervously. "Damned if I know what to make of you, boy. You're a mighty cool hand. Seems like you must be having something up your sleeve."

Drew felt Katie struggle in good earnest. "Do you expect me to whimper at your feet like a peasant?" asked Drew contemptuously. "I know how to die. But if I'm dying on her account, it would be justice for me to enjoy her first."

"All right, all right, I'll do it!" said Guy, his voice strained with excitement. He gestured with his pistols toward the far warehouse. "Bring her along then. But quickly now! No, no, you walk ahead, that's right. And I don't mind telling you, boy, that you're the most depraved young whelp I've ever chanced upon."

"And you wouldn't do the same, in my situation, I suppose?" asked Drew simply. He had scooped the pitiful trembling Katie into his arms, keeping one hand clamped tightly across her mouth. They were nearing the far warehouse. It was a dilapidated barn-like building whose high boarded windows proclaimed its abandoned status. One side door hung open on rusted hinges, exposing an old but serviceable bolt on its inside. They reached the door and Drew turned back toward Guy, and said, "It's dark inside. There might be glass. You have a lamp? You'd better light it."

Chilworthy had an oil lamp hanging from his belt and Guy watched as his partner made to light it. It was a small distraction but it was enough for Drew. He threw Katie into the warehouse, ran in after her and smacked the door shut, ramming the bolt home. Within seconds there was the sound of pounding from the other side and Guy's unintelligible screaming.

"Keep it up, you bastard," said Drew quietly. "I only hope that you make enough noise for Lesley to hear." There was a shallow light from the rotted window boarding and Drew looked down at Katie who had sank into a shivering heap at his feet. He offered her his hand. "Come on. Up. These hinges won't take much battering from that ghoulish henchman of your cousin's."

Katie didn't move. "I thought . . . I thought . . ."

"I know what you thought and I can't say that I'm too damned flattered. Your cousin is stupid and crazy. But you," he said grimly, "are just stupid."

Katie covered her face with her hands, and Drew felt the anger flood from him. He bent down to take her hands, to clasp them inside his. "There. And everyone says I'm the even-tempered one of the family. That was just what you needed today, wasn't it? More unkindness. Listen, you were smart not to trust me. I wouldn't trust me either if I'd had your experience with men." He laughed.

"And if you can decipher that sentence, you're in better shape than me." Drew put his hands under her arms and pulled Katie to her feet. "C'mon Peaches, help me save your life. Or how will I ever face Lesley?"

There was only one door out of the wide dirt-floor room and Drew headed toward it, tugging Katie's stumbling form behind him. The door led to a small airless shaft with a steep flight of steps leading up into darkness.

"Stairs. Good. These ought to slow down our fat friend some. I hope to God they don't lead to a locked door. Let me go first, Katie. Some of these boards are probably rotten. Smells like it."

The stairs went up and up. Twice they came out of the dark stairway onto a landing with faint light stealing in through cracked air venting, but there was no door out. Katie heard Drew mutter that they were on Jacob's Ladder. His quiet laughter floated back to her as he added, "Complete with an angel."

They climbed another flight of stairs and reached another landing but this time with a difference. The stairs stopped before a narrow wooden ladder leading to a trapdoor in a dusty ceiling. Drew scampered up the ladder with monkey-like ease while Katie stood with her head bowed and her hands on her knees trying to choke some air back into her aching lungs. Drew shoved on the trap-door and it landed open with a thud, causing the late evening sky to be framed in the gathered dark of the landing. Drew turned and pulled Katie up after him and then they stood together on the roof, gasping in the warm evening air after their exertion. Drew looked around them. It seemed as though they could see all of London. The slate gray rooftops were ablaze in an orange light and the sun was shooting giant tentacles of fire into the darkening sky, fingering the altitudinous clouds in a blood-red gesture of farewell. Far in the distance, the Tower of London stood like a dire sentinel of the night that was soon to follow. Swallows and bats were darting spirits above the city, squealing and whistling.

"Beautiful. If we were of a mind to admire the landscape. A romantic setting, a girl pretty enough to make your heart turn over, and Guy the Gorgon on your heels. My luck. Will your shoulder make it, Peaches?"

"The shoulder . . ." said Katie, between panting breaths, "is the least . . . of my . . . problems."

Drew knelt by the trapdoor and tugged at the ladder. "Running up three flights of stairs when you're barely off the sicklist isn't nothing, is it? Damn. This thing won't . . . no, here it comes." Drew hauled the ladder onto the roof. "Got your wind again? Let's go."

Drew started off across the roof toward the next building, the ladder held under one arm. Broad rain pools that had somehow escaped drying in the day's heat were scattered over the roof, teeming with vermin and dead leaves, reflecting pale orange and white from the evening sky. Katie saw a nightjar swoop low over the roof giving a triumphant churring thrill as it captured an insect.

"I wish we could fly from these rooftops like the swallows," she said.

"If we did, I wouldn't put it beyond Guy to turn into a buzzard and flap after us," said Drew. "That fellow talks like the arch-villain in a shilling shocker. I'm not stating the case too strongly when I tell you that you're sadly unfortunate in your relatives." They reached the roof's edge. About three feet above them and four feet away lay the roof of the next building. Drew settled the ladder, bridge-like across the void.

"You can't be serious," said Katie, her heart bumping up to her throat.

"No? All right then, don't be serious. Pretend we're ten-year-olds playing pirates. Time to walk the plank." Drew hopped on the roof's foot-high edge-wall, paused a moment, and ran lightly across the horizontal rungs, his arms gracefully outstretched for balance.

"See, nothing to it," he said. "You're a bird, remember? A swallow. You can't fall."

There was a series of confused scrambling thumps from below and behind them. "Damn!" said Drew, "Katie, they're on the stairs. If you can't walk across then get down on your hands and knees and crawl. Look, I'm holding the ladder steady. That's right. Good girl."

Katie was over and in his arms for a brief second before he let her go. He swung the ladder away from the lower building and then sent it on a reeling journey to the ground where it landed with a splintering crash.

"Why'd you do that?" asked Katie.

"Burning our bridges. Guy can't get any use out of it now, and anyway, the thing was so rickety that it wouldn't have been safe for us to use for another crossing."

Katie gasped. "Why didn't you tell me that before I crawled across on it?"

"Stupid question. Because you would never have

crawled across on it if I had. Come on, you can sort the logic of that out later."

They were on the roof of what once must have been an office house, judging from the forest of smokestacks that rose from its tiled surface. The clay shingles were dry with age, and most had worked their way loose. They clattered and clanked under Drew's Hessians and poked uncomfortably into Katie's feet through her thin slippers. She could hear Ivo Guy shouting something to Chilworthy far behind.

"Drew," said Katie, her breath coming quickly in her throat, "do you think Lord Linden will hear them? Or that he'll come out and find the grooms tied up and look for us?"

" 'The miserable have no other medicine, but only hope.' "

"That's not quite what I wanted to hear but it's very clever. Did you make that up?"

"No. Shakespeare made it up." They stopped at the tiled roof's far side and stopped. Drew looked across the level three-foot space to the next building and nodded with satisfaction. "Good. We can jump it."

"Worse and worse and worse," groaned Katie. "Drew, can't we stay here and scream for help? You threw the ladder down and Guy and Chilworthy have no way to follow us."

"They'll find something. That old barn is full of wood. All they need is one plank."

He took some steps backward, ran and leaped across.

"Jump, Peaches. You could clear twice this distance. If this was on the ground, you'd think nothing of it." He opened his arms. "See, I'll catch you."

Katie peered across the open space and forced herself to jump, colliding sharply with Drew's hard body as she landed. But her purchase gave way and for one terrible instant there was nothing underneath her. A small torrent of broken masonry was falling away.

"I've got you, Peaches, it's all right. Damn crumbling parapet." He pulled her after him, past a jutting air vent, past a pile of roofing material. Katie's blood was roaring in her ears. She glanced over her shoulder in time to see Chilworthy break into the open on the many-chimneyed roof. He loped across to the gap, covering ground rapidly on his gangly legs. Drew had seen him as well and yanked her after him as she gave a small despairing whimper. Without breaking stride, Chilworthy leaped confidently into the air, arms spread wide, only to do a ridiculous dance step as the parapet gave way beneath him and he disappeared into eternity, leaving behind a disbelieving howl.

"That's one less to worry about," said Drew callously.

"Oh, Drew, he must have been killed!" said Katie, her face shocked and pale in the dim light.

"What do you want to do, stop and have the obsequies?"

They picked their way across the roof. The sun had left them, taking with it the orange highlights from the sky, leaving them to flee through a deep blue atmosphere. The lamplighters were beginning to make rounds; tiny points of yellow light were popping into their field of vision. Another warehouse was looming ahead of them.

"Drew, look!" she said excitedly, pointing. "Isn't that the warehouse where my father is?"

"Of course it is, sweetheart. Did you think we were plunging headlong to nowhere? Unfortunately, it's a bloody twelve-foot jump from here, and the room where they are is on the other side." He bent to scan the wall below him.

"Drew, be careful."

"We have to get off of this roof," he said. "The only way appears to be through that window."

Katie looked over the edge and saw a small black rectangle positioned about four feet below them. Far down on the ground she could see the coach and four and three saddled hacks still chewing at the straggly grass.

"It's impossible, unless we grow wings," said Katie with certainty.

"No, it'll be all right," said Drew. "I'll lower you by your wrists and you swing into the window."

"Never!"

"Listen, we don't have time for me to convince you. We don't know where Ivo Guy is; he could be right behind us, taken a short cut. This is better than getting shot, isn't it?"

"No, it's not," replied Katie. "I've already been shot, I know what it's like, and this is much worse. She lowered her voice. "Think of Chilworthy."

"Think of Ivo Guy." He grabbed her wrists, lifting her bodily, and swung her over the edge of the roof. She cried out, feeling herself fall and then jerk to a stop, her legs dangling fruitlessly.

"It's right in front of your feet," he urged.

"I . . . I can't find it," she moaned, frightened.

"It's down there," he said encouragingly. "Swing your feet a little to the left and you'll have it." Katie did as he suggested. Her feet landed solidly on the windowsill.

"Now, hook yourself in there and you're safe." She let herself go with a little push and found herself, after a brief, terrifying moment of suspension, sitting firmly on the windowsill from which, with a great sigh of relief, she dropped to the floor. She had never been so glad to have done with a task. Drew followed her easily.

They were standing in a large, exotically scented storeroom, lit by flickering smudgepots. The sickly greenish-yellow glow from the pots reflected off ropes of garlic draped from the ceiling, and loose, fragrant piles created dark, random masses on the floor. Pipes of rum were standing in the far corner.

"Drew, what is this place?"

"Spice warehouse. Of the West India Company by the looks of it. See, they use smudgepots to keep off the humidity." They headed across the room to the only door. He tried to open it, without success, and turned to Katie, setting her gently onto a pile of jute sacks stuffed with rice. Drew put his arm around her shoulders.

"I have a confession to make," he said. "Now that I've gotten us in here, I don't know how to get us out. The door's bolted from the outside."

"What do we do?"

"We wait. They're not going to leave the smudgepots unattended. Must be a watchman coming around to check them."

As if in answer to his surmise, there was a scuffling of footsteps outside the door. The bolt scraped and the door swung open to reveal—a heavily panting Ivo Guy, training a pistol on them with one hand, wiping his foam-flecked mouth on the back of his other wrist.

"Winded, Guy?" taunted Drew. "Don't shoot yourself while you're cleaning up."

"You little rats," he said, his voice cracking with exhaustion. "Which one of you wants to die first?"

Drew stood and put Katie behind him. "You'll have to kill me to get to her."

"Stop being noble," Katie said, wretchedly trying to wiggle out of his arms.

"I'm not being noble, just conventional," he said. "My upper class instincts. Guy, look behind you!" Drew pushed Katie face downwards into a pile of dried basil leaves while Ivo Guy wheeled. There was a rapid succession of deafening explosions and a fog of discharged gunpowder added its bitter scent to the room. A heavy thump shook the floor, followed by an exhale of air as Katie's cousin breathed his last pomposity.

Katie lifted her head to see Lord Linden lowering his small pistol. Streamers of smoke were meandering upward from the barrel and lock, turning a sinuous lime green in the light from the pots.

Drew covered her eyes and shoved her face back down. "Don't look, Katie, you'll get sick. Wait 'til he's covered up."

There was a rustle of cloth and Linden walked across the room to them. "Andrew, you've earned yourself a night at the most expensive bawdyhouse in London. On me."

The rest of the evening passed for Katie in a procession of odd, disjointed impressions. There seemed to be a dozen people asking questions; her father, Zack, Winnie, Lady Brixton's coachman with a bruise on the side of his face. Then they were home and it was Lady Brixton and Suzanne floating before her. Linden handled them all.

"Just put her to bed," he snapped at Suzanne. "And let her sleep."

So they bathed her and put her to bed, with a small nightlight and a call bell beside her.

Katie stared for a long time at the Montgolfier air balloon chandelier and then drifted unknowingly into sleep.

The next morning brought a cool breeze from the north and London sang with relief. Sparrows trilled in the trees of Hyde Park, puppies left off their panting and began to play, Lady Brixton's housemaids waged war on the infinitesimal dust that had gathered on a day's remove from their feather dusters. Katie woke in the same way she had fallen asleep, lying still on her back, staring at the ceiling. In her dreams she had tried to cross the wooden ladder to Drew, but it had stretched before her like a desert. No matter with what desperation or speed she crawled, she would get no closer to the other side. Katie rose and stood gazing out her side window at the garden. Thus she was found by Suzanne and Lady Brixton who had had the full tale last night from Drew. These ladies fairly bristled with compassion, and fussed over Katie like a mother over a favorite child with measles.

Katie sat quietly under their ministration, let them feed her breakfast, and dress her in a white muslin gown blazing with royal blue ribbons. She tried to let their generous comfort cover the painful echoes of last night, the thud of Guy's body hitting the floor, Chilworthy's scream as he fell from the parapet, her father's voice as he told her kindly that he didn't want her, no one wanted her, she should become Lord Linden's mistress. The words clung to her, stinging like hot sand. Dear God, must it have been so public? How much more vivid it had made the words to see them met with Zack's expression of resigned condolence, Andrew's angry pity, and Lord Linden's—well, Lord Linden had simply looked angry.

It was nearing eleven o'clock when a footman appeared with the intelligence that Lord Linden was below and requested the favor of Miss Kendricks's company. Katie walked into the hallway and down the elaborately carved oak staircase. Short figures of playing children surmounted each column along the balustrade and Katie touched their cool hardwood bodies as she padded down the stairs, the sharply pointed steps mewing curtly under the weight of her slippered feet.

Lord Linden, she found, was in the green drawing room leaning against the mantel, dressed with careless elegance in a russet coat, whipcord breeches, and black leather boots. Katie crossed the room to him.

He said her name once, "Katie . . ." as if it were a greeting, and reached up to caress the base of her throat with his knuckles, feeling the rhythm of her pulse increase under his touch. "Katie, I meant it last night when I said that I'd protect you," he said softly.

She stepped back, raising her palm to cover the spot where he had touched her, as though to preserve its warmth. "You have, my lord," she said, a sweet uncertainty in the flower-petal eyes. "From Ivo Guy. He can't hurt me now, so I don't believe that I need to be protected anymore. I've been thinking this morning that perhaps your grandmother might have a friend who would hire me as a maid? Or Miss Steele might? Not a lady's maid, I know I'm not qualified for that, but perhaps something helping out a cook, scrubbing pots and such things, or dusting?"

"Or maybe Zack would buy you back if I gave him fifty pounds," snapped Linden. "Or, if we're committed to that course, we could sell you to Andrew. I could probably turn a nice profit and you'd be much better taken care of."

Katie retreated another step from the temper in his restless sable eyes. She stood still and fragile, like a porcelain fashion doll. "I'm sorry I made you angry," she whispered.

"I'm not angry, damn it." He reached out, drawing her to him, his arms tightening around the slight body, as though he could pull her inside himself. "Be still. Rest quietly against me. God, you're fearful with me today. Does it frighten you to feel how much I want you? No? Then . . ." He stood back, studying her thoughtfully.

"Katie, was it something your father said to you last night? I see. And now you're afraid that I'm about to make a dishonorable proposal? Oh, God, is that all? I thought for a minute it was something serious."

Katie fought free in a flash, but when she looked up, she saw his eyes were light and smiling. Linden took Katie's head between his hands, placing them tenderly over her ears, his fingers spread. He tilted his hands slightly, lifting her face.

"My bonny Kate, if you had sprung from a large family who was devoted to furthering your interest, I might have been able to seduce you with a clear conscience. Though I doubt it. As things stand . . . Katie, will you marry me?"

She stared at him. It seemed as though the very beat of her heart stopped with surprise. "You . . . but you must be saying that because you think you've compromised me."

Linden kissed her eyelids, feeling the feathery touch of the lashes against his lips. "Katie, I've been compromising girls since I was Andrew's age. If I'd asked them all to marry me, I'd have a harem like the Grand Turk." He moved his thumb to caress her jawline, then her lips, which curved into a feeble smile.

"You're only being kind," she said bravely. "I know you are."

Linden made a sound something like a groan and brought his mouth down on Katie's. "Kate. Sweet Kate. The prettiest Kate in Christendom. There's no help for it," he murmured, his lips moving against hers, "you'll have to marry me because I'll never be able to bring myself to stop compromising you."

Katie turned her head to the side so he cradled her against his chest, one hand on her cheek, his lips brazing over her curls. "You can't . . ." faltered Katie. "Your family, your friends, what will they say?"

"They'll say you've redeemed me from a life of corruption and dissipation," Katie could hear the smile in his voice. "If I know anything about *Grandmère*, I'll wager she's upstairs writing our betrothal notice for the *Gazette*." His long fingers slid under her hair to explore the fine skin of her neck. Then he stroked back the hair that covered her dainty ear and kissed its tip. "Katie?" he whispered. "Listen. This is the first time I've ever said this to anyone. God, I hope I don't choke on it." His arms tightened around her. "Katie. I love you." He looked down at her, smiling. "I love you." He recaptured her face in his hands, and turned it gently from side to side, dragging her lips across his, saying it again and again until he felt her arms slide around his neck and cling to him, her lips dilated and pliant. She pressed herself closer to him of her own accord, moving against his hard body in innocent unconscious arousal.

He laid one hand firmly on the back of her neck, and his other hand floated gently down her back, touching his fingertips at random intervals, feeling her trembling body, until his hand came to rest on the full swell of her hip. He became aware then of her own small white hand, laid flat on his chest with just a hint of pressure. "I feel your heartbeat," she said, her voice quiet and interested. She was so close to him now, her eyes luminous, and suddenly their lips met in a clinging kiss, deep, passionate, and free, and they were holding onto each other tightly, trying not to fall, trying not to remain standing, but above all else, trying to be close.

"You're so beautiful," he breathed. "Love me. Katie, hold me." He led her to a low couch nearby, and she felt supported and safe and close as he lowered her there and his mouth met hers again in a biting liquid search.

There was the quiet clack of a well-oiled door handle turning and a hesitant footstep, followed by Andrew's intensely apologetic voice.

"You wouldn't believe how sorry I am," he said, "but I've been compelled to, er . . . keep you company. By *Grandmère*."

There was silence from the low couch. Katie whispered something and then Andrew heard his brother's rueful laugh.

"No, I'm all right, Katie," said Linden, his voice still slightly thick. "'Time in its aging course teaches all things.' I should have locked the door. Andrew, take your hands off your eyes, you look ridiculous. What did *Grandmère* threaten to do, come in here herself? God, that would have aged me ten years. What did she say?"

Drew placed a light armless chair backwards, close to the couch. He straddled it, folded his arms across its crested top rail and grinned. "She said, 'I won't have any innocent young lady under my protection debauched by a notorious libertine. Take yourself down those steps, boy, and into that room before Katie becomes the first girl ever to lose her virtue on my drawing room floor.'"

It was three months later when Kathleen Janette Byrne, Lady Linden, found herself snuggled in the depths of a great tent bed in her husband's ancestral mansion. He had pulled her tight against his chest, his arms entwined about her neck, his fingers tracing shifting sensual patterns over the smooth flesh of her back. Katie felt the hard, steady flow of his heart under her cheek.

"Lesley?"

"Mmmmmm?"

"Do you know, it wasn't as bad as I feared it would be."

"Thank you," he said. Then, "Your expectations, I collect, were not high."

Katie giggled. "Not *that*, that was wonderful. I was talking about our wedding this morning." She let her hand stray through his hair; it was a silky delight beneath her fingers. "You really have an enormous family, don't you? I mean, twenty first cousins! But I'm afraid that Lady Brixton did not at all like it when Papa slapped her backside."

"No. But everyone else did."

Katie strained the onyx curls through her fingers. "Do you think Papa will like it in America?"

"He'd better like it. The ticket I bought him was only one way. Come here."

Katie laughed again, though this time the sound came from deeper within her throat. "I'm here already."

"Closer." He rolled onto his back, drawing her gently over on top of him. He stroked the little freckled nose above him.

"Did I tell you where I got my nightgown?" asked Katie. "Laurel sent it to me! Lady Brixton said it wasn't a fit garment for a decent woman to wear and it ought to have been white but Suzanne said she thought it would be just the thing and that Laurel ought to know. Did you like it?"

"Yes."

"Oh. I thought you might not have noticed it much, you snatched it off me so quickly."

"Poor Katie." She felt his finger's gentle urge beneath her chin, and raised her lips obligingly to his.

Between kisses she said, "I'll bet when we met at the Maidenhead that you never thought we would ever be like this, together?"

"Mmm? Like this? I'm afraid, my innocent, that it was one of the first thoughts that occurred to me."

"It's very pretty of you to say so! But am I not too heavy for you?"

"Lord, no. Lie on me forever if you like."

"I would, but we'd present a most unconventional appearance at your grandmother's *soirée* for the prince next Thursday. Lesley, dearest Lesley, I'm so happy!"

"Good. It's too late for an annulment." His voice was muffled by the cascade of her auburn curls as he pressed his lips to her throat.

"Les-ley?"

"Mmmm?"

"I wondered—who do you like this better with . . . me or Laurel?"

"God. The things you say." His voice was soft with tender amusement. "You. Of course you, Little Star."